JIGSAW

Recent Titles by Anthea Fraser

The Detective Chief Inspector Webb Mysteries
(in order of appearance)

A SHROUD FOR DELILAH
A NECESSARY END
PRETTY MAIDS ALL IN A ROW
DEATH SPEAKS SOFTLY
THE NINE BRIGHT SHINERS
SIX PROUD WALKERS
THE APRIL RAINERS
SYMBOLS AT YOUR DOOR
THE LILY-WHITE BOYS
THREE, THREE, THE RIVALS
THE GOSPEL MAKERS
THE SEVEN STARS
ONE IS ONE AND ALL ALONE
THE TEN COMMANDMENTS
ELEVEN THAT WENT UP TO HEAVEN *
THE TWELVE APOSTLES *

Other Titles

PRESENCE OF MIND *
THE MACBETH PROPHECY *
BREATH OF BRIMSTONE *
MOTIVE FOR MURDER *
DANGEROUS DECEPTION *
PAST SHADOWS *
FATHERS AND DAUGHTERS *
BROUGHT TO BOOK *

* available from Severn House

JIGSAW

Anthea Fraser

This first world edition published in Great Britain 2004 by
SEVERN HOUSE PUBLISHERS LTD of
9–15 High Street, Sutton, Surrey SM1 1DF.
This first world edition published in the USA 2004 by
SEVERN HOUSE PUBLISHERS INC of
595 Madison Avenue, New York, N.Y. 10022.

British Library Cataloguing in Publication Data

Fraser, Anthea
    Jigsaw
    1.   Women biographers - Fiction
    2.   Detective and mystery stories
    I.   Title
    823.9'14 [F]

    ISBN 0-7278-6065-8

Typeset by Palimpsest Book Production Ltd.,
Polmont, Stirlingshire, Scotland.
Printed and bound in Great Britain by
MPG Books Ltd., Bodmin, Cornwall.

One

'How much do you know about Buckford?' Rona Parish asked suddenly.

Her twin sister raised an eyebrow. 'What is this, A-levels?'

'Seriously; if someone asked you, what would you say?'

Lindsey reflected as she sipped her coffee. They were seated at the kitchen table in the basement of Rona's tall Georgian house. Beyond the open glass door, the small patio garden was ablaze with colour and Gus, her golden retriever, lay dozing in the sunshine.

'Well?' Rona prompted.

'Well, it's the county town, of course, and goes back yonks. Isn't it about to celebrate its nine-hundredth anniversary or something?'

'Eight-hundredth. Go on.'

Lindsey frowned, reviewing her scanty knowledge of the town. 'I know some important people were born there, though offhand I can't remember who – a poet, I think, and some general or other – oh, and one of the nineteenth-century prime ministers. Then there's the school, of course, which is why most people outside the county have heard of it.' She paused. 'And I must confess to being even hazier on its more recent history; in fact, all I remember is that murder a couple of years ago, that hit the headlines.'

She gave a little laugh. 'You know, it's ridiculous, but I don't think I've been back since that school trip when we were about eleven.'

'Lord yes, I remember; we had to find a list of exhibits in the museum, and then draw them.'

'So!' Lindsey sat back and looked at her challengingly. 'Have I passed my exam?'

'Borderline,' Rona adjudicated.

'You, presumably, know a great deal more.'

'Actually, no, but I soon shall. I'm thinking of writing a series about it, to coincide with the celebrations.'

'That's a great idea!' Lindsey exclaimed. 'Something you can really get your teeth into!'

Rona smiled ruefully. A few months ago she'd had to abort a promising biography, since when she'd done nothing more enterprising than write a few articles for the Sunday supplements. Obviously, her twin expected more of her.

'Nothing's been decided yet,' she warned. 'I'll have to sound Barnie out first.' Barnie Trent was the features editor of *Chiltern Life*, a prestigious glossy magazine for which Rona wrote on a freelance basis. He was also a friend. 'It won't be a straightforward history,' she went on. 'I'm thinking more of a quirky look back over the centuries, picking out places and people that were slightly out of the ordinary.'

Lindsey reached for some grapes. 'Sounds great; I was beginning to wonder when something would grab you. I mean, it's not as though you've been short of offers, is it? Max was telling Pops you've been inundated with requests to write bios or look into unsolved crimes.'

Rona laughed. 'A slight exaggeration, though I've been approached, yes.'

'Thanks, no doubt, to the Theo Harvey débâcle.'

The reason for dropping the biography had been Rona's inadvertent discovery that its subject, thought either to have drowned accidentally or committed suicide, had, in fact, been murdered; an outcome that had led indirectly not only to two more deaths, but to the reappearance on the scene of Hugh Cavendish, Lindsey's ex-husband, a development with which the family was less than happy.

As he came into her mind, Rona asked involuntarily, 'What's the position with Hugh?'

'No change.'

'Which means?'

'That he's still trying to get a transfer back here, but in the meantime comes up every weekend.'

'And stays with you,' Rona said flatly.

'Don't be stuffy, Ro, it doesn't suit you.'

'It's not that,' Rona defended herself. 'I just think it's unfair on him; he's obviously hoping to be taken back permanently.'

Lindsey shrugged. 'No harm in hoping, but I'm not rushing into anything. Once bitten, twice shy.'

Twice bitten, too, Rona corrected silently, remembering her sister's last disastrous liaison. Lindsey needed a man in her life, and loneliness had warped her judgement.

'Anyway,' she was continuing, 'it has its advantages, seeing each other only at weekends. As you should know.'

Rona's husband, Max, was an illustrator and part-time art tutor, and since they both worked from home, friction had arisen when it transpired that he liked to have music playing at full volume while he painted, whereas Rona needed complete quiet in which to write. The solution had been to buy a cottage ten minutes' walk away, where Max set up his studio and played his loud music to his heart's content. And since he held evening classes three times a week, and Rona frequently worked late to meet deadlines, it seemed sensible on those occasions for him to stay there overnight, an arrangement that had initially horrified Rona's parents – who foresaw imminent divorce – and gave rise to Lindsey's dubbing him Rona's 'semi-detached husband'.

Lindsey looked at her watch. 'I must be going,' she said, pushing back her chair. 'I'm seeing a client at two thirty.'

Rona also rose. 'I'll walk part of the way with you and call in at *Chiltern Life*. Might as well make a firm commitment before I change my mind.'

Gus, hearing the word 'walk', raised his head, ears cocked hopefully.

'Come on, boy,' she confirmed. He bounded inside, tail wagging, and, having closed and locked the door, she followed him and her sister up the basement stairs to the hall.

Unlike Lindsey, whose flat was a fifteen-minute drive away, Rona lived in the centre of town, her road parallel with Guild Street, the main shopping district. They walked in companionable silence along the pleasant, tree-lined avenue, turning up Fullers Walk in the direction of the shops and then, two thirds of the way along, branching off into Dean's Crescent and following its curve towards the eastern end of Guild Street.

The Crescent contained not only the offices of *Chiltern Life*, but Dino's Italian restaurant, regularly patronized by Rona, who never cooked if she could avoid it. She paused now to glance at the menu in its glass case. This was one of Max's class nights and she would be eating alone.

'One of the perks of living in town,' Lindsey observed. 'You can either dine here in splendour or slum it with a choice of takeaways. If *I* don't feel like cooking, I have to rely on convenience foods.'

'But you *always* feel like cooking,' Rona pointed out equably. 'Obviously, you snaffled all the culinary genes.'

'I'm just not lazy!' Lindsey retorted.

Round the next curve they could see the main road ahead of them, clogged with traffic, and, just short of it, the imposing building that housed *Chiltern Life*. Lindsey's office was on Guild Street, some fifty yards round the corner.

'Thanks for lunch,' she said, as they came to a halt.

'Such as it was.' It had, in fact, been a selection of cold meats and salads. Rona's dislike of cooking did not prevent her eating well.

'Love to Max when you see him.'

Rona raised a cryptic eyebrow. There was a state of armed

neutrality between the two of them that she had done all in her power to overcome, to no avail.

'And good luck with the Buckford idea,' Lindsey added more sincerely.

Rona nodded an acknowledgement as she pushed open the door. Polly, the receptionist, came round her desk and took Gus's lead out of her hand.

'Let me look after him, for the sake of Barnie's files.'

Rona smiled, undeceived by the pretext. True, the dog's plumed tail had more than once dislodged piles of papers, but Polly was unashamedly devoted to him and took every opportunity to have him to herself.

'Thanks, Poll.'

Gus was already trotting behind the reception desk. Polly kept a supply of biscuits in a drawer, and had never failed him yet.

'Rona!' Barnie Trent came to greet her, planting a smacking kiss on her cheek. 'Long time no see! How goes it?'

'Less than brilliantly,' Rona admitted, taking the chair he indicated.

He nodded in sympathy. 'It was damned bad luck, being left high and dry like that. Specially when you'd geared your-self to the prospect of two or three years' work.'

'It cast a long shadow,' she admitted sombrely. She had indeed lost a lucrative contract, but what had plagued her these last months was that her work had precipitated one of the deaths. 'However,' she went on, brightening determinedly, 'I've come up with an idea I'd like to run past you. It's to do with Buckford's octocentenary.'

'Yes?' His shrewd eyes examined her from beneath bushy brows.

'I wondered if you'd be interested in a series of articles? Not a chronological spiel – there'll be plenty of those over the next year or so. I was thinking more of cherry-picking.'

'Go on.'

'Well, each would be complete in itself, but taken together they'd be a record of the town from its earliest beginnings – its architecture and how it developed, the foundation of the school and its slot in the development of education generally. Like a giant jigsaw really, starting with a handful of jumbled pieces and fitting in the different bits to make a complete picture. As far as possible, I'd like it to be people-based, concentrating on interesting or eccentric inhabitants over the centuries and their effect on the town.'

'Yes,' he said slowly, 'I like the sound of that. How many articles do you envisage?'

'That's up to you. I could start with half a dozen, and see how we go. I thought we might do them as a central pull-out and offer a binder or something, so they could be kept as a souvenir.'

'Good thinking. You'd need photos, of course. Then and now.'

She nodded. 'The "then" will be in the archives, but I'd like to borrow Andy for the modern stuff, if that's OK?'

'Sure, no problem. It'll be good to have you back on board.'

Taking that as dismissal, Rona retrieved her bag from the floor. 'How's Dinah?'

Barnie grimaced. 'Up to high doh about the expected grandchild.' The Trents' only daughter, who lived in the States, was awaiting her second baby.

'Of course, it must be getting close now.'

'Still eight weeks off, but Mel's blood pressure's causing concern.'

'That's bad luck,' Rona sympathized. 'Look, why don't you come to dinner, for a bit of light relief? We've been meaning to ask you for ages.'

'Sounds good.' He gave a lopsided grin. 'I take it Max will do the honours?'

'Very definitely.' Rona fumbled in her bag for her diary. 'Let's make it a Friday, so we can all relax. Next week?'

Barnie leafed through his appointments book. 'I'm free, but I'll need to check with the boss.'

Rona replaced her diary and stood up. 'I mustn't take any more of your time.'

'Keep me posted on the articles, and I'll come back to you about Friday.'

She'd burned her boats, she thought, as she ran down the stairs. Now there was no going back, no more procrastinating. It was high time she put the traumas of the biography behind her and embarked on a new project. And this, she thought, her spirits rising, should be just the one.

'I have a proposition for you,' Rona told Max, when he phoned that evening.

'Sounds promising.'

'How would you like to go to Buckford for the weekend?'

'What a let-down! You're going ahead with those articles, then?'

'Yes, I saw Barnie today and he's in favour. I'd like to have a look round and get the feel of the place. It's ages since I was there.'

'I thought the anniversary wasn't till next year?'

'It's not, but plans are already under way, and if I time it right, the articles should extend into the new year.'

'You'll have a fair bit of competition, love; there'll be any number of people wanting a piece of the action.'

'I know, but mine will be slanted differently.'

'That, I don't doubt!'

'Seriously, is the weekend OK? Up on Saturday, back on Sunday?'

'Fine, if that's what you want.'

'Oh, and I've invited Barnie and Dinah to dinner next Friday.'

'OK. Anything else you've let me in for?'

'No,' she answered serenely, 'that's all for the moment.'

He laughed. 'I must go. The class starts in ten minutes and I still have things to prepare. Love you.'

Max Allerdyce replaced the phone and went up the open staircase to his studio, his mind still on his wife. It seemed that at last she was getting back on her feet, he thought with relief. He'd been surprised it had taken so long, when initially she'd appeared unscathed – on a high, perhaps, from unearthing facts the police had missed. Of course the loss of the contract was a blow, but she'd always bounced back before. In fact, it had been her supreme self-confidence that first attracted him, and though at times it could irritate, it was still the quality he most loved in her. And to be fair, he conceded as he set up the easels, it was hardly surprising she'd suffered some reaction, when she'd twice narrowly escaped death herself.

The front door bell interrupted his musings and, whistling softly to himself, he ran down the stairs to let in the first of his students.

The following day was a Friday, and Rona spent it at the local library, going through archives and old newspapers and making numerous photocopies.

It wasn't until mid-afternoon that, almost guiltily, she fast-forwarded a century or two, to reports of the murder Lindsey had mentioned. It was, as her sister had said, part of the town's recent history, but Rona admitted to herself that her own brush with murder had left her with a morbid curiosity.

The story she read was a tragic one: four-year-old Charlotte Spencer had been knocked down and killed by Barry Pollard, whose blood/alcohol level was found to be just over the limit. His drinking – apparently totally out of character – had been a direct result of receiving his divorce papers, and he had broken down in court, overcome with guilt and remorse. His relatively light sentence caused predictable outrage, and within days of his release, he was attacked outside a pub and stabbed to death. Charlotte's father was convicted of his murder.

Rona's heart contracted as the child's photograph appeared on screen, a curly-haired little girl laughing at the camera. Abruptly she switched off the monitor, collected her papers, and went out into the warm sunshine.

'I invited both girls to Sunday lunch,' Avril Parish said flatly, 'but they don't want to come.'

Her husband lowered his newspaper. 'I'm sure they never said that.'

'Oh, they made excuses, of course. Lindsey's expecting Hugh – *again* – and Rona and Max will be up in Buckford.'

'What are they doing up there?'

'Rona's taken it into her head to write about the town for its eight-hundredth anniversary, which, mind you, isn't till next year, so I don't know what the rush is. You'd think they could have put it off for a week.'

'Well, the invitation was rather short notice, love,' Tom said placatingly. 'They'll have made plans.'

'That's right, take their side, as usual.'

He sighed, took off his reading glasses and polished them. If this was a foretaste of retirement, he'd rather stay on at the bank. Trouble was, he hadn't the option. The heart attack he'd suffered a few months back had sapped his strength and he still tired easily. Though he'd fought against it, it had been decreed that early retirement was the sensible course, but as the weeks remorselessly ticked past, the prospect filled him with increasing dread.

What would he *do,* for God's sake? It wasn't as though he'd a host of hobbies he was longing to indulge in. He wasn't much of a golfer, nor particularly interested in stamp collecting, though he still had a few albums he'd embarked on in his youth. For nearly forty years his life had been intrinsically bound up with the bank, involving daily inter-action with a host of people, many of them coming to him for help or advice. He revelled in its bustling activity, the challenge of meeting targets, discussions with senior staff

9

– in short, holding a position of authority; unlike at home, where he was frequently made to feel useless and in the way.

And that, he admitted to himself, as he replaced his glasses and retreated once again behind his paper, was the crux. How would he and Avril get on, when they were thrown together all the time? As it was, the weekends were more than enough, and, to his shame, by Sunday evening he was longing to escape back to work.

He glanced surreptitiously at his wife, who was flicking through a magazine with patent lack of interest. How had they come to this? he wondered sadly. They'd been in love when they married and, as far as he remembered, for quite a while after. There had been happy family holidays with the twins, evenings when they booked a babysitter and went out for meals or to the theatre. But over the years, without really noticing, they'd drifted apart. For a long time now their love-making had been practically non-existent and they no longer seemed to have anything to say to each other. His illness had briefly brought them closer, but as soon as it was clear he wasn't going to die, she'd retreated again. It occurred to him, with a jolt, that Avril might be dreading his retirement just as much as he was.

Laying aside his paper, he went to look at the photographs arranged on the corner table. Almost obscured at the back was their official wedding group and he reached to pick it up, experiencing a welter of emotions as he looked down at his radiant bride, and at his younger self, smiling nervously and holding tightly on to her hand.

'What on earth are you doing?'

He jumped. 'Looking at our wedding picture.'

'Why?'

To remind himself of past happiness? He answered obliquely, 'We were two different people, weren't we?'

'A couple of innocents,' she agreed acidly, 'who believed in Happy Ever After.'

He turned to face her, the photograph still in his hand. 'And haven't you been?'

For a long minute she held his eyes before turning back to the magazine. 'Oh, you know what they say: "Into each life some rain must fall."'

'*Are* you happy, Avril?' he persisted, suddenly, urgently, needing to know.

But she wouldn't be drawn. 'What's happy?' she asked rhetorically. 'I reckon we've done as well as most people. At least we're still together.'

'When I retire,' he said on impulse, 'we should do something really special. Go on a world trip or something.'

She looked at him in amazement. 'Tom Parish, what has got into you today?'

'Seriously, would you like to? It's ages since we did anything – exciting.'

'That's true enough.'

'So?'

'So we'll wait and see what your package is before we decide how to spend it.' And, ending the discussion, she determinedly picked up the magazine.

Dispiritedly he replaced the photograph and returned to his chair.

Mum really didn't need to be so negative all the time, Lindsey thought irritably as she turned on the shower. Pops was a saint to put up with her.

The thought, taking her unawares, gave her pause. It had never occurred to her to analyse her parents' relationship; they were simply themselves, unchanging over the years while she and Ro had grown from babies to schoolgirls to wives. And ex-wives, she added ironically. Men may come and men may go, but they went on for ever. Except that they didn't, of course. Pops's heart attack had been an indication of that. They were mortal, and one day, unthinkable though it might be, they would die. So – eat, drink and be merry, and all the rest of it.

11

She was thinking in clichés this evening, but nevertheless, now that she considered it, there didn't seem much merriment in her parents' marriage. Soaping herself vigorously, she examined this new and disturbing idea. Of course they were *fond* of each other; look how Mum had panicked when Pops was ill. Perhaps it was just that they took each other for granted. Perhaps, after a certain number of years, all married couples did; she wasn't in a position to know.

But Mum always seemed so discontented these days, making no attempt to look her best. It was years since she'd worn make-up except on special occasions, and without it her pale skin and colourless brows lacked definition. Nor did she dress smartly any more; all her blouses and skirts looked the same, and she simply flung an old duffle coat over them to go out.

Admittedly, her mother's latest grievance, and the cause of all this analysis, was at least understandable: namely, that instead of dutifully going home for Sunday lunch, she'd be spending the weekend with Hugh. Lindsey conceded that she had a point; she herself knew, better than anyone, that she was playing with fire in taking up with him again. Their marriage had been a disaster, a see-sawing emotional maelstrom from which, at the time, she had been thankful to escape. He had a furious temper that could spring up from nowhere, and though he'd never actually hit her, he'd come close to it several times. The only reason she'd stayed so long was the strength of the physical attraction between them, and it was that same attraction, infuriatingly undiminished, that made it so hard to withstand him now.

When they split up, he'd arranged a transfer to the Guildford branch of his accountancy firm and there had been no further contact between them until, earlier this year, he had written to say he'd made a mistake and wanted her back.

She lathered shampoo into her long dark hair, massaging her scalp and lifting her face to the stream of water as she recalled the panic she'd felt, the determination not to let him back into her life. But events had overtaken them, giving him the opportunity to gain a foothold which, so far, she'd been unable – or unwilling – to dislodge. One thing was certain, though: she didn't want him transferring back to Marsborough. As she'd hinted to Rona, the present situation suited her well enough, though she accepted it could not continue. Ro was right; it wasn't fair to Hugh to let him rearrange his professional life, and then shut the door in his face. She owed it to him to make plain there was no future for them, and to do so before he achieved a transfer.

She stepped out of the shower, towelled herself dry and padded through to the bedroom. Still, there was no time to plan any speeches now, she told herself, switching on the hairdryer; there was still the pastry to make, and he'd be here in an hour. Time enough to work it out on Monday – which, as she ruefully admitted, was what she told herself every week.

Max was cooking the meal, as he always did when he was home.

'How did you get on at the library?' he asked Rona, who was leaning against a counter watching him as she sipped her customary vodka.

'I unearthed some nuggets that might be worth following up. One thing I'd like to look at while we're there is the parish church; some Royalists barricaded themselves in it during the Civil War.'

'Have you decided how you'll plan the series?'

'A few ideas. Nothing more.' She watched him slurp a generous amount of wine into the sauce.

'Pity it's not Marsborough celebrating its eight-hundredth. You'll be wearing a track up and down, and it must be a good two and a half hours' drive.'

'I've been thinking about that,' she admitted. 'I think I'll spend a couple of nights a week there, at least in the early stages.'

He turned to look at her, wooden spoon in hand. 'Planning to desert me, are you?'

'Not at all; you spend Monday and Tuesday nights at Farthings, and I'll be home on Wednesday. You won't notice the difference, and it would only be for about four weeks, while I do the initial research. After that, the odd day-trip should suffice.'

He grunted, turning back to the cooker. 'Have you booked us in anywhere for tomorrow?'

'Yes, the Tavistock, right in the centre of town.'

'Hope it's not too noisy.'

She laughed. 'Don't be such an old fuddy-duddy. It's only for one night.'

'Is that where you'll base yourself?'

'At that price? Hardly; I'll find a B&B.' She sniffed appreciatively. 'That smells good.'

'It will be,' he said complacently. 'Now make yourself useful and lay the table. It's nearly ready.'

'Yes, Chef.' She reached up and kissed the back of his neck.

'And don't interfere with the cook, or he won't be responsible for the consequences.'

'Promises, promises!' she said, and went to do as he asked.

Two

For the last few weeks, since she'd been feeling unwell, the events of a few years ago had been preying on her mind, and, for the first time, Edna Rosebury began to question whether she'd been right to keep silent.

At the time, it had seemed that passing on what she'd seen would simply have caused trouble and benefited no one. What was done was done, and nothing she could have said would have changed anything. But the niggling doubts that she'd suppressed were now resurfacing to torment her.

With both hands on the arms of her chair, she eased herself upright and stood for a moment, stretching her back. It did her no good to sit still for too long; her old joints seized up and made walking painful. And if she couldn't walk, she reflected, life wouldn't be worth living. It had been one of her passions all her life, and with her great friend Maisie she had over the years covered most of the county, its hills, its moorlands and its valleys. But Maisie had been dead these ten years or more. Now, most of her walking was done late at night, when there was no one around to approach her, to ask if she was all right and if she'd like them to see her home.

She loved the old town when it was sleeping, when the only movement apart from her own was the sleek shadow of a cat on its nightly prowl, the only sound the occasional hoot of an owl from the trees in the churchyard. Sometimes, in the warm summer nights, she'd come upon a couple of young lovers huddled in a doorway, oblivious of her presence, and

15

would be touched by a fleeting sadness. True, she had never known a man's love, but her life had been filled with children, generation after generation of them, whom she had taught at Sunday School and who, for the most part, had kept in touch and later sent their own children into her care.

And it was, of course, on one of these nightly rambles that she had seen . . . She clamped her mind shut on the unwelcome memory. Had Maisie still been around at the time, she would have had someone with whom to discuss it, and together they might have reached a different decision. But it was too late to worry about that.

The stiffness having eased, she made her way across the room and, supporting herself on the sill, stood at her window looking out across the square. With the church, the post office and the pub, it was the heart of the old town, virtually untouched by the modernity that intruded on the outskirts, and the view from this house where she'd been born hadn't changed over the years. The pub sign, with its familiar face, long dark hair and goatee beard, had been her weather guide for over sixty years, since she could gauge by the angle of its swing the direction and strength of the wind. Glancing at it now, she wondered, as she often did, if anyone else appreciated the poignancy of its name – the King's Head – when, over four hundred years ago, the king depicted on the sign had lost his.

As she watched, Gordon Breen emerged from his front door, crossed his garden to the gate in the fence, and let himself into the churchyard. She glanced at her watch. Just after eleven. Nuala would have finished cleaning by now, and would shortly be coming across to check on her. She was a good girl and Edna was fond of her, but she did so wish she wouldn't fuss.

She was turning from the window when a couple on the pavement outside caught her eye, bent over a map of some sort while their dog sniffed interestedly at a lamp post.

Tourists, no doubt. She moved aside as the woman glanced in her direction, unwilling to be caught studying them, and after a moment they crossed the road and went through the gateway into the church grounds. They were in luck; Gordon was always ready to answer questions about his beloved church and its history.

Smiling to herself, Edna returned to her chair and prepared to await her niece's arrival.

'How old do you think it is?' Rona asked, as they walked up the long, curved path to the church.

Max shrugged. 'Eight hundred years, if the town's anything to go by, though some parts will be older than others.'

'Amazing to think it's stood here, virtually unscathed, throughout wars, famines and pestilence.'

'Pestilence?' Max repeated with a laugh. 'Where did you dig that up?'

'Plague, then.'

'Whatever, but I bet you we'll find that it's locked.'

They crossed the tiled porch and Rona lifted the latch on the heavy oak door, which swung inwards.

'I should have taken you up on that,' she told him.

An odour redolent of churches everywhere met their nostrils, compounded of polish and musty old hymn books and strongly scented flowers. Sunshine was streaming through stained-glass windows and lying in pools of crimson and blue on the black and white tiled floor. Rona stared about her at the arched ceiling, the glowing wood of ancient pews, the brilliant colours of the glass.

'It's beautiful!' she murmured, awestruck, and turned quickly as a voice behind her answered, 'Thank you!'

A grey-haired man in sports jacket and flannels, wearing a dog collar, came forward with a smile, his hand held out. 'Always good to hear unsolicited praise,' he said. 'You're most welcome to St Giles's. I'm Gordon Breen, the vicar. Do feel free to look round.'

'Is it all right to bring the dog in?' Rona asked tentatively.

'Of course. Hello, old fellow.' The vicar bent to pat Gus, who waved his tail ingratiatingly.

'We were wondering how old the church is,' Max said.

'The first building on the site was wooden, and burned down in the fourteenth century. They lost no time in starting on this one, though not everything you see is that old, by any means. There've been various alterations over the years, some more sympathetic than others.' He nodded towards a table laden with pamphlets. 'There's a booklet over there, if you're interested.'

'Didn't Royalist soldiers take refuge here during the Civil War?'

'They did. We have one of Cromwell's cannon balls in the vestry, if you'd like to take a look at it.'

'Thank you, we should. I'm Rona Parish, by the way, and this is my husband. The reason we're here is that I'm planning to write a series of articles on Buckford, to coincide with next year's anniversary. I hope you'll let me interview you at some stage on parts of the church's history that aren't in the guide book – scandal among the clergy, and so on?'

He laughed. 'Plenty of scope there! Seriously, though, you'll have stiff competition. I've already been approached more than once.'

'I'm sure, but I want to concentrate on unusual or little-known facts. Each article will have a different theme – the town itself, then its churches, schools, and so on.' She smiled. 'You haven't such a thing as a Fount of All Knowledge, have you? Someone who knows all there is to know about the place, and would be willing to talk to me?'

'Oh, we've several of those. Old Miss Rosebury, across the square, has lived here all her life. I'm sure she'd be delighted to have a new audience for her stories. As to the schools, Catherine Bishop would have been your best bet, but she retired and moved away. She was head teacher of the local primary, which, under one guise or another, dates back several centuries. She actually compiled an archive on it – a kind of scrapbook crammed with all kinds of weird and wonderful facts. It was such a success, she was asked to do one for the grammar school and the college as well.'

'She sounds ideal. Have you any idea where she went?'

'All I remember is that her mother was an invalid and Catherine left to look after her. I could probably find out her address.'

'If you could, it would be fantastic. I wonder – but we've already taken up enough of your time. I'm sure you have things to do.'

'As it happens, Saturday's my day off. I only came in to see if our cleaner had finished.'

'Then we're imposing on your free day,' Max apologized.

'Not at all. If I can help in any way, I'll be delighted.' He turned back to Rona. 'You were going to ask something?'

'It's just that we live in Marsborough, which is rather a long way to commute. It seems more sensible to stay up here for a couple of nights a week, just while I'm gathering material, and I wondered if you could recommend any-where?'

'Oh dear, I'm afraid I don't—' He broke off, frowning and rubbing his chin. 'On second thoughts, though, perhaps I could, though I'd have to check first. How long are you here?'

'We're staying overnight at the Tavistock and driving back tomorrow.'

'Oh, I should be able to let you know by lunchtime. I'll leave a message if you're not there.'

'Thank you, that's very kind.'

'Actually, if it comes off, it might benefit others as well. Now, if you'll excuse me I should be getting back; my wife wants me to look at some new curtains for my study, though I'm not convinced I need them. Stay as long as you like,' he added. 'We usually have church welcomers on hand, but Mr Talbot, whose shift this is, is on holiday. I look forward to meeting you again, Mrs Parish.'

19

He shook hands with them both, and left them to their wandering.

'You'll have to disabuse him of that,' Max commented drily. 'Ms Parish or Mrs Allerdyce, he can take his pick.'

'I hadn't thought of that; the hotel won't know who he means.'

Max laughed. 'They'll look at us in a new light. In the meantime, I suggest we move on. Our time is limited and you want a look at the school, don't you? You'll have plenty of time to prowl round here later.'

'He might expect us at tomorrow's service,' Rona said tentatively.

'No harm in expecting,' Max returned, and held the door open for her.

Buckford College was one of the oldest schools in the country, and renowned worldwide. It was situated a couple of miles north-west of the town, in grounds of several acres that prevented much of the building being seen from the road. In the distance, a game of cricket was in progress.

'No question of just wandering in there,' Max commented. 'Very definitely by appointment only, I'd say. So where next?'

'Let's go back to the hotel, leave the car, and forewarn the receptionist about the vicar phoning. Then we can mooch around till lunchtime. Gus could do with a walk, and I'd like to explore some of those old courtyards and alleyways. I bet they all have a tale to tell.'

In fact, by the time they'd found a slot in the hotel car park and reached the reception desk, Rona was just in time to take the call herself. As she crossed the foyer, she heard the girl say, 'Parish? I don't think—' and hurried forward with a vaguely explanatory smile to take the phone from her.

'Mrs Parish? Gordon Breen here. I'm glad I caught you; I've spoken to the young woman concerned, and she'll be happy to talk to you about the possibility of letting her spare room. Her name is Mrs Nuala Banks, and the address is Two Parsonage Place. If you've a pen handy, I'll give you her phone number.'

Rona fumbled in her bag and wrote it down. 'Thanks so much, Mr Breen, it really is most kind of you.'

'Well, as I said, it might work to everyone's advantage. I hope you'll find it suitable. Oh, and before I forget, my wife tells me Catherine Bishop moved to Marsborough. Isn't that where you live?'

'It is indeed. How very convenient!'

'I hope you manage to track her down. And let me know when you'd like to interview me; I'm usually around.'

Rona guided Max outside again, taking out her mobile as she went. 'A Mrs Nuala Banks. I'll ring her now, and perhaps we can go round straight away.'

'Never one for letting the grass grow, are you?' Max said resignedly.

Nuala Banks agreed to the suggestion and gave directions to the house, a five-minute walk from the hotel. As they'd guessed from its name, Parsonage Place lay behind the church, approached via a footpath that ran between it and the pub.

'Very handy,' Max commented, as they picked their way over the uneven cobbles, 'but I trust there's another entry for motor vehicles. I don't want you parking in some multistorey and having to walk down here at night.'

'Let's not anticipate problems,' Rona said lightly.

Parsonage Place led off to their left, a stone post barring all but pedestrian access. On their right stretched a terrace of some dozen houses, each double-fronted, with a small lawn in front of it and a neatly painted gate. On their left, a low wall ran the length of the road, and parking places were marked out on the tarmac in front of it. Most of them were occupied. Over the wall they could see the church and, farther along, a garden that must belong to the vicarage. The main entrance to the road was indeed at the far end, and it seemed to be from there that the houses were numbered.

They walked the length of the terrace, noting the individual touches that distinguished almost identical houses. Some front doors were glazed, some painted in bright colours. One garden had been paved over, with a terracotta pot in pride of place. Others displayed varying degrees of care, some of the grass being in need of a cut.

Number two, almost at the end, had a solid wooden door and its garden was simply lawn, with no flowerbeds. Rona's knock was answered at once, by a woman about her age with dark, straight hair and a sweet smile. She held out her hand.

'Mr and Mrs Parish?' she said. 'I'm Nuala Banks. Do come—' She broke off as she caught sight of Gus. 'Oh, I'm sorry – would you mind leaving him outside? Unfortunately my son's allergic to dogs. Perhaps you could tie his lead to the gate?'

'Of course.' Max did so, but Rona felt a shaft of disappointment; it seemed she wouldn't have Gus's company during her visits to Buckford.

They found themselves in a narrow hallway, with stairs rising in front of them. There were a couple of doors on the right and one on the left, while beyond the stairs the passage continued to what was presumably the kitchen. Nuala Banks opened the left-hand door and showed them into a long room that extended the depth of the house. The far end doubled as a dining room, and through the French windows they could see a garden with a swing and climbing frame.

'Please sit down.' As they did so, she turned to Rona. 'Mr Breen said you'd be coming for a couple of nights a week?' she began hesitantly.

'Yes, just for a month in the first instance. I don't know if he told you, but I'm a journalist, and I'm planning to write some articles about Buckford. Since we live in Marsborough, it seems sensible to spend some days up here while I'm doing my initial research. And I should explain that Rona Parish is my professional name, which, admittedly, I use most of the time, though officially I suppose I'm Mrs Allerdyce.'

Nuala Banks nodded. 'I think I've heard of you,' she said. 'Perhaps I've read something of yours?'

Rona avoided Max's eye, knowing he disliked the publicity which, earlier in the year, had catapulted her into the headlines. She said obliquely, 'I write for *Chiltern Life*.'

'Then I must have seen it at the dentist. But I owe you an explanation, too: you'll be my first paying guest, so this is by way of an experiment.' Her eyes dropped. 'My husband left me three years ago, and things have been a bit straitened lately. When you said you were looking for somewhere, Mr Breen kindly thought it might help.'

Nuala Banks had been more honest in her explanation than she had, Rona thought ruefully. 'I'm so sorry. You have a little boy, you said?'

'Yes, Will. He's ten. My father lives with us, too. Since his accident, he can't go upstairs, so he has the room across the hall as a bedsitter. That's why, though we have only three bedrooms upstairs, there's one spare. Perhaps you'd like to see it?'

They followed her up the steep staircase to the first floor, where she opened the door to one of the front rooms.

'It's a bit basic,' Nuala said apologetically. 'All Dad's furniture moved downstairs with him. Still, the washbasin's handy. We have only the one bathroom, I'm afraid, though there's a loo and shower room downstairs.'

'It looks very comfortable,' Rona said. The room was large and square, with a double bed under an old-fashioned candlewick spread. The only other items of furniture were a wardrobe, a dressing-table with a frilled valance, and an armchair. She walked to the window and leaned on the sill. Over to the left she could see the church set in its grounds, while immediately opposite, at the end of a long, rambling garden, was the handsome stone house they'd assumed to be the vicarage. Nearer the wall, about a third of the way down the garden, an overgrown summerhouse nestled against the hedge.

'There's a clock radio by the bed,' Nuala was saying, 'and if you'd like television, you could borrow the small portable from the kitchen.'

'I think I can manage two nights a week without one,' Rona smiled, turning from the window. 'I spend most evenings working, anyway. What would be useful, though, would be a small table for my laptop and an upright chair, if that's possible.'

'Of course – no problem.'

'Well, if you're prepared to take me on, I'd be more than happy to come.'

'We haven't mentioned finances,' Nuala began tentatively, 'but I've not really had time to—'

'If it would help, I could pay for the whole week,' Rona offered, and as Nuala started to protest, she went on quickly, 'You'll be holding it for me even when I'm not here, which means you can't let it to anyone else.'

'I wouldn't even consider it,' Nuala said firmly. 'As I said, this is a new venture, and no one's likely to be queuing up.'

'If you're sure then. Incidentally, will it be bed and break-fast, or would an evening meal be available? If not, it doesn't matter; I'm sure I could eat at the pub.'

Nuala lifted her shoulders helplessly. 'Again, this has all happened so quickly, I've not thought it through. But you'd be welcome to eat with us, if that would help?'

'It'd be fine, if you don't mind. I don't want to impose on your family life, but as I said, I'd spend the evenings working in my room so I shouldn't get in your way. As to your charges, why don't we leave it till you've had a chance to discuss them with someone?'

Nuala Banks looked relieved. 'That would be great, thanks. I'll let you know in a day or two. Have you any idea when we can expect you?'

Rona glanced at Max. 'It won't be this coming week – I've a few things to sort out. How about a week on Monday, which will be – what? – the sixteenth? It'll always be Monday and Tuesday nights that—'

She broke off as a voice from downstairs called loudly, 'Mum? There's a dog tied to the gate. Did you know?'

They smiled at each other and moved out on to the landing, looking down at the boy who stood with a foot on the bottom stair. He had his mother's dark hair and eyes and was dressed in some kind of camouflage outfit.

'Jungle warfare,' Nuala Banks explained softly. Then, raising her voice, 'This is Mr and Mrs Allerdyce, Will, and the dog belongs to them. Mrs Allerdyce will be staying with us for a couple of nights a week, though she'll leave the dog at home. Say hello to her.'

'Hi,' the boy said, suddenly shy.

'Hello, Will. And it's Rona, if that's OK?'

He nodded, standing aside for them as they came downstairs. Rona handed Nuala her card, and it was agreed that the terms should be decided by telephone over the next few days.

They were halfway down the path when Max turned back to ask about a parking space across the road.

'Officially there's one per house, and three set aside for visitors, but not everyone has a car. There shouldn't be a problem.'

With the final detail settled, they untied the patently relieved Gus and made their way back to the pub for lunch.

'Apparently that woman who did the school archives lives in Marsborough,' Rona said, spearing a rogue tomato.

'Fate!' Max returned, with his mouth full.

'I'll look her up in the phone book when we get back.'

'What do you want to do this afternoon?'

'We never got our mooch, did we? And we certainly owe Gus a walk, after the indignity of being tied to the gate.'

'Talking of Gus, I suppose you want me to dog-sit while you're up here.'

Rona shrugged. 'I'd much prefer to have him with me, but it seems we've no choice.'

Someone had left a copy of the local paper at the next table and, having finished his lunch, Max reached across for it.

'Anything that could be useful?' Rona enquired idly.

'Typical local rag, by the look of it. Death and disaster on every page.'

'Literally?'

'Well, you know, the usual spate of burglaries and muggings and people dropping dead at their Golden Wedding party. That kind of thing.'

'No murders?' Rona asked lightly, and Max shot her a glance.

'Not that I can see, thank God.'

'There was quite a well-publicized one some years back. Lindsey mentioned it, and I came across it in the library archives.'

'Came across it, or specifically looked for it?'

Rona smiled. 'A bit of both,' she admitted. 'No need to be apprehensive, though; this time it was all cut and dried and the murderer's safely behind bars. Rather a sad case, actually. A drunk driver killed a child, got a light sentence, and was murdered by the child's father on his release.'

'So the court favoured the drunk driver over the bereaved father?'

'"Cold-blooded" and "premeditated" figured a lot in the reporting, which I suppose is fair comment. He must have been dreaming it up all the time the driver was inside.'

'And now his wife has neither her child nor her husband.'

They were both silent for a moment, then Max tossed the paper back on to the chair.

'Come on,' he said, 'let's go and have that walk.'

Marsborough, developed during the eighteenth century, had the spacious elegance of Bath or Cheltenham. Buckford, several hundred years older, was quite different. According to the tourist brochure, there was an Old Town and a New

Town, though as Rona remarked, they merged into one another and it was hard to tell where each started and ended.

'For instance,' she said, 'the square we've just left is, it says here, at the heart of the old town, bordered by St Giles's Church, the King's Head pub and an ancient building now housing the post office. But more modern houses have been slotted in, haven't they, such as the vicarage and the terrace in Parsonage Place, which I'd guess are both Victorian.'

Beyond the square there was less ambiguity, and they found a maze of narrow streets and alleyways, hidden court-yards, and worn stone steps leading from one level to another. In many cases, the owners of the buildings had renovated their properties and, though careful to preserve their old-world charm, had turned them into boutiques, galleries and coffee shops.

Max and Rona wandered through the streets, pausing to look at an ancient well, two buildings that met across a narrow alley, the Counting House and the town hall. Another square, with a stone cross in the centre, was the site of the weekly market, and sprawled down one side of it was St Stephen's Primary School – presumably, as Rona remarked to Max, the one where Catherine Bishop had taught. The original building was unprepossessing, of dark stone and with small, high windows, but new classrooms had been built in the play-ground, with, doubtless, all the modern equipment education now demanded. St Stephen's Church, its original sponsor, had, according to the guide book, collapsed back in the nine-teenth century and the public library now stood on the site.

'And here we are, back in the twenty-first century,' Max commented, as they emerged from the cobbles to find them-selves facing a glassed-in shopping mall. 'Something to suit all tastes, I suppose.'

'I think it melds together rather well,' Rona said. 'After all, building went on continuously over the centuries, so the changes were gradual. Our hotel dates from the 1920s, and even that's old hat now.'

27

'There's certainly enough here to keep you busy,' Max said. 'You won't forget you've a home to come back to, will you?'

'No chance of that,' Rona assured him, squeezing his arm, and added with a twinkle, 'I'd miss Gus too much!'

Beth Spencer stood at the window of her sitting room, watching her two sons racing round the garden. Saturday afternoon, and all over the town – the world, she thought wildly – families would be together, gardening, shopping, going to the cinema, spending what the newspapers called 'quality time' together. If she went out, she'd see fathers everywhere, pushing prams or carrying toddlers on their shoulders. That was why she stayed home on Saturdays.

Would life *ever* get back to normal? she wondered. Even when Alan was eventually released, could they take up where they'd left off? When he'd been found guilty, she had wanted to scoop up the boys – her precious, remaining children – and flee the country. She couldn't, of course. For one thing, the prison was here in Buckford, and Alan needed her as never before. For another, Harry had just joined Josh at the college, which, to her surprised gratitude, had been endlessly supportive of both them and her. And even more importantly, if she'd run away, everyone would have assumed she believed Alan was guilty, which was not and never had been the case.

Admittedly, Lottie's death had put an almost unbearable strain on their marriage, and instead of bringing them closer, seemed to have forced them apart. It was chiefly her fault, Beth acknowledged; because Charlotte had been with her father when she was killed, Beth had held Alan responsible, thereby adding to his own burden of guilt. Ironically, it had taken the death of Barry Pollard and Alan's conviction for his murder that had brought them close again.

Briefly, she wondered how preparations for the appeal were going. The trouble, as her solicitor had explained, was the weight of evidence against him – his undeniable motive, his presence at the murder scene, and – most damning of all – their own kitchen knife, smeared with the man's blood and hidden in their garage.

She put her hands to her head, fingers clutching her scalp. She *must* stop reliving it, or she'd go crazy. Tomorrow was a visiting day, and she must be her outwardly bright, optimistic self. All three of them depended on her for that.

She turned from the window, and her eyes fell on the framed photograph that had been in all the papers: Lottie on her fourth birthday, with the whole of life before her. How could they have known, as they snapped her laughing at them, that her life was already almost over?

With dragging footsteps, Beth went through to the kitchen to sort out the children's tea.

Three

It was a tradition that Edna came to tea on Sundays, and as always she'd declined Nuala's offer to collect her in the car. 'I hope I'm capable of walking that far,' she'd retorted, as she always did.

Today, though, she was looking older and decidedly more frail, Nuala thought anxiously. That spark that had always been so much a part of her seemed to be missing. She glanced from her aunt to her father, sitting in the chair with his Zimmer beside him, and held down a sigh.

'I've a spot of news for you,' she began brightly. 'Guess what? I'm going to be a landlady!'

Edna looked at her blankly over her teacup. 'I thought that was only in wartime,' she said.

'Not land*girl,* Auntie, land*lady*: I'm going into the B&B business.'

Her aunt frowned, and Nuala went on quickly, 'A couple from Marsborough were up for the weekend; the wife's a journalist and she's going to write about the town for the anniversary. Anyway, they were talking to Gordon in the church, and she asked him if he could recommend anywhere for her to stay a couple of nights a week, while she did her research. And he thought of me and the spare room. Wasn't that kind of him?'

Edna looked worried. 'But things aren't that bad, are they, dear? Financially, I mean?'

'They're not desperate, no, but a little extra always comes in handy.'

Edna turned to her brother-in-law. 'What do you think of this, Jack?'

He lifted his shoulders. 'Can't see the harm in it, and if it helps finances, why not? As Nuala says, it's only two nights a week, and she'll be out all day.'

Edna frowned. 'I don't like the thought of strangers in the house.'

Nuala smiled. 'Only one, Auntie, and she's perfectly respectable, I assure you! In fact, her name sounds familiar. Rona Parish? Does it ring a bell?'

Edna shook her head.

'Well, anyway, I showed her the room and she seemed to like it. I'll ask Jonty Welles tomorrow what I ought to charge.' Nuala smiled. 'Gordon says she's going to dig up all the local scandal!'

To her surprise, her aunt's face darkened. 'I trust she'll stick to what's safely in the past.'

Nuala's eyebrows went up. 'Has there been something recent, then?'

Edna gazed into her teacup and did not reply.

'Auntie? You know something? Come on, out with it!'

Before Edna could reply, the door burst open to admit Will.

'Hello, darling,' Nuala greeted him. 'I've saved you some currant cake, but wash your hands first and change your shoes.'

As he went under protest to obey, she turned quickly back to Edna, but the moment was lost, and whatever her aunt might have told her lost with it.

'More tea, Dad?' she asked resignedly, and at his nod, went to collect his cup and saucer.

The phone was ringing as they opened their front door, and Rona lifted it to hear her mother's acid tones.

'You're home, then,' she said without preamble. 'Did you enjoy yourselves?'

'Hello, Mum. Yes, thanks, and what's more, I made some useful contacts.'

'That's all right, then. Well, since your weekends are so busy nowadays, perhaps you can spare the time to come for supper on Wednesday? That's not one of Max's work evenings, is it?'

'No.' Rona raised questioning eyebrows at Max, who'd heard the invitation. He shrugged resignedly, and she went on, 'Thanks, Mum, that would be fine. About seven thirty?'

'Yes, and don't be late, or the meal will spoil. Lindsey's agreed to come too, since Hugh won't be around.'

Rona pulled a rueful face at her husband. 'Look forward to seeing you, then. Love to Pops.'

'That'll be a barrel of laughs,' Max commented, as she replaced the phone.

Rona sighed. 'I don't know what's got into her. It's as if she has a permanent grudge against us these days.'

He picked up their cases and started up the stairs. 'Quite a social whirl we're having; isn't it this Friday the Trents are coming?'

'Lord, I'd forgotten that. Yes, Barnie rang to confirm it.'

'You'll be off to Buckford for a rest,' Max teased.

'Hardly. Thanks for coming with me, love. At least I'm not venturing into unknown territory, and I know I've a bed waiting for me.'

To Rona's frustration, there was an entire column of Bishops in the local phone directory. Four had the initial 'C', but she didn't strike lucky with any of them.

'I'll have to ask the vicar if he can be more specific,' she said.

'I thought it sounded too easy,' Max remarked, switching on the kettle. 'Anyway, it's not a number-one priority, is it, seeing this woman?'

'It would be a good way to ease myself into the project.'

'She mightn't want you cribbing her research.'

'I've no intention of cribbing,' Rona retorted hotly. 'I was just hoping for a kick-start. Still, I'll have to manage without her for now.'

Rona spent the following day devising a working outline of the articles she planned. She'd intended to start with education, but since she'd been unable to contact Mrs Bishop, turned her attention to the development of the town. In any event, the order in which she wrote the articles wouldn't govern that in which they appeared.

She took out the photocopies she'd made at the library and reread them, finding them more interesting now she could picture the places they described. She was particularly intrigued by the history of the King's Head pub, where she and Max had lunched. It had already been an ancient building when Charles I's men refreshed themselves there.

The research, as always, engrossed her, and it was only when Gus whined from the foot of the stairs that she realized it was past five o'clock and he'd not had his walk. Reluctantly she put away her papers and they set off together up the alleyway to the park above the town.

As the dog romped ahead over the grassy slopes, Rona's thoughts began to fall into shape, as they so often did up here. It was always a restorative to stride along the paths with the wind in her hair and the town laid out below, giving her a sense of distance, both physical and mental, from current problems. Down there, family commitments and a dozen responsibilities awaited her, while up here there was just herself and the dog and the wide open spaces.

Mentally, she reviewed the people she'd met during the weekend: Gordon Breen, the vicar; Nuala Banks and her dark-eyed little boy; the landlord of the pub. No doubt a few weeks from now she'd know them all better, and maybe revise her initial opinions of them. She pictured the bedroom that would be hers during her visits, its window giving on to the church and the vicarage garden with its oddly shaped

summerhouse. And she thought of the sprawling school buildings near the market cross, where Catherine Bishop had
compiled her own archives. Might she, as Max had hinted,
resent Rona's project? She could only hope not.

Back home again, she fed Gus and, deciding against a
take-away, phoned Dino's to book their usual table,
explaining she'd be dining alone.

'We look forward to seeing you, Signora,' came the deeply
accented voice. Lindsey maintained that Dino had been born
Joe Bloggs and taken his name from Dean's Crescent, the location of the restaurant; but while Rona conceded the name might
be suspect, she was convinced the man was genuinely Italian.

Two hours later, she was duly escorted to the alcove, and
Gus settled in his accustomed place under the table. Dino
himself, full of effusive welcome, spread a snow-white
napkin on her lap, set a small dish of olives in front of her,
and handed her the menu. She had barely started to read it
when a familiar voice accosted her.

'Rona! We were wondering if we'd find you here!'

'Magda – and Gavin!' She stood up to receive their greet-
ings. 'I didn't realize you were back.'

'We barely are,' Magda told her. 'We only landed this
morning. I was just saying I must give you a buzz; it's ages
since we spoke.' She glanced at the single place-setting. 'Max
not coming?'

'No, it's one of his teaching evenings.'

'Then may we join you?'

'Of course; I'll be glad of the company.'

An extra chair was brought and places laid, and Rona
watched as her friends settled themselves. They were a
striking couple, both tall and thin, she just under six foot,
he just over. But while Gavin's thick hair was ash-blond,
Magda's, curving into her cheeks in a casual bob, was as
black as a crow, as were her large, heavy-lidded eyes and
thick brows, a legacy from her Italian mother.

The three of them went back a long way; Magda had been

Rona's closest friend at both school and university, and probably still was. Often caustic and astringent, she made a point of speaking her mind, and had lost not a few friends in the process. They'd had their spats over the years, but mutual affection always drew them back.

As for Gavin Ridgeway, he was the first man Rona had loved, and she'd been considering his proposal when she met Max. It was a memory that still embarrassed her, though the rest of them took it in their stride. As Magda pointed out, in a town the size of Marsborough, everyone had been out with everyone else at some stage.

Rona glanced across, trying to view him dispassionately. His features were too irregular to be handsome, but they had an angular virility that women – herself included – found attractive. Briefly, their eyes met and in his was the usual hint of amused speculation. Rona quickly looked away.

Magda was studying the menu. 'Good, I see they're still doing their *affettati misti*. I'll start with that.'

They made their selections, and when the hovering waiter approached, Magda relayed them in Italian. 'So,' she began, turning to Rona, 'what have you been up to? I haven't seen any of your articles lately.'

'No, it's – taken me longer than I expected to get going again.'

'After the Harvey fiasco?' Magda had missed the drama, having been abroad on a lengthy buying trip. She owned a string of boutiques dotted round the county. 'But you're working now, surely?'

Her tone made Rona thankful she had plans to outline, and she told them about Buckford and the weekend she and Max had just spent there. 'A town as old as that,' she finished, 'is sure to have its legends – heroes, ghosts, miscarriages of justice. All I have to do is unearth them.' She glanced at Magda. 'You've got a boutique there, haven't you?'

'Yes, but I'd be no help on the history angle. My interest in the place is limited to movement of stock and sales figures.'

The drinks were brought, followed by their first courses. 'Now,' Rona invited, as they took up their forks, 'tell me about the trip. Gavin certainly looks the better for it.'

Earlier in the year, he had succumbed to a viral infection that took its toll before finally fizzling out, and the holiday had been intended to put him back on his feet. Judging by his clear eyes and healthy tan, it had worked admirably.

'It was totally wonderful,' Magda enthused, spearing a fig. 'Perpetual sunshine, interesting food and nothing to do but please ourselves all day, being as lazy or adventurous as the mood took us. Imagine, Ro, we actually sailed on Lake Titicaca – remember doing it in Geography? – and were lucky enough to be in Rio for one of their fiestas.'

'Then we went on to the States,' Gavin put in, topping up their glasses, 'and flew over the Grand Canyon in a helicopter. It was pretty breezy, and to be honest, I was glad to be back on terra firma. The views were magnificent, though, and it was great seeing more of the country than just the usual stopovers in New York and Washington.'

'The Yanks always sound so aggressive, don't they?' Magda observed reflectively.

Rona raised an eyebrow. 'Do they?'

'Think about it: we *turn off* the ignition, they *kill* it; we *pick up* the phone, they *grab* it; we *press* the bell, they *punch* it; we *take to* the road, they *hit* it. Not to mention that ghastly punching-the-air gesture that's overtaken the more sportsmanlike raised arm. Perhaps they just like to seem tough. Still –' she pushed back her plate – 'I love them in spite of it. So tell me about the family: how's that enigmatic husband of yours?'

Rona smiled; Max and Magda were established sparring partners. 'Fine. He's working on a commission for postage stamps at the moment.'

'Gummed or self-adhesive?'

Gavin gave a bark of laughter. 'Ignore her, Rona. It sounds most impressive.'

Magda shrugged. 'Can't say I'd care for black franking all over my works of art, but *chacun,* as they say. And twin sister? What's she up to these days?'

Rona grimaced. 'Dallying with Hugh again.'

'Never!' Magda gazed at her in astonishment. 'I thought she couldn't wait to see the back of him?'

'So did we all. But he decided it was all a mistake and he wanted her back. She withstood him for a while, but then he rode to our rescue in the Harvey affair, and since then he's been coming up every weekend and is angling to be moved back here.'

'If she gives in, history will repeat itself,' Magda said darkly. 'Leopards don't change their spots.'

They lingered over coffee and *petits fours,* and it was after eleven when they rose to leave. To Rona's embarrassment, Gavin insisted on paying for her meal.

'It's no big deal, for heaven's sake,' he insisted, refusing her attempts to contribute. 'Anyway, you added to our enjoyment, didn't she, Maggie?'

'Of course she did.' Magda kissed Rona's cheek lightly. 'Love to the family, and let me know how the Buckford project proceeds.'

They separated on the pavement, the Ridgeways to collect their car and Rona, declining their offer of a lift, to walk home with Gus.

'Magda and Gavin are back,' she told Max when, as always, he phoned to say good night. 'They came into Dino's, so we sat together.'

'Has Gavin recovered from that bug?'

'Yes, he seems fine. They've had a fantastic holiday, by all accounts, in South America and the States. Do you know, Max, I've just worked out that I've known Magda nearly thirty years! Isn't that frightening? I can still remember her first day at school; Sally Tompkins pulled her pigtails, and Magda went for her!'

Max laughed. 'And she's been going for people ever since!'

Rona remembered his words as she sat reading in bed, and, laying down her book, she let her thoughts drift back across the years to her first meeting with Magda, when they were both ten years old. She'd been a new girl at the beginning of the summer term, and consequently had to brave a class where everyone else knew each other. However, Rona's initial twinge of sympathy rapidly dissipated as it became clear the newcomer could fend for herself. After the episode with Sally, Magda seemed to regard them all as potential enemies and made no attempt to form friendships. Even then, she stood out from the others, in the way she spoke as much as in her looks. Thinking back, Rona realized that her clear diction and impeccable grammar came from having learned English as a second language.

The turning point came one day when Lindsey had been kept at home with earache, and Rona just happened to walk out of the school gates alongside Magda. Among the familiar, homely figures of the other mothers was an exotic creature in scarlet skirt and white lacy top who, to Rona's alarm, swept down upon them, catching them both up in her enthusiastic embrace.

'Ah, *cara*, this is one of your friends?' She bent down to smile into Rona's face. 'You will come home for tea, yes? There are some *copate*, which I am sure you will enjoy.'

Rona glanced wildly at Magda, whose face was as scarlet as her mother's skirt. 'Mama—' she began, but her mother was already shepherding them both down the road like a mother hen with her chicks. 'We will telephone to your mother and tell her where you are,' she declared. 'Then she will not worry, no?' She had said *mahzzer* and *wahrry*.

Magda, meanwhile, was in a turmoil of embarrassment. 'Mama is Italian,' she whispered to Rona, as though that explained everything.

And it probably did. Over the following months Rona came to idolize Paola King, revelling in her vibrant colours, her full-bellied laugh and her obvious joy in life, all of which were such a stark contrast to her own mother. The Kings' house was a semi-detached, to a passer-by no different from its neighbours; but once inside it became, to Rona's young eyes, an Aladdin's cave. The furniture was subtly foreign, religious pictures and crucifixes hung on the walls, and the floors were spread with brightly coloured rugs instead of carpets. And overlaying it all was its distinctive aroma of exotic breads and pastries, rich meat sauces and succulent pastas.

It became her retreat from teenage angst, disagreements with her mother, exam nerves. With or without Magda, Paola always welcomed her, listened with sympathy to her problems, and sat her down at the kitchen table to whatever delicacy she was in the process of making. The magic always worked, and an hour or so later, Rona would return home with her equilibrium restored, able to face the world again. Looking back, she saw that those times with Paola were some of the most formative of her adolescence, and the only ones she'd not shared with Lindsey. It was only much later that she'd wondered whether Magda's reserve had been a subconscious reaction to her mother's gregariousness.

On that first visit she had duly made her phone call, and Avril, having established she was only in the adjacent street, had raised no objection to her delayed return. 'As long as you do your homework,' she'd added as an afterthought. Then Rona was seated at the table opposite Magda and given a bright-blue mug of milk and the promised *copate,* which turned out to be delicious little wafer-like cakes.

'I'm so glad to meet a friend of Magdalena,' Paola declared, joining them at the table and studying Rona with frank interest. 'She does not make friends easily, eh, *cara mia*? I worry about that.'

'But Magda has lots of friends,' Rona said, with more loyalty than truth, and was rewarded with a flash of gratitude.

'That is so? I am so happy to hear it! My husband always say I fuss too much.'

39

'Is he Italian too?' Rona asked, gaining confidence.

'No, he is as English as you are. We met when he was working in Italy, but he has been moved back here now.' Mrs King glanced ruefully at the cloudy sky outside the window. 'I miss the sunshine,' she said.

And that was how it began. Rona's obvious appreciation of her mother and her home, not to mention her support on the subject of friends, penetrated Magda's prickliness and they did indeed become friends and, apart from a clash or two, had remained so ever since.

Rona smiled sleepily, rearranged her pillow, and turned out the light.

Avril Parish stood at the kitchen sink and stared unseeingly through the window. Tom had already left for work, with that air of suppressed eagerness that both hurt and infuriated her. She knew, though he hadn't said so, that he was dreading his retirement – and so, heaven knew, was she. There were so many things they hadn't discussed. Would she be expected to be home each day to cook his lunch? What of her trips to town, her bridge, her hours at the charity shop? Would she be forced to 'retire' simply because he had?

She turned on the taps, remembering a similar panic when the girls left home for university. How, she'd wondered, would she face the long evenings when Tom dozed over his paper, without their lively chatter to enliven them? Still, the courses had been of limited duration and she was proud of her daughters' achievements. The sense of rejection came later when, though both were working in Marsborough, they elected to share a flat instead of living at home. But they'd always been as thick as thieves, whispering secrets together from early childhood and, whether deliberately or not, making her feel excluded.

She squeezed in the washing-up liquid, her mind still broodingly on her daughters. They hadn't turned out as she'd expected. In fact, nothing had. To start with, they were too independent by half. Rona's downright refusal to take Max's name on her marriage had been bad enough – and raised not a few eyebrows at the bridge club – but when they decided to live apart half the week, she gave up on them. No amount of explanation could make her accept the logic, though Tom, after the initial shock, had come round to it. And admittedly they still seemed happy together. Despite what Lindsey termed their 'semi-detachment', at least they hadn't formally separated, as Lindsey herself had from Hugh.

And that was another bone of contention, Avril thought, determinedly scrubbing at a pan. God knows, Lindsey had put them all through it during the lead-up to her divorce – tantrums, storms of tears, total unreasonableness. But she'd come through it, been offered promotion in her job, and now had her own nice little flat out at Fairhaven. And into this restored harmony Hugh had had the damned nerve to reappear. Even more unbelievably, Lindsey had let him, arousing in her mother an overpowering urge to shake her.

'Haven't you any pride at all?' she had ranted. 'You let that man walk all over you! If you've forgotten what he put you through last time, you've a shorter memory than the rest of us.'

Lindsey's mouth had set in the familiar mutinous line. 'He comes up on my terms, Mum. I know what I'm doing. I've never said I'll take him back.'

'He's as good as back already. Well, don't expect us to pick up the pieces next time, that's all I ask.'

'Don't keep on at her, love,' Tom had said later, in his maddeningly patient way. 'You'll only make her more determined to go her own way.'

'What makes you think she pays a blind bit of notice to anything I say?' she'd retorted. 'I'm only her mother.'

He had put an arm round her waist. 'I know you're worried for her – so am I. But we learned early on, didn't we, that's not the way to win the twins round. They're apt to bolt if too much pressure is applied. We worried about Rona, too, but everything seems to be going swimmingly.'

'If that's what you call spending only half the week with your husband.' Even as she said it, Avril felt a twist of unacknowledged envy, which only added to her irritation. '*Why have they turned out like this?*' she'd cried, shrugging away from his arm. 'It's not the way we brought them up.'

But he had only shaken his head and wandered out of the room. Well, they'd be here this evening, Rona, Max and Lindsey, though thankfully not Hugh. And if she didn't get a move on, the butcher would have sold out of the best cuts of beef. Avril tipped the foamy water out of the bowl, dried her hands, and reached for her old cardigan. *Sufficient unto the day,* she thought gloomily as she let herself out of the house.

Nuala was shampooing the spare-room carpet when the phone rang and, propping the machine against the wall, she went into her bedroom and picked up the extension, her mind still on preparations for her guest.

'Hello?' she said.

'Well, hello there. How are things?'

A wave of heat suffused her and her hand tightened on the phone. 'Clive?' she stammered.

'The very same. Nice to hear your voice after all this time.'

'I wish I could say the same,' she retorted, shock giving way to anger. 'What do you want, Clive?'

'Just phoning to see how you and Will are.'

'After three years?'

He gave a low laugh. 'I was warned off by your father, if you remember. "Never darken our doors again" and all the rest of it. So I didn't darken your phone, either.'

'Where are you?' she asked evenly.

'In Chilswood at the moment, but I've no permanent base.'

'Very wise.'

'Don't be like that, sweetheart. Point is, I want to ask a favour.'

'Ah!'

'Nothing drastic, just a bit of storage space. With being on the move, I need somewhere to leave a few things for a while.'

'What kind of things?'

'Just a couple of suitcases. If I dump them in the spare room, they won't be in anyone's way.'

'That's where you're wrong; I have a paying guest coming next week.'

There was a brief silence. Then he said, 'Pull the other one.'

'I'm not the one who tells lies, Clive.'

'You're actually going to have someone living in?'

'Yes.' No need to tell him it was only for four weeks.

'A man?' There was suspicion in his voice.

'What's it to you?' But it was pointless being childish, and she added, 'Actually, it's a woman. A writer.'

'Well, I'm sure she wouldn't object to the odd suitcase on top of the wardrobe.'

'She might not, but I would. I don't want anything of yours here, Clive. For all I know, they could be full of drugs or stolen goods.'

He gave a mirthless laugh. 'You've too much imagination, my love, that's your trouble. It's all perfectly innocuous, I assure you; I just—'

'Then put them in a left-luggage locker,' she said crisply. 'I have to go, I'm busy. Please don't call again.'

She put the phone down and stood, heart hammering, looking round the bedroom she'd once shared with her husband. God, he was *still* her husband! She tended to forget that. At the time of his departure she'd been too trauma-tized to face divorce proceedings, and as the months passed and nothing was heard from him, she'd kept putting it off. In any case, she hadn't known how to contact him. Now he'd turned up again, all the old fears came back. Perhaps she should—

43

'Nuala? Did I hear the phone? I'm expecting a call.'

She went on to the landing and looked down at her father standing in the hall.

His voice sharpened. 'What is it, girl? You're as white as a sheet.'

'That was Clive, Dad.'

He stiffened, leaning more heavily on his Zimmer. 'What in God's name did he want?'

'To use us as a left-luggage office.'

'For what?'

'Some suitcases, contents unspecified. He suggested leaving them in the spare room, "out of the way". I told him it was impossible.'

Jack Stanton was silent for a minute. Then he asked, 'How did he sound?'

'The same as ever.'

'He didn't – threaten you in any way?'

'I didn't give him the chance.'

The old man shook his head. 'I don't like it, him surfacing like that. It can only mean trouble. Suppose he doesn't take no for an answer?'

'We'll face that hurdle when we come to it. In the meantime, though, I'll go and see Frank Jeffries and start divorce proceedings. That should nip it in the bud.'

'He'd still have access to Will.'

'He's never made the slightest attempt to see him,' Nuala said hotly. 'Why should he now?'

'To cause problems,' Jack Stanton answered flatly.

She shrugged. 'I've wasted enough of my life worrying about Clive, Dad; I'm not going to let him get to me again. Now, I'm going to finish cleaning this carpet and then I'll see about lunch. OK?'

He held her eye for a moment longer, then nodded slowly and turned away. Nuala drew a deep breath and, determined to abide by her resolution, returned to her work.

* * *

Avril's forte was plain English cooking, at which she excelled, and it was for this reason that she preferred the family to come to Sunday lunch, with its traditional roast. Deprived of that option, she had settled on smoked salmon, followed by grilled steak and gooseberry fool. It had been Paola King who'd given Rona her taste for spicy foods, and made her a regular visitor to Dino's.

Lindsey was tense that evening, no doubt anticipating a tirade against Hugh, and to safeguard her, Rona monopolized the conversation with her plans for the Buckford articles.

'We found a very pleasant B&B up there,' she said, 'recommended by the vicar, no less. Actually, he was helpful in other ways, too. He gave me the name of a woman who's lived there for years and is a mine of information, and another who was a headmistress and compiled histories of the local schools. Believe it or not, she retired to Marsborough, but I can't find her in the phone book, which is frustrating.'

'What's her name?' Avril asked, passing round the vegetables.

'Bishop, Catherine Bishop.'

Tom looked up in surprise. 'I know Mrs Bishop. She has an account with us.'

'*Has* she, Pops? What a stroke of luck! What's she like?'

'Well, I've hardly spoken to her, but she struck me as quiet and unassuming. I'd no idea she used to be a headmistress.'

'Could you let me have her phone number?' Rona asked eagerly, but her father was shaking his head.

'Against bank policy, love. Next time I see her, though, I'll ask if she'd mind your contacting her.'

'But she mightn't come in for ages,' Rona protested, 'and I really need to speak to her.'

'Sorry, that's the best I can do.'

Rona bit her lip in frustration, but she knew that note in her father's voice, and accepted that nothing she could say would sway him.

'What about the other person?' Lindsey asked, coming in her turn to Rona's rescue.

'Which other person?'

'The one who's a mine of information. Can't you start with her?'

'I suppose I'll have to,' Rona said ungraciously.

'Rona saw the Ridgeways the other evening,' Max remarked into the uncomfortable silence. 'Apparently Gavin's finally fit again.'

Rona, aware that both her sister and her husband were trying to rally her, flashed them a shamefaced smile and emerged from her sulk. 'They've been living it up in Brazil,' she volunteered, and the conversation settled back on an even keel. Between them, they kept it going, ensuring there was no pause in which Avril could insert the subject of Hugh, and as a result the remainder of the evening passed without incident.

'Thanks, guys,' Lindsey said outside on the pavement. 'That went better than I'd dared hope. Mum opened her mouth purposefully once or twice, but each time one or other of you leapt nobly into the breach and cut her off.'

'All part of the service,' Max said lightly.

Four

As it happened, Catherine Bishop called at the bank the following day. Mindful of his promise, Tom had asked the chief cashier to advise him of her next visit, and a little after eleven, his phone rang.

'Mrs Bishop has just come in, Mr Parish,' the cashier told him. 'She's purchasing some foreign currency.'

'Thank you, Charles. Would you ask her to come and see me when you've completed the transaction?'

Five minutes later there was a tap on his door and she was shown into the room. Tom rose to his feet and held out his hand, which she gravely took.

'Nothing wrong, I hope, Mr Parish?' she asked quietly, seating herself at his invitation.

'No, not at all.' He glanced down at his hands clasped on the desk, aware of the unusualness of his request. 'I'm wondering if I could possibly ask you a favour,' he began, and saw her eyebrows arch.

'My daughter is about to start on a series of articles to coincide with Buckford's celebrations next year, and your name was given to her as a source of information.'

Catherine Bishop frowned. 'Given by whom?'

'Er – the vicar, I believe.'

'Gordon Breen?' Surprise rang in her voice.

'I'm afraid I don't know his name. Look, if you'd rather—'

'No, please, tell me more about this project. She's a journalist, your daughter?'

'Basically she's a writer. She works freelance for *Chiltern Life* but her main interest is biographies. She—'

Mrs Bishop held up a hand. 'Just a moment – biographies?' A look of enlightenment crossed her face. 'Your daughter's not Rona Parish, by any chance?'

'Well, yes, but—'

'How silly of me not to have made the connection. I've read several of her books. You must be very proud of her.'

'Yes, I am,' Tom said simply, and they both smiled, simultaneously aware of each other not as stereotypical bank manager and customer, but as two human beings. A check on the computer had revealed that Catherine Bishop was a widow in her fifties; now he found himself compiling a more personal dossier. Quiet and unassuming was how he'd described her, but that, he was realizing, left a lot unsaid. The first thing he'd noticed as she crossed the room towards him had been her impeccable grooming, hair sleek, shoes highly polished, and linen suit miraculously uncreased. The second, as she sat across from him, was her deportment, straight-backed and with feet neatly together – a posture that had no doubt served as an example to her pupils.

For the rest, her face was unremarkable – pale skin, steady grey eyes, very little make-up, hair simply styled, light brown fading to grey. But there was an air of what he could only describe as stillness about her that he found oddly restful. He sat back in his chair, unconsciously relaxing.

'I didn't know you'd been a headmistress,' he said.

She took the non sequitur in her stride. 'Yes indeed, for twelve years. I was widowed when I was forty, and teaching was my anchor. It was also a lifestyle ideally suited to having a young son; I worked the same hours he did, and was home during the holidays.'

'So what brought you to Marsborough?'

'My mother; she suffered a stroke two years ago and was no longer able to look after herself. I took early retirement and moved down here.'

'It must have been a wrench.'

'Yes.'

'And now?'

'Sadly she died last year, but there's nothing to take me back to Buckford. My son's married and living in Cricklehurst, so I see quite a bit of him and his wife.' She paused, and added with a smile, 'We seem to have strayed from your original request. What was it you wanted to ask me?'

Tom flushed. 'I'm sorry, I didn't mean to interrogate you. It was just that Rona would very much like to meet you. She was told you'd done a lot of research on the history of the schools up there.'

'I suppose I have. It started as a project for eleven-year-olds and just – took off.'

'Would you have any objection to meeting her?'

'Of course not, I should be delighted. As I said, I've admired her work for some time.'

'Then may I give her your phone number? She couldn't find it in the book.'

'The directory came out while I was at my mother's.' She opened her bag, extracted a card, and handed it across to him. 'I'll be in Paris for the weekend – I've just been collecting some euros – but perhaps we could arrange something for next week.'

'Paris? I envy you,' Tom said. He had a sudden vision of her walking in the Tuileries Gardens, sitting at pavement cafés, going to museums and art galleries. Her visit, he felt sure, would not be the frenzied shopping trip he'd endured with Avril on their sole visit to the French capital twenty years ago. He felt a twinge of disloyalty, and cleared his throat to free himself of it.

'Yes,' she said, unconsciously echoing his thoughts, 'I'm hoping to see the Matisse exhibition.' She closed her handbag and stood up, smoothing down her skirt. 'I look forward to hearing from her.'

'Thank you.' Tom had risen with her, casting about for ways of detaining her but unable to think of any. He took the hand she held out.

'Have a good trip,' he said fatuously, and rang for a clerk to see her out. As the door closed behind her he sat down again, feeling oddly flat. A charming woman, he thought, and wondered suddenly who was accompanying her to Paris. The telephone on his desk shrilled sharply, and he turned to it with a sense of undefined relief.

'Tom Parish,' he said.

Catherine thought over the meeting as she walked back to her car. She seldom went to the bank, and as far as she could remember this was the first time she'd spoken to the manager. He seemed a pleasant man, touchingly proud of his clever daughter – and with reason. Rona Parish had a gift for making readers empathize with her subjects; though frank about their faults and eccentricities, she was non-judgemental, illustrating instead how those traits had made them the characters they were and contributed to their enduring places in history. Catherine always finished one of her biographies feeling that the subject was a friend.

Emerging from the car park, she turned right rather than continue over the junction into the clogged thoroughfare of Guild Street. She drove as she did everything else, competently and calmly, and, having negotiated Alban Road, wove her way unhesitatingly through the maze of little streets to her new bungalow.

'Good God, Mother!' Daniel had exclaimed on his first visit. 'You need a map and compass to find this place!'

For herself, she preferred her home to be tucked away in a close, rather than on a busy main road, as her mother's had been. It afforded her the sense of privacy that, over the last fourteen years, had become so essential to her. Odd, really, to think how her character had changed since her husband's death. When Neil had so tragically and so unbelievably died at forty-two, the torrent of emotions she'd felt had seriously alarmed her, and for a while she had feared for her sanity. Anguish, fury at the fates and searing loneliness had vied for supremacy, but for the sake of twelve-year-old Daniel she succumbed to them only when alone.

During those terrible months she'd grown increasingly paranoid about allowing anyone other than her son to come close. Even her mother, whose open weeping for Neil at first embarrassed and then irritated her, had been held figuratively at arm's length. She had been, she now admitted, selfish in her grief, resentful of anyone else expressing a sense of loss, and gradually family and friends had stepped back, withholding open expressions of sympathy in admiration for what they saw as her courage and strength of character. They knew nothing of the endless nights she'd spend ranting in impotent fury and soaking her pillow with her tears. And gradually, month by month, year by year, the calm front she presented to the world had become grafted on to her personality, screening her from any involvement that might, in some unforeseen way, inflict future hurt. She could not withstand it a second time.

No one suspected, either, just how bitterly she'd resented having to leave St Stephen's and come back to Marsborough to nurse her mother. In fact, she thought now, the bank manager, whom she barely knew, was the only one who'd expressed understanding. 'It must have been a wrench,' he'd said.

Indeed, the sense of loss in giving up a true vocation to nurse a fretful and ungrateful old woman had been insupportable. But then they'd never been close. Mary Jessop, fifteen years her husband's junior, had played the part of child bride until her death at seventy-six, and in her teens Catherine had frequently been embarrassed by her 'little girl' attitude, her kittenish behaviour towards her husband and – to be frank – any other men with whom she came in contact.

Regrettably, therefore, she had shed few tears at her

mother's death. Perhaps she'd gone to the other extreme and her detachment had become cold-heartedness. Whatever, it had allowed her to go dry-eyed through her mother's effects and put up for sale the house in which she'd been born. Its position on the main road, coupled with its nearness to schools and the station, had ensured a quick sale at what Catherine considered a phenomenal price, and she had found the bungalow with a minimum of fuss.

She'd not had a home of her own since leaving Buckford; her personal things had been in storage during the eighteen months that she'd nursed her mother, and she enjoyed having them about her again. The Buckford house hadn't been large, and almost everything fitted in here. The few pieces that had not found homes – a wardrobe, a wall mirror and a wrought-iron table – Daniel and Jenny had been pleased to take.

She turned into her driveway and garaged the car, pausing as she walked up the path to survey the small garden over which she'd been labouring. It was at last beginning to repay her efforts, and the effects of months of neglect under previous ownership were being overtaken by a profusion of scent and colour.

And now, she thought as she closed the front door, she must decide what to take with her to Paris. She went into her bedroom and had just taken down her suitcase when the phone rang.

'Mrs Bishop?' said an unfamiliar voice. 'This is Rona Parish. You were kind enough to give my father your number.'

Catherine sat down on the edge of the bed. 'Yes of course, Miss Parish. I believe you'd like to talk about Buckford?'

'If you wouldn't mind.'

'I'd be delighted. As I told your father, I'm off to Paris for a long weekend, but I'll be free on Tuesday, if that would suit you?'

Rona hesitated. 'Actually, I'll be spending half the week in Buckford for the time being. Could we possibly make it Thursday, a week today?'

'Of course. If you've a pen handy, I'll give you my address.' She did so, but when she started on directions, Rona cut her short.

'It's all right, I know where it is. I have friends in Barrington Road.'

'Fine; about ten thirty, then? In the meantime, if you're going up to Buckford is there anything I can help with? Names and addresses, for instance, of people you're hoping to contact?'

'That's very kind of you,' Rona said slowly. 'As it happens, I'd been hoping to start with education. It's not straightforward histories of the schools I'm after, so much as interesting sidelights – an eccentric headmaster, famous former pupils, and so on. It'll have to be condensed into one article, since that's all I can spare on any one subject, but I hope to give each school a mention.' She gave a little laugh. 'I suppose there aren't any scandals you can regale me with?'

'Not without consulting my lawyer! Seriously, though, I can give you their addresses and suggest whom you should contact.'

'That would be great. How many schools are there?'

'Let's see; there's a private kindergarten, a Roman Catholic primary, St Stephen's, of course, two secondary schools and a sixth-form college, though that's relatively recent. And, of course, the estimable Buckford College. I'm pretty sure the names I have are up to date; I keep in touch with friends up there, and I'd have heard if there'd been any changes. If you think it would help, you could mention my name.'

Immediately after the call, Rona rang her father.

'I've just been speaking to Mrs Bishop, and she was great,' she reported. 'She's given me a string of names and addresses so I can arrange appointments at the schools.'

'I'm glad she could help,' Tom said. 'She's a fan of yours, by the way; she's read several of your books. I'll be interested to hear in due course what you think of her.'

'Thanks so much for putting in a word for me, Pops. I do appreciate it.'

'It was a pleasure,' Tom replied. Which, in every sense, was true.

Friday evening was warm and sunny, and Max had elected to have a barbecue.

'I don't think we've been in summer before,' Dinah said, looking approvingly round the patio garden. 'How very attractive you've made this, with all the pots and statues.'

'It's not much more than a backyard really,' Rona answered deprecatingly. 'Nothing like your glorious garden.'

'But a lot less trouble, I'll bet!' Barnie put in feelingly.

'I particularly like the way you've contrasted shapes and colours,' Dinah continued. 'And scent! Just smell those stocks! I've always wanted a walled garden.'

'Now she tells me!' Barnie said humorously.

They all laughed, but Rona was acutely aware of the tension just below the surface. 'How's Mel?' she asked quietly.

The Trents exchanged glances.

'Not good,' Barnie admitted. 'Dinah's considering flying out there.'

'We were going anyway when the baby's born,' Dinah added, 'but I'm wondering if I'd be more use now. She's having to take a lot of bed rest, and poor little Sam doesn't understand why she can't play with him.' She looked down at her hands. 'It's very difficult, being so far away.'

Rona murmured understanding. She'd never seen Dinah so subdued. A small, dynamic woman with wiry black hair and a surprisingly deep voice, she was usually a whirlwind of energy, sweeping everyone along with her enthusiasm. The Trents were a good ten years older than Max and herself, but Barnie, renowned at *Chiltern Life* for his short fuse, had been kind to her when she first joined the magazine, and after she met Dinah at an office party, a deep friendship had developed which, before her marriage, had involved frequent invitations to supper at their home. She still went over occasionally when Max was working, and Gus had a longstanding truce with the couple's Siamese cats.

Max had lit the barbecue and Barnie was helping him carry trays of prepared meat, fish and vegetables out to the waiting table.

'Barnie tells me you're about to visit my home town,' Dinah said, sipping her drink, and, at Rona's enquiring look, added, 'You didn't know I come from Buckford?'

'No, I didn't. I'll be able to pump you, then.'

Dinah shrugged. 'I doubt if I'd be much use to you. I haven't lived there for thirty-odd years.'

'But it's the history I'm interested in,' Rona pointed out.

'Thanks! That makes me feel my age!'

'Seriously, Dinah. For instance, where did you go to school?'

'A local kindergarten, and then the college.'

'*Buckford* College?'

'Don't sound so surprised! Actually, we were the first proper intake of girls. They'd only been allowed into the sixth form before.'

'Who was the head?'

'A man called Peter Rillington. He kept parrots, would you believe?'

Rona clapped her hands delightedly. 'That's *just* the kind of thing I want!'

'One day the wretched things got out, and he had us all scrambling round the grounds trying to catch them.'

'And did you?'

'Some of them, and the rest made their way back when they got hungry. Needless to say, the head's nickname was Polly.'

'That really is great. Would you mind if I popped round one day with a tape recorder?'

'Not at all, if you think it's worth it.'

'Come on, girls!' Max called. 'The steaks are nearly ready.'

What with Catherine Bishop and now Dinah, Rona reflected as she picked up a plate, she could probably have saved herself the trouble of staying in Buckford.

Lindsey had booked seats for that evening at the Darcy Hall, where a visiting Russian ballet corps was performing *Swan Lake*. As she walked into the foyer with Hugh, she was reminded of the time she and Rona had met Rob Stuart, a man she'd subsequently fallen for, and who had turned out to be very different from what she'd supposed. God, *why* did she have such bad luck with her men? she wondered irritably. Why couldn't she be like Rona, and settle happily with the right one?

Hugh was looking good this evening; his blue shirt matched his eyes, and his usually pale face had a wash of colour. Though whatever his appearance, she thought wryly, the attraction between them never faltered. How much simpler life would be, if that weren't so.

The magic of music and dance enfolded her, and Lindsey relaxed, putting her worries on hold. It wasn't until much later, after their love-making, in fact, that they reappeared in full force. Hugh's fingers had been moving gently over her and she was on the edge of sleep when he said softly, 'I've some news for you, darling; I've been saving it till the time was right, and it seems to me it couldn't be better.'

She frowned drowsily. 'What kind of news?'

'Our period of rationing is over; soon we'll be able to make love any time we want.'

Suddenly awake, she moved her head sharply to face him. 'What do you mean?'

'My transfer's come through, sweetheart; I'm moving back to Marsborough at the end of the month.'

She said stupidly, 'But – you can't.'

He gave a short laugh. 'What do you mean, I can't? I can and I am. I thought you'd be pleased.'

'But – where will you live?'

His fingers stilled on her body. 'You *are* joking?'

'No, Hugh, I'm not.' Lindsey heard her voice rising and made an effort to control it. 'I've said all along that we can't get back together.'

'Just what the hell do you think we've been doing, every weekend for the last three months?'

'I mean not permanently. I'm not going to marry you again.'

'I don't remember asking you,' he said nastily. 'Well, I must say, this isn't the reaction I expected.'

'Then it should have been. I've made it perfectly clear from the start.'

'What you've made clear, my love, is that every time we meet, you can't wait to tear my clothes off.'

'It works well as it is,' she said, humbled by the truth of his words. 'Why change it?'

He snorted. 'If you imagine I'm going to settle for a Rona–Max solution, you're very much mistaken. We belong together, Lindsey. You know it as well as I do, so what's the point in fighting it?'

'I don't want to live with you,' she said stubbornly, hearing her voice tremble.

'You'll get used to it.'

'No, Hugh, I won't. This is my flat, and I don't want you here. Not permanently.'

'And what the hell would I tell the firm? Here I've been, moving heaven and earth to come back to my loving ex-wife, and now she refuses to have me.'

She sat up, clutching the sheet to her breast. 'I think you'd better go.'

'At one in the morning? Don't be bloody ridiculous.'

'To the guest room, at least; the bed's made up.'

'I'm not going to any bloody guest room,' he said furiously.

'Then I will.' She slid her feet to the floor and stood up. 'I'm sorry, Hugh. I did tell you, you know I did.'

'That was in the early days. Anyway, I've changed.' He stretched out a hand and she took a step backwards, out of his reach. 'I know I have a temper, it goes with my red hair, but it doesn't mean anything. Being away from you made me realize how much I miss and want you, and you might as well admit it, you want me, too.'

'Not permanently,' she repeated weakly. Since he was making no move to get up, she added, 'I'll see you in the morning,' and, catching up her robe, hurried out of the room. A shaft of moonlight lit her way as she ran across the landing, half-expecting to hear him coming after her. She reached the guest room, closed the door, and stood listening, heart thumping. There was no sound, and after a moment she moved woodenly to the bed, pulled back the covers, and crept between the cold sheets. What in the name of goodness was she going to do now?

The doorbell rang at ten o'clock the next morning, while Max and Rona were having a lazy breakfast in their dressing gowns.

'Who the hell can that be?' he grumbled. 'The post's been, hasn't it?'

Rona nodded. 'You go; you're more respectable than I am.'

He got up and with bad grace went barefoot up the basement stairs. Rona heard voices in the hall and a minute later Max called, 'Rona? I think you'd better come up.'

Rona frowned, put down the paper and followed him upstairs, to find Lindsey in the hall.

'What are you doing here?' she asked in surprise. 'I thought Hugh was coming up?'

Lindsey burst into tears. Rona looked helplessly at Max, who shrugged his shoulders, said, 'I'll leave you to it,' and thankfully disappeared back down the stairs.

'I'm sorry to spoil your Saturday,' Lindsey sobbed, 'but I'm frantic, Ro. I don't know what to do.'

Rona took her arm and led her into the sitting room, where the curtains were still drawn and last night's coffee cups on the table.

She pulled back the curtains, motioned Lindsey to the sofa, and sat down beside her. 'Now, tell me what's happened.'

'Hugh's transfer's come through. He's coming back to Marsborough.' Lindsey looked at her tragically with swimming eyes.

'Oh God,' Rona said flatly. 'And I suppose you never got round to telling him in so many words that you didn't want him back?'

Lindsey shook her head. 'We had the most awful row last night. I – I slept in the guest room. This morning he was all white and po-faced and I told him to leave.'

'And did he?'

'Eventually, but he made it clear this isn't the end of it. He says he'll be a laughing stock, having moved heaven and earth, as he put it, to get back here. Go on – tell me it's my own fault.'

'Well, you did want to have your cake and eat it,' Rona reminded her, aware of sounding pious.

'And what's wrong with that?' Lindsey demanded rebelliously.

'Nothing, if you can get away with it.'

They looked at each other for a minute then, unwillingly, Lindsey smiled.

'That's better. In the meantime you've sent him packing, and at least he's not in any doubt any more.' She paused. 'When's he moving back?'

'The end of the month. But suppose he turns up as usual next Friday? What should I do?'

'Arrange to be out,' Rona said crisply. 'Better still, go away for the weekend.'

'Where?'

'Oh, for heaven's sake, Linz! Stay with a friend, go to a health spa – anything to be out of Marsborough.'

'But I can't go away *every* weekend,' Lindsey said plaintively.

'At least it will give you time to decide what to do.'

Lindsey nodded and slowly got to her feet. 'OK. Thanks for the advice.'

'There's no need to rush off. Come down and have some coffee.'

She shook her head. 'Max doesn't want interrupting with my woes. I'm all right. There's some work I could be doing, anyway. Don't worry, Ro, I'll survive. I just wanted a bit of TLC, that's all.'

Rona gave her a hug. 'Any time, you know that. I'll ring you this evening and see how you're doing.'

'OK. Are my eyes red?'

'Not very, but as your car's at the gate you've only got to get down the path, and I doubt if any film directors are hiding in the bushes.'

'Hugh?' Max asked resignedly, without looking up from his paper.

'Hugh,' Rona confirmed.

'What now?'

'He's moving back, and Linz has taken fright.'

'She should have thought of that before.'

'Not much help telling her that, is it?'

'I guess not. Ah well, no doubt they'll sort it out between them.'

'What a convenient philosophy,' Rona commented, and started to clear the table.

Beth Spencer reread the paragraph in the *Courier.*

Rumours have reached us that biographer Rona Parish will be adding to the wealth of material already commissioned for next year's celebrations. Parish made headlines earlier this year during her aborted biography of

60

thriller writer Theo Harvey, when she uncovered the fact that, appropriately enough, he had himself been murdered. It will be interesting to see what skeletons she can unearth in our cupboard!

Beth raised her head and stared unseeingly through the window. This woman had apparently solved one murder. She was a journalist, and no doubt had contacts not available to herself. Was there, Beth wondered, the slightest possibility that she would listen to her insistence that Alan was innocent, and help her to prove it? It had to be worth a try.

Five

Rona had left home at eight thirty, but heavy traffic in and around Marsborough caused the usual delays, and it was almost eleven when she arrived at Buckford.

She had arranged with Nuala Banks that on arrival she would, if possible, claim a parking space and drop off her suitcase at the house. Nuala herself was out at work, but her father, leaning heavily on a Zimmer, answered her ring and, having left the case in her room, Rona went straight out again. Max had warned her that B&B owners did not want you in their homes between nine and five. In any case, after speaking to Catherine Bishop she'd phoned the local schools and arranged a series of appointments beginning at eleven thirty.

However, the day proved not to be as interesting as she'd hoped. Back in her room that evening, she tried to sort out a mélange of impressions of corridors, chalky blackboards and slightly harassed heads in overcrowded studies. The private kindergarten – presumably the one Dinah had attended – alone stood out clearly, since it was in a converted private house, the graciously proportioned rooms mutilated by makeshift divisions to form a series of classrooms. It seemed some of the tots boarded; Miss Pierson, the headmistress, told her they were the children of army or diplomatic families based abroad. She provided Rona with a prospectus and a copy of the school magazine, neither of which contained much that she could use. However, she promised the school would receive an honourable mention, and that a photographer would be in touch later.

She had decided to leave St Stephen's until after speaking to Catherine Bishop, but there seemed little to choose between the rest of them. Her query about former pupils or unusual incidents for the most part produced blank looks, and clearly several of the heads thought she was wasting their time. Consequently she was feeling slightly dispirited when she went down to join the Banks family for supper.

Nuala's father, whom she'd met briefly that morning, added little to the conversation, whether from shyness or a taciturn nature Rona could not be sure. His face was deeply furrowed, possibly from pain following his injuries, possibly from the strains of life generally. Young Will was also quiet – unusually, Rona suspected. No doubt he would open up when he felt he knew her. It was therefore left to Nuala to make conversation, and this she gallantly tried to do.

Supper was home-made leek and potato soup, followed by pork pie and salad. In deference to the guest, dessert was a rather elaborate trifle.

'Mr Breen mentioned some people who might be willing to help me,' Rona began, breaking a short silence. 'I've tracked down one of them in Marsborough, but the other was an old lady who I think he said lived opposite the church.'

That caught the attention of the other two, who both looked up, Will exclaiming, 'Auntie Edna!'

Rona turned to Nuala, who explained, 'That would be my aunt, Miss Rosebury. She's lived here all her life and not much escapes her. Or at least, it didn't used to.' She paused. 'As a matter of fact, we're a little anxious about her. She's become increasingly frail since Christmas, and she didn't arrive for tea yesterday, as she always does on Sundays. When I went to find her, she said she thought it was Saturday, and seemed very vague and disorientated. I'm wondering if she's had a minor stroke, but she refuses point-blank to see the doctor.'

Rona felt a stab of disappointment, mixed, after her less than satisfactory day, with frustration. She hoped all her leads weren't going to fizzle away. 'I wouldn't want to worry her if she's not well,' she said tentatively.

'Actually,' Nuala replied, 'it would probably do her good. A new face might stimulate her, and talking to you could help her to remember things. In any case,' she added frankly, 'I'd be glad of your opinion. If you also think she's not well, I'll ask the doctor to call round. I'll phone later if you like, and ask if she'll see you. Would tomorrow be all right?'

'The morning would be fine, thanks.'

The local paper was lying on the table as she crossed the hall and, seeing her glance at it, Nuala handed it to her.

'I kept this for you, because there's a paragraph about you. I thought I'd heard your name before, and of course I remember where, now.'

'What does it say?' Rona asked uneasily.

'That you discovered that writer had been murdered, and they wondered what skeletons you'd find in our closet.'

Rona made a face. 'What a reputation!'

Up in her room, she ignored the reproachful laptop and settled in the armchair with the paper, finding the relevant paragraph on the third page of the main section. There was no byline, and it contained little more than Nuala had said. The front page was given over to the crime wave that had hit the town; someone had been attacked and mugged over the weekend, making it the second incident in as many days, and this time the victim had ended up in hospital.

The rest of the paper covered a wide range of local-interest subjects including school concerts, the opening of a new supermarket and a batch of weddings. Conscious of the hours to fill until bedtime, Rona read every paragraph, ending with a reread of the one on herself. It would do no harm, she thought, to have a word with the reporter who had written it.

She stood up, stretched, and leant on the window sill, looking out across the road to the garden beyond the wall.

Immediately, however, she drew back; Gordon Breen was

walking there with a blonde woman who was doubtless his wife. They seemed to be having an animated discussion on the flowers in the border, and Rona could hear the faint sound of their voices through the open window. She watched them for a moment, then reluctantly turned away and returned to the chair. It was only eight thirty, another hour before she could phone Max. If only she'd had Gus with her, she could have taken him for a walk, but she couldn't be bothered to make the effort for herself. She'd spent most of the day walking round Buckford anyway. Perhaps, she thought ruefully as she retrieved her library book from her case, she'd been too quick to decline the offer of the kitchen TV.

An hour or so later, just as Rona judged Max's classes would have finished, Nuala tapped on her door. 'I've spoken to my aunt and she says she'll be pleased to see you. It's possible, though, that she'll have forgotten by tomorrow, so I'll take you over and introduce you on my way to work.'

Rona thanked her, assured her she had everything she needed, and, as the door closed behind her, took out her mobile.

'How's Gus?' she asked, when she'd filled Max in on her day.

'OK, but he's obviously expecting you to arrive any minute to collect him. His ears prick every time someone walks past. He'll be fine; I'm just about to take him out for a run.'

'There's a snippet about me in the local rag,' Rona said, and immediately wished she hadn't.

'What did it say?' Max's voice had sharpened.

'Oh – just that I was going to add to the mass of writing about the octocentenary.'

'And no doubt happening to mention that you'd unmasked Theo Harvey's killer?'

'Well, something along those lines.'

'God, when will people forget that? Just as well your local murderer's safely behind bars.'

'This is an entirely different scenario,' Rona assured him. 'I'm not personally involved this time.'

'Mind you stay that way.'

It was still early when they finished speaking, but Rona was tired after her long day. The bathroom was likely to be vacant at this time; she'd have a bath to relax her and take the chance of an early night.

'You said you're on your way to work,' Rona remarked, as she and Nuala walked the length of Parsonage Place and turned into the cobbled alleyway. 'Is that the church cleaning?'

'Goodness no; there's a rota for that, and I only do it once a month. I have a part-time job, temping for a secretarial agency. It's varied and interesting, and as I only work nine thirty to twelve thirty, I'm home to cook lunch for Dad and be there when Will gets in. Occasionally there isn't any work – there wasn't last week – but that gives me a chance to get on with the housework. I'm sorry it's an early start for you, but it won't worry Aunt Edna. She's up at six every morning.'

As they crossed the square towards the little house with its dipping eaves, Rona thought she made out a figure at the window, but it had gone by the time they reached the pavement. Nuala had a key, and after a warning press on the bell, she opened the door and called out, 'Auntie? I've brought someone to see you.'

No one came into the hall, and Nuala led the way to the door on the right that opened into the front room. A gaunt, bent figure was standing just short of the window, staring across the room at them, and Rona's heart sank. Nuala went quickly over, took the old lady's arm and led her slowly back to her chair. 'Auntie, this is Mrs Allerdyce – I mean Ms Parish.'

'Well, which is it?' the old lady demanded waspishly. 'There's only one of them that I can see.'

Rona smiled and came forward. 'I know it's confusing, Miss Rosebury. Officially I'm Mrs Allerdyce, but since, as my father says, I'm too independent for my own good, I prefer to be known by my maiden name – which I also use professionally. Please just call me Rona.'

Miss Rosebury pursed her mouth, which might be taken as disapproval, and Nuala said uncertainly, 'You'll be all right, Auntie? Ms Parish would like to hear the tales you're always telling us, about how it was when you were young, and the ghosts and things. Perhaps even that scandal!' she added with a smile.

The old woman's head reared up. 'What scandal? What are you talking about?'

'The one you mentioned last week, that happened recently. I'm sure she'd like to hear about it.' Nuala waited, but when there was no reaction, said quietly to Rona, 'I must go, or I'll be late. I'll see you this evening, but if you need to contact me –' her eyes flicked towards her aunt – 'Dad has the number that'll reach me.'

She bent to kiss the unresponsive figure and a minute later the front door closed behind her. An old clock ticked loudly into the silence. Rona drew up a chair and sat down opposite her hostess.

'May I switch on the recorder, Miss Rosebury, so I don't miss anything? It won't worry you, will it?'

The old lady nodded, then a quiver crossed her face, her eyes refocused, and to Rona's surprise she leant towards her, smiling.

'My dear, you don't know how good it is to see you! For some reason, I thought you'd died.'

Rona stared at her, coldness crawling up her spine. 'Miss Rosebury, I'm—'

'I wanted your advice, you see,' the old voice continued, speaking clearly now. 'Should I have mentioned it, or not? Seeing them together, I mean, in view of what happened after? At the time I decided no good would come of it, especially after the child and everything, and reporting it would only lead to more suffering.'

Was this the scandal Nuala had teased her about? Rona

laid her hand on the dry, wrinkled one. 'Miss Rosebury, I don't want to speak to you under false pretences. My name is Rona Parish, and we've never met before. I was hoping to ask you—'

'I was sure I'd done right until that policeman came on television. He was asking people to come forward if they'd heard or seen anything at all unusual, even if it didn't seem relevant. But I kept quiet. It was his poor wife I was thinking of; she'd suffered enough. You see, it wasn't only the once; I came across them several times. They never saw me – at least, I don't think they did. They were too engrossed in each other, kissing, you know, and – oh dear me.' She broke off, obviously distressed. 'It was so difficult, knowing both families.'

'It must have been,' Rona said over her hammering heart.

'I still see her about the town and she's always so pleasant. "Hello, Miss Rosebury, how are you today?" It would be a different story if she knew what I'd seen.'

The old eyes stared into space. Rona said desperately, 'Shall I make you a cup of coffee? Or hot milk, perhaps?'

There was no answer, but it was claustrophobic in that dim, stuffy room and she needed some space. She went out into the hallway, where dust motes danced in the sunshine, and turned towards the back of the house. The kitchen was totally unmodernized, but contained all the essentials. After opening various cupboards in search of pans, cups and saucers, she was able to produce two cups of milky coffee and, finding an old tin tray propped in a corner, she carried them through.

Miss Rosebury turned sharply as she entered the room. 'Who are you?' she demanded, alarm in her voice. 'What are you doing here?'

Rona set down the tray on a piecrust table, switching the recorder back on as she did so. 'I'm Rona Parish,' she said steadily, passing the old lady her coffee. 'Nuala introduced us, remember?'

A frown. 'She might have mentioned you on the phone.'

'That's right. I'm going to be writing about Buckford, and would love to hear some of your stories.'

The old eyes regarded her uncertainly. Then she nodded. 'There's no denying I have plenty of those, as has everyone my age. You'd think we'd learn from experience, wouldn't you, but we go on making the same mistakes.' She took a sip of coffee, glancing at the ring on Rona's finger. 'As you'll have gathered, I never married, my dear. I used to regret that when I was young, but I fancy I saved myself a lot of heartache. Such an unsuitable young man – I never trusted him.'

Rona waited, unsure to whom she was referring. An erstwhile suitor from the distant past?

'I warned her not to marry him, but I should have saved my breath.'

Someone else's suitor, then.

'Do you believe in ghosts?' Miss Rosebury demanded abruptly. Startled, Rona hesitated, but she was already continuing. 'Buckford's full of them, like any self-respecting town its age. Monks and white ladies, Roundheads and Cavaliers, and more recent ones, who don't yet realize they're dead. I can't think why people have such difficulty in accepting them. It stands to reason when you think about it; the human spirit is pure energy, and as any scientist will tell you, energy is indestructible.' She paused, gazing reflectively into her coffee cup. 'I came across a little boy once, down Clement's Lane, crying for his mother. I bent down to comfort him, and my hand went straight through him. I knew then it was better not to interfere.'

Rona moistened her lips, unsure whether a comment was called for, but apparently not. Miss Rosebury was off at another tangent.

'If it's history you're interested in, we had witch-ducking in the seventeenth century. If they drowned, they were innocent, if they floated they were guilty, and were hauled out to be burned at the stake. Not much of a choice. They still call it Witch's Pond. Behind the almshouses it is, but nowadays children feed the ducks there, which I suppose is as it should be.'

'Nuala says you've lived here all your life,' Rona prompted, as she fell silent.

'Indeed yes, in this very house. We were born in the front room upstairs, my three sisters and I. Florence – Nuala's mother – was the youngest and I the eldest – fifteen when she was born. But they're all dead and I'm still here. Odd, how life works out.'

She drank some more coffee, wiped the corners of her mouth with her handkerchief, and switched topics again.

'I was a milliner, you know, with a nice little shop off Thackeray Street – where that monstrous mall is now. We made special hats for weddings and presentation at Court, but our bread and butter trade was everyday hats, in the days when people wore them. It all changed after the war. Still, my most satisfying work was teaching at Sunday School for thirty years, often several generations of the same family. All those children.' She shook her head. 'For the most part they grew up to lead ordinary, blameless lives – or at least as blameless as any life can be. But you could tell, even at that age, the ones that would go to the bad. It might be politically incorrect to say so, but I was reading the other day that scientists have found some gene or chromosome or whatever that indicates how a person's character will develop. I could have told them years ago that it existed.'

Rona hoped fervently she wouldn't wander again; she'd be a goldmine of information if she could be kept on the right track.

'You must have known quite a few vicars during your lifetime,' she prompted.

'Over the road there? At least half a dozen, and there've been some shenanigans, I can tell you. Fights with the organist, the choir going on strike, the Mothers' Union up

70

in arms. At least no blood was shed in my day, as it had been earlier. You know about the siege?'

'I did hear, yes.'

'Poor Charles; people blacken his name nowadays but I've always felt sorry for him. He and I nod to each other every day.'

For a moment Rona thought she was back among her ghosts, but Miss Rosebury jerked her head in the direction of the window, and she realized she was referring to the pub sign. She was planning her next question when Miss Rosebury said suddenly, 'Would you excuse me? I'd like my nap now.'

Rona felt a spurt of frustration; after a shaky start, the interview had been going well and she was loath to abandon it.

'Of course,' she said, since there was no help for it, and removed the cup and saucer from the old lady's hand as her eyelids started to droop. She carried the tray back to the kitchen, where she washed and dried the crockery and put it away. By the time she returned Miss Rosebury's head had fallen forward, which would doubtless result in a stiff neck. Gently, Rona propped a cushion behind her, and the old lady settled more comfortably, murmuring, 'Maisie? Is that you?'

'It's all right,' Rona said softly. 'Go to sleep now.'

And moving almost on tiptoe, she let herself out of the house.

The meeting left Rona with a feeling of unease. According to Nuala, Miss Rosebury had been alert and on top of everything until recently; now it seemed her alertness was only spasmodic. *I thought you'd died*, she'd said. Rona, walking in the hot sunshine, repressed a shiver. She didn't, however, feel it sufficiently urgent to phone Nuala at work; time enough to report back this evening.

She was impatient to replay the cassette, analyse it, and as the privacy of her room was denied her, her first priority must be to establish a base in which to work between appointments. The library was the obvious choice.

She and Max had passed it last week, but for a moment she couldn't recall its whereabouts. Then she remembered it stood on the site of the defunct St Stephen's Church, in Market Square. Retracing the steps they'd taken, she made her way along narrow Clement's Lane – keeping a weather eye open for ghostly little boys – past the town hall and the Counting House to the square with the cross in its centre.

Directly opposite her, the buildings of St Stephen's Primary occupied the entire side of the square, and to her left, as she'd remembered, stone steps topped with an ornate balustrade led up to the public library. She was about to approach it when she was distracted by the irresistible aroma of roasting coffee, which, turning instead to her right, she traced to the door and bow window of St Stephen's Coffee Shop. Without hesitation Rona went inside, selected a window table and sat back with a sigh of relief. At Miss Rosebury's, she'd had to chip stale instant coffee out of its jar, and it had left a disagreeable taste in her mouth. She ordered a cappuccino and, spoiling herself, a Danish pastry. Then she took out a notebook and began an aide mémoire.

Almost immediately, voices from the counter reached her and she looked up. The woman standing there had her back to her, but Rona noted enviously the cut of her green silk dress – designer, for sure – and the height of her elegant heels. 'I'll try the Blue Mountain again,' she was saying in a high, well-educated voice, 'but I hope it's better than the last batch, which had no flavour at all.'

'I'm sorry, Madam.' The assistant sounded flustered. 'It was from our usual supplier, but if you have any more trouble, please don't hesitate to return the packets and we'll look into it.'

The customer nodded and turned from the counter, slipping her purchases into her shopping bag, and Rona, interested to see her from the front, was not disappointed. A cloud of auburn hair surrounded an oval face, with a full mouth and finely delineated eyebrows. As the woman looked up, eyes of an unusually dark blue met and briefly held Rona's. Then she was out of the door and tapping quickly away down the pavement, leaving Rona, feeling like a schoolgirl in her cotton dress, to return to her notes.

The approach of the waitress was a further interruption, and as her coffee and pastry were set down, Rona heard continuing voices from behind the counter.

'She's always complaining,' the assistant was saying in a low voice. 'Perhaps she thinks we'll knock something off her next purchase if she makes enough fuss. Well, hard luck. I always tell her to bring it back if she's not satisfied, but she never does.'

Her colleague laughed. 'Thinks she can browbeat the peasants, does she?'

One of the girls, suddenly aware of Rona within earshot, nudged the other and they moved to the back of the shop. Not good policy to criticize your customers, she reflected, particularly when others were present. Magda would have sacked them on the spot, and briskly overridden claims of unfair dismissal.

A couple of young men in suits came in and sat at a table near her, discussing a business appointment, and when the waitress came to serve them, Rona asked for her bill. As she waited for it she glanced through the lunch menu, deciding to return later. It was convenient for the library and the menu looked appetising.

At the library she made her way to the reference section, selected a table at the far end and took out her laptop, recorder and earpiece. The morning wore on as she transcribed verbatim all the interviews she'd done so far, with the heads of the various schools yesterday and, finally, with Edna Rosebury. Out of context, and without the old lady sitting opposite, her opening words sounded even more bizarre. Rona would have given a lot to know what she'd decided to keep quiet about, and so, from what she'd said, might the police. How long since she had seen those illicit lovers? From the way she'd jumped from one century to another, it could have been either last week or twenty years ago. Yet Nuala had mentioned a *recent* scandal. Was it that which was preying on Miss Rosebury's subconscious?

At twelve thirty Rona packed up her belongings and returned to the coffee shop, considerably more crowded now, where she enjoyed hot chicken salad and a spritzer. She'd an afternoon appointment at Buckford College, and needed to keep a clear head. As suggested by Mrs Bishop, she had phoned the school secretary, who, having established she wasn't a prospective parent, had agreed to allocate her an hour of her time, to include a quick tour of the school. When, however, Rona tentatively enquired about meeting the headmaster, she had received short shrift. Apparently Mr Maddox did not speak to journalists.

Having collected her car from Parsonage Place, she drove out of town and along the road that led to the college. This time she could legitimately turn into the gateway, and she made her way up the winding drive and round the back of the buildings, following the signs to the car park.

The building itself, large and handsome in red brick, looked to be Victorian. It was surrounded by green lawns and flowerbeds, but from behind a screen of trees came the unmistakable sound of leather on willow, and in the distance white-clad figures could be seen on tennis courts. It seemed that afternoons were devoted to sport.

Her ring was answered by a neatly dressed young woman, who conducted her to Miss Morton's study. The school secretary, efficiently bespectacled, came forward to meet her.

'Miss Parish? Joan Morton. How do you do?'

'I'm so grateful you could spare me the time,' Rona said, taking the hand she held out. 'It would be impossible to write an account of Buckford without mentioning the college, and there's no substitute for seeing it yourself.'

'I must warn you that its history has already been well chronicled,' Miss Morton said, waving Rona to a chair and reseating herself behind her desk. 'It might be hard to find a new angle.'

'I realize that. In fact, I was wondering if it would be possible to see the account Mrs Bishop did a few years ago?'

Miss Morton frowned. 'I'm not sure I could lay my hands on it. In any case, it was little more than a scrapbook. You'd do better to study more authenticated versions.'

'But it's the anecdotal material I'm after.' Rona held up her recorder with a raised eyebrow and Miss Morton nodded. 'As you say,' she continued, switching it on, 'there are plenty of other sources for the factual history. I'm aiming for more general interest – famous pupils, school ghosts, anything of that nature. For instance, when a friend of mine was here, the headmaster kept parrots.'

Miss Morton allowed herself a small smile. 'That would be Mr Rillington. Admittedly he was a little – colourful – but I'm afraid you'll find most of them have been earnest academics.'

'What about the present one?' Rona asked bluntly. 'Mr – Maddox, is it?'

'Definitely one of the latter. Eton and Cambridge, double first.'

'No exotic pets?'

'I'm afraid not.'

'How long has he been here?'

'Eight years; he succeeded Mr Palfrey.'

'Has he any family?'

Miss Morton stirred. 'I can't really see—'

'Surely his CV appears in the prospectus? Parents must want to know—'

'As you say, it's no secret.' Miss Morton's voice was clipped. 'Mr Maddox has two sons from his first marriage. And no, he was not divorced; his wife was killed in a car crash twelve years ago.'

'But he'd remarried by the time he came here?'

'Yes; married headmasters are a requisite. And before you ask, there are no further children. You mentioned ghosts,' Miss Morton continued smoothly, steering the conversation away from the personal. 'Allegedly the science block is haunted. The boys amuse themselves by hiding there at Hallowe'en.'

'Who's the ghost?'

'A boy in the nineteenth century, who quite literally blew himself up while carrying out an experiment. All nonsense, of course, but the imagination plays strange tricks. And there's also the wounded soldier.'

Rona raised an enquiring eyebrow.

'During the First World War the building was used as a convalescent home for the troops. One of them committed suicide by throwing himself out of a window. The sound of his stick is heard tapping along the top-floor corridor.' She permitted herself another smile. 'Or so it's said. The window is still referred to as Perkins' Drop.'

'That's great!' Rona exclaimed enthusiastically. 'Just what I was after! Thank you.'

'A thumbnail history of College, before I show you round: it originated in a small house in the centre of town in 1560, moving several times as it grew larger. Finally, in the nine-teenth century, a trust bought this land, the building was purpose-built, and both day boys and borders moved here in 1840. As to famous pupils, there have been quite a few: Jerome Fitzsimmons, the Victorian prime minister; the poet Frederick Lancet and Seymour Leonard, the silent-movie star, among others, but they're all listed at the back of the booklet I've put out for you.

'Now, if you'd like I'll take you on a quick tour of the building. We'll avoid the few classrooms that are in use, but most of the pupils are out on the games fields.'

The fact that his brief was a school rather than a stately home had not swayed the architect from his grand design.

Jigsaw

Sweeping staircases led to prefects' studies and staff rooms resplendent with wood-panelled walls; vaulted ceilings arched over well-stocked libraries, and in the beautifully proportioned classrooms the banks of computers seemed an anachronism. Only the Science Wing had of necessity been modernized, and though, as Miss Morton had indicated, the supposedly haunted lab still existed, its sad ghost would barely have recognized it.

Back in the main entrance hall, highly polished boards listed the names and dates of headmasters since the college's earliest beginnings. Rona stopped to read them, and had reached the last name, Richard Maddox, as he himself came down the staircase beside them.

Since he could hardly ignore them, he paused with an enquiring smile and Miss Morton said quickly, 'Headmaster, this is Miss Rona Parish, whom I told you about. She's researching Buckford for the octocentenary. Miss Parish, Mr Maddox.'

He was a tall and imposing figure, with dark hair touched with grey at the temples and deep lines between his eyes. His black gown, hanging loosely from his shoulders, gave him an air of effortless authority.

'Miss Parish.' He held out a hand that was cool and dry.

'How do you do, Mr Maddox. I've been admiring your splendid school.'

'I'm sure Miss Morton will supply you with all the information you require. We have a well-illustrated prospectus that is full of facts.'

'I've put one out ready for her,' Miss Morton murmured.

Rona thought it wise not to repeat her interest in ghosts and eccentricities. 'Thank you,' she said dutifully, and, with a nod, Richard Maddox went on his way. She would not, she reflected, like to cross swords with him, and spared a thought for the boys sent to his study for a reprimand. Corporal punishment might be frowned on these days, but it was clear Richard Maddox would have no need to resort to it.

They returned to Miss Morton's study and while she

extracted the promised literature, Rona glanced through the window in time to see a car draw up outside and the driver get out. To her surprise, it was the woman from the coffee shop.

'Is that a member of staff?' she asked quickly.

Joan Morton looked up, turning to follow her gaze.

'No,' she replied, her eyes on the retreating figure, 'that's Mr Maddox's wife. Why?'

'I – saw her in town this morning.'

'Here are the brief history and guide, and the latest prospectus. I hope you'll find them useful.'

'Thank you. And there's really no chance of seeing Mrs Bishop's account?'

'I'm sorry,' Miss Morton said firmly. 'I'm not even sure we still have it.'

Rona swallowed her frustration. 'Well, thanks for your help,' she said.

Having secured her parking place opposite the house, Rona walked back to the library where she transcribed the latest interview, discovering to her consternation that the cassette had run out. However, it seemed all she'd missed was Miss Morton's identification of Mrs Maddox. Odd that she should have seen her twice in one day, Rona thought. They seemed a spiky couple, the headmaster and his wife. She found herself wondering, with a writer's curiosity, what had brought them together.

With relief, she saw that the hands of the library clock were approaching five o'clock. It was like being an exile, she thought ruefully, to be shut out of her temporary home during working hours. Possibly, when she knew Nuala better, she might ask if the rules could be bent. Or possibly, since this was Nuala's first venture into B&B, she had no such rule. Rona should have checked instead of taking Max's word for it. She resolved to do so before her return next week.

She put away her things and, with a smile of thanks to the librarian, made her way thankfully back to Parsonage Place.

Six

Nuala was in the hall when Rona let herself into the house with the key she'd been given.

'How did it go with Aunt Edna?' she asked at once.

Rona hesitated, aware of Will doing his homework at the kitchen table.

'Would you like to come up and listen to the tape?'

'You recorded it? Oh yes, please, I would.'

With the bedroom door closed, Rona rewound the machine to the beginning of the interview. Nuala caught her breath as her aunt's halting voice filled the room, and when Rona switched off where she'd gone to make coffee, her eyes were full of tears.

'I'd no idea she was as bad as that,' she whispered.

'The odd thing is that she wasn't, the rest of the time. She didn't know who I was when I went back with the coffee, but after I'd explained she spoke quite lucidly, if a little disjointedly. She was positively eloquent on the subject of the Sunday school; talked about genes and chromosomes, for heaven's sake.' Rona flashed a look at her companion. 'That first bit, though: what did she mean about *coming across* the couple?'

'It would have been during her night walks. She wanders all round the town after dark. It frightens us even to think about it, but she's done it ever since Maisie died and so far she's come to no harm.'

'Maisie?' Rona repeated sharply. 'That's what she called me, just as I was leaving.'

Nuala nodded. 'I gathered that's who she thought you were. They were friends all their lives, till Maisie's death ten years ago.' She paused, then, avoiding Rona's eyes, added hesitantly, 'She mentioned a child.'

'Yes; I suppose the woman, whoever she was, must have become pregnant. Perhaps she lost the baby – or got rid of it.'

Nuala didn't reply and after a moment Rona prompted, 'You think it might be something else?'

'I don't really see how it can be. It doesn't make sense.'

'What doesn't?'

Nuala looked up miserably. 'It was when she mentioned the police.'

At Rona's blank face, she went on, 'We had a tragedy here a few years ago; a little girl was run over and killed.'

Rona said slowly, 'And when the driver came out of prison, her father murdered him.'

'You heard about it? Yes, it was terrible – it knocked the whole town for six.'

'And you're wondering if *that* was the child she was referring to?'

'Well, after the driver was murdered, the police did make an appeal, as Auntie said, though the following day they charged Mr Spencer. How could anything she saw possibly tie in with that?'

'Could there be a connection with that scandal you mentioned?'

Nuala looked alarmed. 'God, I hadn't thought of that.'

'What do you know about it?'

'Absolutely nothing. It was just that when I told her about your coming, and that Gordon had said you were interested in scandals, she said she hoped you'd stick to those safely in the past.'

'Safely in the past,' Rona echoed thoughtfully.

'So I asked her if she knew of a more recent one, but Will came in at that point and we never got back to it. Oh God!' she said again.

'Have you any idea who the couple might have been?'

Nuala shrugged. '*If* it was to do with Lottie – and it's a big "if" – I suppose it must have been one of her parents – her father, since Auntie talked about "his poor wife".'

'It could have been the driver.'

'If it was before he went to prison, yes. The trouble is we've no idea when this was taking place. But you're right – it could have been virtually anyone; it was only her mentioning both the police and a child that made me think of Lottie, though I can't imagine how an affair could be relevant.'

'That was just your aunt's idea, and it *was* during her less rational phase.' Rona slid out the full cassette and put in a new one, while Nuala watched in silence. 'Anyway,' she added, 'whoever was involved, it's nothing to do with us, so we might as well forget it. I only played you that bit to show her state of mind.'

'Yes, and I'm grateful. I'll pop round and see her after supper.'

Remembering her feeling of confinement the previous evening, Rona checked in the local paper for cinema times, deciding that an evening there would be preferable to her own company. She should be in time for the main feature if she left straight after supper.

Nuala informed her that the cinema was at the far end of town, near the shopping mall, and strongly advised her to take the car. 'With this spate of muggings, it's not safe after dark,' she warned. Max had said something similar.

Despite Nuala's efforts to speed up the meal, it was seven forty-five before they had finished. Rona ran upstairs, scooped car keys, pen and house key from the table into her handbag, and hurried from the house. In her haste she'd not closed it properly, with the result that when she juggled with it to open the car door, it fell to the ground and spilled its contents in an annoyingly wide arc.

Swearing under her breath and aware she was already late,

she darted about retrieving comb, purse, mobile and keys, and felt quickly under the car in case anything had rolled there. Then, sure she had everything, she jumped into the car and drove off.

The auditorium had already darkened when she was shown in, and she felt her way down the aisle to a vacant seat and sat back, trying to catch her breath. The film was not one she would have chosen, but it was interesting enough and she was sufficiently caught up in the plot for the time to pass pleasantly, which was all she asked of it.

Back in the car, she saw there was a message from Max on her mobile, and promptly rang him back.

'And where have you been until eleven at night?' he greeted her.

'To the cinema, for want of anything better.'

'Good film?'

'It was all right. Brad Pitt.'

'Ah!'

Rona laughed. '"Ah" nothing; there was a limited choice and it seemed the best bet.'

'You're not getting bored up there already?'

'Not really, though it's unsettling having to stay out all day. I've been haunting the library. Had some interesting interviews, though, one of them up at the college.'

'Are you back at the house now?'

'No, in the cinema car park. I thought you might have rung, so checked my mobile.'

'You've a parking space near the house, though?'

'Yes, don't fuss!'

'Just checking,' he said. 'See you tomorrow, then.'

'Yes; I'll be leaving about four, to be back around the same time as you.'

'Fine. Sleep well. Love you.'

'Love you too,' she replied, and with a little sigh, switched off and drove back to Parsonage Place.

* * *

She had decided to spend the next morning familiarizing herself with the town. First, though, she phoned the news editor at the *Buckford Courier*, identified herself, and asked the name of the reporter who'd written the previous week's paragraph. She was told it was Lew Grayson, that he'd be in the office all day, and would be pleased to see her if she'd like to drop in.

Having slipped notebook and recorder into her bag, she set off and had actually passed her car when something she'd subconsciously noticed made her turn. She'd not been mistaken: a small sheet of paper was tucked under the wipers.

Surely it couldn't be a parking ticket? she thought irritably as she extracted it; she was legitimately parked in a space reserved for visitors. She unfolded it, but since she'd been expecting an official notification, it took a minute for the words to sink in. Then, with a tightening of the throat, she read it again: INTERESTING CASSETTE! ANY THOUGHTS ON WHAT THE OLD BIRD MIGHT HAVE SEEN?

Rona turned and ran back up the path, her fumbling fingers needing several attempts to fit the key in the lock. Back in her room, she looked wildly about her. What had she done with the cassette? Feverishly she pulled open the table drawer. It was not there. Nor was it with her laptop, or among her notebooks. Heart hammering, she forced herself to be calm, to think back. When had she last seen it?

She'd taken it out of the machine after playing it to Nuala, and inserted the new one. So when she went down to supper, she must have left it on the table next to the keys she'd dropped there when she and Nuala first came into the room. And in her haste later to scoop up the keys, she'd have swept the cassette into her handbag with everything else – and dropped it by the car. All she could think was that it must have slid underneath, beyond her reaching fingers, and she'd not had time for a thorough search. But God, she thought now, she should have *made* time!

She forced herself to sit down at the table and steady her breathing. First, she mentally ran through its contents. As well as the interview with Edna Rosebury, it contained those at the various schools and at the college. Thank heaven she had at least transcribed them and had them safely on disk. Nevertheless, they had been vouchsafed to her personally, and although those interviewed knew she'd be using the material for later publication, that was very different from handing over their actual voices to a person or persons unknown.

She shivered at the sinister implications of the phrase, and another, even more unpleasant, thought struck her. Whoever had the tape knew to whom it belonged! He must have seen her drop her bag and noticed it lying in the road when she drove off. And – her heartbeats quickened – either come back later to leave the note, or – worse – never left, if, as was certainly possible, he lived in this street. So what would his next move be? To leave similar cryptic messages at the homes of those on the recording? The addresses of the schools and college could easily be ascertained – what of frail Miss Rosebury? Her name had been mentioned more than once, and if he didn't know her, he had only to look in the phone book. God, suppose he frightened her in some way?

He. She was thinking of the note's author as male, but that wasn't necessarily the case. The capital letters gave no hint of gender. She smoothed the crumpled paper with her fingers, turning it over for some clue as to its origin, but without success. It was torn from a small, spiral notepad, much like the one she'd been using herself, though hers, thank God, was safely in her bag.

So – what should she do? No point in going to the police; the cassette wasn't commercially valuable, nor, she thought with relief, was there anything confidential on it. Strictly speaking, it had not even been stolen, and from what Nuala had said, the police already had their hands full with mugging victims. Should she then warn the people she'd interviewed that she'd mislaid it? She couldn't see any advantage; some would be annoyed, some, perhaps, worried, and they would all think her irresponsible – as, indeed, she had been.

The best course, she told herself, moistening dry lips, was to do nothing, put the whole thing out of her mind. She was going home today, thank God, and the unknown watcher would soon get bored when her car didn't return. If, of course, there *was* a watcher. She'd been in too much of a hurry to notice anyone around, but perhaps some boys using the road as a short cut had seen what happened, and decided to play a trick on her. Surely that was the most likely explanation? She'd been over-reacting, she told herself; no real harm was done.

She set off again, flicking a wary eye up and down the street. No one else was in sight and she walked quickly and purposefully past the row of houses, inscrutable behind their windows, to the cobbled pathway leading to the square. At the end of it, instead of turning left as she usually did, towards the pub and Clement's Lane, she veered right, past the church. Someone was mowing the grass and a coffee stall had been set up in the porch. Rona hesitated, but decided to continue with her exploration.

However, she'd gone only a few paces, bringing her level with the vicarage garden, when a voice from behind the hedge hailed her and she turned to see the blonde woman she'd spied from her bedroom window. She was wearing jeans and a T-shirt that had seen better days.

'You *are* Mrs Parish, aren't you?' she continued, approaching the gate. 'Staying with Nuala Banks?'

'Yes, that's right. At least, I'm Rona Parish.'

'Lois Breen.' The woman eyed her keenly, reaching over a hand, which Rona took. 'But not Mrs?'

'Parish is my professional name,' Rona explained; 'I'm actually Mrs Allerdyce, though I don't think of myself as that.'

'I see.' Mrs Breen surveyed her for a minute, digesting this. 'You're a writer, I believe? My husband was telling me about you.'

'He was very helpful, putting me in touch with Nuala.'

'To your mutual benefit, I'm sure,' Lois Breen said briskly. Her short blonde hair framed a face that consisted of keen grey eyes, a long nose and a large mouth. Rona's instant impression was of a woman who spoke her mind, who, though compassionate, did not suffer fools gladly and stood for no nonsense. It would be interesting to see if her assessment proved right.

'Have you actually started yet?' Lois Breen enquired.

The lost tape flashed through Rona's mind but she answered steadily, 'Yes, I've had one or two interviews. People are being generous with their time.'

'Shall I also be coming under the spotlight?'

Rona smiled. 'I'd be delighted to interview you, if you wouldn't mind.'

The grey eyes showed amusement. 'Don't look for any revelations, though. The vicar's wife has to be the soul of discretion.'

'Then we'll keep it strictly factual. Perhaps you could fill me in on previous incumbents?'

'Done! Why don't you come round to supper this evening, so we can get to know each other?'

'That's kind of you, but I'm driving home this afternoon. I'm only here two nights a week.'

'Your next visit, then? Monday?'

'Thank you, I'll look forward to it.'

'Where are you off to now?'

'I thought I'd explore a bit, try to get the feel of the place.'

'Wednesday's market day, did you know? You might find that interesting. You know where Market Square is?'

'Yes, I spent a large part of yesterday at the library.'

'Worth a look, anyway. Well, enjoy yourself, and we'll see you about seven thirty on Monday.'

She turned away and walked back up the garden and Rona, abandoning her planned route, retraced her steps in the direction of the market. It was going to be a hot day; although still early, the sun already blazed in a cloudless sky, and the narrow confines of Clement's Lane were unpleasantly airless.

The square when she reached it looked very different from her last visit. It had been closed to traffic and its centre was a mass of colour as people thronged the aisles between the various stalls, stopping now and then to feel the fruit and vegetables, sample the display of cheeses, and riffle through the racks of clothes and stands of crockery, while above the sea of moving humanity the ancient stone cross rose lofty and apart. Along two sides of the square traders had parked their vans, some of which were being used for direct sales. There was a queue for fish at one, Rona noticed, and another, seizing on the bonus of a hot day, was dispensing ice cream. Anyone not visiting the market was confined to the narrow footpaths that ran round the square, and even there they were likely to be jostled.

Seeking a bird's-eye view, Rona climbed the steps to the library and leaned on the balustrade, unashamedly people-watching. Just below her, two traders were vying with each other, each shouting the value of his wares at the top of his voice. To her far left, safe behind their railings, the children of St Stephen's chased each other round their playground, and to her right she could see the bow window of the coffee shop, and two women seated at the table she'd occupied the previous day.

She made a note to speak to someone about the market; ask how long it had held its charter and whether any inter-esting events had befallen it in its long history. Idly she ran her eyes over the throng below her – and was disconcerted to find that she, the watcher, was being watched. Her observer was a slight, dark man who was leaning against a lamp post on the corner of the square. As their eyes met, he gave a slight smile of acknowledgement and she looked quickly away, ostensibly turning her attention to the stall immedi-ately below her. When, several minutes later, she again glanced in his direction, he had disappeared.

A sudden shout rose above the general clamour, and at the far side of the square a scuffle broke out. Rona saw a figure break away and run off down one of the side roads, with another in hot pursuit.

'What happened?' she asked a fat woman who'd just reached the top of the steps and was pausing to regain her breath.

The woman glanced behind her. 'Bag-snatcher,' she replied laconically. 'Happens every week. You'd think people would be on their guard.' And, shaking her head at their stupidity, she disappeared into the library.

Keeping a tight hold on her own handbag, Rona descended the steps, and immediately became engulfed in the crowd. She strolled up and down for a while, stopping to buy a can of lemonade and enjoying the generally good-humoured atmosphere. Eventually, when the heat generated by so many bodies became too much, she manoeuvred her way out of the square in search of the *Buckford Courier*. She'd checked their address when she phoned, and located it on the map she and Max had bought. Even so, it took several minutes to run it to earth, by which time, despite the cooling properties of the lemonade, she was uncomfortably hot again.

The newspaper was housed in a three-storey building with a private car park alongside. A placard bearing the paper's masthead was fixed to the wall above the door and she pushed her way inside, finding herself in a small foyer furnished with a couple of desks – one bearing a computer screen – a sofa and several armchairs. From behind one of the desks, a girl smiled a greeting.

'I'm Rona Parish,' she introduced herself. 'I've come to see Lew Grayson, if he's available?'

'If you'd like to take a seat, I'll phone through.'

Rona seated herself on the sofa and looked about her. Potted plants were dotted around and on the walls blown-up photographs recalled past local events. Three doors led off the foyer, and as she glanced at them, one opened and a man came towards her. He wore a red, open-neck shirt and his face, hardly less red, had beads of perspiration at the hair-line.

'Rona Parish? Hi, I'm Lew Grayson. What can I do for you?'

'I wanted to thank you for the plug last week,' Rona said diplomatically, 'and I was wondering if there's any way we might be of use to each other.'

Someone else had entered the building and was speaking to the receptionist.

'It's more peaceful upstairs,' Grayson said. 'We'll use the editor's office – he's out today.'

He led her through a security door and up some stairs. At the top, a corridor led to what, as far as Rona could see, was the newsroom, an open space where people sat at desks staring at monitors. Grayson, however, had stopped short of it and, opening a door, ushered her into a small office, where he motioned her to a chair and seated himself behind the desk.

'Delusions of grandeur!' he said with a grin. 'Right – shoot.'

Rona explained that she was working freelance for *Chiltern Life*, and briefly outlined her plans for the articles. 'I want them to be from the human-interest angle – the development of education and architecture, yes, but principally how they affected the population. And I'm anxious to collect as many anecdotes as I can about eccentric or famous personalities over the years. Would there be any objection to my looking at your archives?'

'No, they're open to everyone, but it would be as well to make an appointment.'

'I realize that. I'm only here for three days a week, so it wouldn't be on this visit. And might it be possible to borrow some old photos – those you won't be using, of course? Obviously we'd credit you with them.'

Grayson lifted his shoulders and let them fall. 'You'd have

to speak to someone else about that, but I don't see why not. We're aiming at an entirely different readership.'

Rona gave an embarrassed laugh. 'It sounds as though I'm simply recycling what other people have done, but I assure you I'm not. What I'm lacking is direct access – a means of obtaining people's memories of different events. How the war affected life in Buckford, how they celebrated VE Day and Royal Weddings – that kind of thing.'

Grayson thought for a minute, pulling at his lower lip. 'I could run another piece, if that would help. Ask people to get in touch with you if they've anything to contribute?'

'Would you?' Rona exclaimed eagerly. 'That would be great!'

He pulled a piece of paper towards him and uncapped his pen. 'Address and contact number?'

She hesitated, remembering the note on her windscreen. 'My mobile would be best,' she said.

'Sure.' He jotted it down.

'I presume you'll be running special editions yourself when the time comes?' she hazarded.

'Yep, but as I said, they'll be slanted differently from yours. There shouldn't be any clash.'

'I really am very grateful,' she told him, rising to go.

He made a dismissive gesture. 'It could work both ways; let us know if you come across any interesting lines.'

'I will,' she promised, and he escorted her back to the foyer.

Outside, the heat lay in wait for her, and to her relief she saw the striped awning of a café a little way down the road. Like a homing pigeon she bore down on it, glad to find that not only were there vacant tables, but each one bore a jug of iced water and some glasses. She hadn't accomplished very much, she thought as she seated herself and picked up the jug, but nevertheless it had been an eventful morning.

When Rona emerged after lunch the heat had intensified, and her recharged energy promptly drained away. It was too hot to do anything outdoors, and since she was up-to-date with her notes there was no point in returning to the library. In any case, she didn't know what time the market ended, and the thought of battling her way through it again was more than she could bear.

She'd go home, she decided with a wave of relief. There was no need to stay until four, as she'd intended; she'd go back to Parsonage Place, pack her case, and set off for home. She'd even be in time to take Gus for a walk.

Unfamiliar with this part of town, she took several wrong turns and it was nearly two thirty when she put her key in the door of number two. Immediately raised voices reached her from the sitting room, and she hesitated. Better to announce her presence, before she unwittingly eavesdropped.

'Nuala?' she called. 'I'm back. I've decided to leave early, so I'll just collect my things, if that's all right.'

She had started up the stairs when Nuala, her face flushed and upset, emerged from the sitting room, pulling the door shut behind her.

'Sorry, what did you say? You're leaving now?'

Rona gave her a bright smile. 'Yes; sorry to barge in like this, but it's too hot to think, so I decided to cut my losses.'

Nuala hesitated, obviously torn between her lodger and the visitor in the room behind her. 'So we'll see you on Monday?'

'Yes. Oh, and Mrs Breen has invited me to supper that evening.'

'One less pea in the soup, then,' Nuala said, with an attempt at a smile.

'Thanks for looking after me, and I'll see you next week.'

She continued purposefully up the stairs and after a minute Nuala said, 'Goodbye, then,' and returned to the sitting room. Rona, intentionally clattering about as she put things in her case, could hear the low hum of muted voices, but the argument or whatever it was had clearly been put on hold till she was out of the house.

After a last quick look round the room, she carried her case and laptop downstairs, called 'Goodbye!' to the closed door, and without waiting for a reply, hurried out to the car. For the moment, she had had enough of Buckford and its secrets.

As she was approaching Marsborough, she phoned Max at Farthings. 'Have you nearly finished there?' she asked him.

'Nearly; where are you?'

'Almost home, thank goodness.'

'Already? You left early, then?'

'Yes, I've done everything I planned for this week.'

'I've just finished clearing up, and was about to take Gus for a walk.'

'Hang on then, and we'll go together.'

'Right; I'll meet you back at the house in – what? – fifteen minutes?'

'About that,' she said.

Gus was overjoyed to see her, jumping up to lick her face, which was unusual for him. 'I've missed you too, boy,' Rona told him, ruffling his ears. She stood in the hallway, looking round the house. 'In fact, I've missed everyone and everything. It's good to be home.'

Max regarded her quizzically. 'You're not usually so effusive. Something go wrong up there?'

'Not really, no.' Since he'd been so anxious over her previous involvement, she didn't mention the lost tape, insignificant though it was. 'It's just that there are atmospheres, hints, you know the kind of thing,' she added vaguely.

'Plenty of that here,' Max told her. 'Shall I take your case up, or do you want to go straight out?'

'Let's go, and you can tell me what's been happening while I was away.'

'It's only been three days!' he reminded her.

They set off along the tree-lined streets and up the alley to Furze Hill Park, their usual destination. Immediately inside the gates were walkways and flowerbeds, fountains and sunken rose gardens, but a path on the left led to the upper area, a stretch of grassland and trees much patronized by joggers and dog-walkers. The main heat of the day had dissipated and a welcome breeze met them as they emerged on open ground.

'So did it go according to plan?' Max persisted, releasing Gus from his lead.

'In as much as I had a plan. I visited the schools, as I told you, and the college. The head's a cold fish, and I wasn't impressed by his wife, either.'

'You met her?'

'Not met exactly, but I saw her in a coffee shop, and gathered that she's always complaining. Stunning looking, though.'

'And the digs are OK?'

'On the whole, though it's a nuisance having to be out all day. The old man's a bit taciturn and the little boy's still cagey with me, but Nuala's friendly enough. She arranged for me to meet her aunt, who's lived there all her life. Believe it or not, she sees ghosts!'

'There's always one,' Max commented, throwing the ball for Gus.

'I also met the vicar's wife, and she's invited me to supper on Monday. I bet she could tell a story or two, but she warned me that her lips are sealed.'

As the ground levelled off they turned, as they often did, to look down over the town spread below them, with its irregular skyline, its steeples and towers. Rona drew a deep breath of satisfaction. There seemed much more space here than she had found in Buckford, for all its impressive history. Or perhaps it was just that Marsborough was home.

'I bumped into Dave Lampeter the other day,' Max remarked. 'Remember him?'

'As if I could forget.'

Dave was an ex-student of Max's, whom, during the

93

Harvey débâcle, he had co-opted to keep an eye on Rona without her knowledge, thereby causing her considerable disquiet.

'He still hasn't found a proper job, poor lad; he's filling in time stacking supermarket shelves. And talking of students, a new one signed on today; youngish married woman, very pale and quiet but a promising watercolourist.' Max had only one afternoon class, specifically for retired people and those at home.

'Should bring down the average age,' Rona said lightly.

They took it in turns throwing the ball, exchanging pleasantries with passers-by, people exercising their own dogs and elderly couples strolling arm in arm. School was out, and the play area lower down the slope was already crowded. Gus's ball retrieval grew noticeably slower and his panting more pronounced and, deciding he'd had enough, they started to retrace their steps.

'I'm beginning to feel hungry,' Rona announced. 'It was too hot to eat much at lunchtime. What's for supper?'

'Salmon marinated in wine and dill, cooked in foil, accompanied by one of my special salads, followed by home-made strawberry mousse. Does that meet with your approval?'

'Very much so. With the best will in the world, Nuala's cooking, bless her, is pretty basic.'

'Look who's talking!' Max retorted.

Seven

Gus was used to being left in the car, but when Rona pulled up outside the bungalow and told him to wait, he whined piteously. Hardening her heart, she locked the door, ignoring his reproachful pawing at the window, and turned to see Mrs Bishop standing in her doorway.

'Bring him in if you'd like to,' she called.

'Are you sure you don't mind?'

'Of course not. I like dogs.'

Rona unlocked the door, and before she could stop him, Gus bounded out and down the path towards the house. She hurried after him.

'I'm sorry, he's not usually so badly behaved,' she apologized, as Catherine bent to pat the dog. 'It's just that I've left him with my husband for the last few days, and now he won't let me out of his sight.'

'Quite understandable,' Catherine said, straightening and holding out her hand with a smile. 'He's done the introductions for us, hasn't he? What do you call him?'

'Gus. Short for Augustus.'

'A splendid name. Now, I thought we might sit outside. It's cool at the back of the house, and the people next door are out, so we shouldn't be overheard.'

Holding Gus firmly by the collar, Rona followed her hostess through the hall and sitting room to the open patio doors. The garden beyond was small and secluded, planted mainly with shrubs whose different-coloured foliage made an attractive frame for the lawn. Such flowers as there were seemed to have been chosen for their scent; jasmine, roses and honeysuckle.

'It's my first summer here,' Catherine explained, 'and I'm waiting to see what comes up before I make any plans.'

'It's lovely as it is,' Rona said. 'We've only a paved garden, but I try to ring the changes with seasonal plants in containers.'

The patio, in the shade as promised, was furnished with two floral-cushioned chairs and a table with a parasol. 'Would you prefer coffee, tea or home-made lemonade?'

'The lemonade sounds wonderful.'

Whether or not due to Gus's precipitate arrival, there seemed none of the initial restraint normally present at interviews. Catherine Bishop had about her an air of quiet self-assurance that smoothed over any awkwardness. At first sight Rona had thought her plain, but she was already revising that opinion. There was character in her face, and although it would have benefited from more liberal use of make-up, its lack was more than compensated for by an impression of what Rona could only describe as cleanliness, apparent in her sleekly shining hair and the understated elegance of her dress, as well as in the immaculate room they had just walked through.

As she disappeared indoors, Rona allowed herself to relax in her chair while Gus, soft-footed, set off on an exploration of the garden.

'Would you mind if I record this?' she asked on Catherine's return, as a crystal jug and glasses were set down on the table.

'Not at all, I was expecting you to. You're just back from Buckford, aren't you?' Catherine handed her a glass which chilled her fingers. 'What were your impressions of it?'

'Oh, it's fascinating; I hope my articles can do it justice.' She took a sip of the lemonade. 'I suppose you'll know all the people I met up there – Nuala Banks and Miss Rosebury, and Mr and Mrs Breen?'

'I do, yes, some better than others. Since there's no St Stephen's Church, we borrowed Gordon Breen for our chaplain and he proved a good friend. Did you manage to get round the schools?'

'I left St Stephen's till after I'd seen you, but the others were helpful, thanks to your introductions. I even had a couple of minutes with the august Mr Maddox.'

'You *were* fortunate.'

'I'd been told he didn't give interviews, but as luck would have it, he came into the hall while I was there. He was perfectly civil, but I'm glad he was never my headmaster.'

'He's a brilliant teacher, by all accounts,' Catherine said neutrally. 'The exam results have improved enormously.'

'Well, it was Miss Morton who attended to me. She gave me a lightning tour and supplied me with various pamphlets, but I've not had a chance to study them yet. She even told me about the school ghosts.'

Catherine smiled. 'Yes, I looked into them while I was doing the history. The sightings seem to have been quite well authenticated.'

Rona bit her lip. 'You must have known Mr Maddox quite well; I'm sorry if I spoke out of turn.'

'Not at all. In fact I didn't have much contact with him; it was his predecessor, Reginald Palfrey, who invited me to do the history, though unfortunately he left before it took shape.'

'It must have been quite an undertaking,' Rona commented.

'Indeed it was. The original one, on St Stephen's, started life as a project for the children; they worked on it for a whole academic year, and the finished scrapbook was on display at Speech Day. That's where Reggie saw it – he presented the prizes that year – and he persuaded me, against my better judgement, to do one for BC. Buckford College,' she added, as Rona looked up enquiringly. 'That's what we called it. But it was a massive challenge, far, far larger in scope than St Stephen's, because of course it's three hundred years older.

Then there was the change of headship, and the fact that I was conscious all the time of the necessity of maintaining prestige. The whole thing became considerably more scholastic – and time-consuming – than I'd anticipated, though I doubt it was academic enough for Richard.' She shot Rona an amused glance. 'You weren't shown it, I presume?'

Rona shook her head.

'As I suspected. It was probably filed in the waste-paper basket.'

'But that's too bad, after all your work!' Rona exclaimed indignantly.

'Oh my dear, I thoroughly enjoyed myself. So much so, that I later did a third compilation for the Grammar School, though Lord knows if that's still in existence.'

Rona felt it politic to change the subject. 'How long were you at St Stephen's?' she asked.

'Twelve years. As you can imagine, it was an important part of my life.'

'Have you always taught?'

'It's all I ever wanted to do. Before Buckford, I was Head of Infants at a church school in Stokely.'

'You never considered teaching older children?'

'I was tempted, yes. In fact, I was offered the headship of a local grammar school, but after a lot of thought I turned it down. In some ways it would have been more stretching, but there's something about forming young minds, teaching them to think for themselves and work things out, that had me hooked. I felt I could do most good by giving them a strong foundation on which to build.'

Rona nodded, making notes on her pad, and Catherine, always intrigued by family relationships, scrutinized her for any resemblance to her father. It was obvious that her height and brown eyes were his legacy; and probably his hair, now steel-grey, had once been as dark as that which swung above her shoulders and flicked up at the ends. Her mouth, though, quirking delightfully at the corners, and the lift of her chin were very much her own. The overall impression was of a confident, independent young woman who knew her own mind, and Catherine, usually slow to form judgements, realized, slightly to her surprise, that she already liked her very much.

Rona, looking up, misinterpreted her gaze and flushed slightly. Her father, she remembered, had described Mrs Bishop as quiet and unassuming. She felt 'watchful' would be a better description.

'I'm sorry,' she said, 'that last bit was rather personal.'

But Catherine was shrugging. 'No matter; St Stephen's and I were pretty intertwined.' She paused. 'Without wanting to seem pushy, I could lend you the histories, if they'd be of interest?' And, at Rona's quick glance, she added, 'Obviously I kept copies for myself.'

Rona's face lit up. 'That would be wonderful, as long as it wouldn't ruffle any feathers. I mean, the college couldn't withhold permission, could they?'

'No, since I own the copyright; but if you're going to use anything, it might be a courtesy to tell them.'

'Then thank you, I'd love to borrow them.'

'I'll look them out before you go. Now, is there anything else I can help you with?'

Rona thought back to Edna Rosebury and her encrypted ramblings. 'Did you know that little girl who was run over?'

Catherine's face clouded. 'Charlotte Spencer? Yes, I knew her. Her brothers were with us before going to BC.'

'So you'd have met her parents, too?'

Catherine nodded. 'I liked Mr Spencer, though I really only knew him from parents' evenings. He was a quiet man, always leaving his wife to do the talking and seldom offering any insight as to his own views. But he was positively the last person I'd have expected to behave as he did, especially after the considerable time-lapse.'

The journalist in Rona came to the fore. 'From newspaper reports, though, the evidence seemed fairly conclusive – motive, means and opportunity.'

'Yes, it was the knife that clinched it: one of the family's kitchen knives with traces of Pollard's blood still on it, hidden in the garage. The defence made the point that since Spencer was arrested on the spot he couldn't have hidden it himself, and that if, as the prosecution alleged, he'd asked someone else to dispose of it, he'd certainly not have told them to put it in his own garage.'

'And what was the reply to that?' Rona asked.

'That he'd not expected to be arrested, and was intending to replace it in the drawer before it was missed.' Catherine sighed. 'But of course, even without that question mark, he was the prime suspect.'

'And he's still in prison?'

'Yes, for the next umpteen years.'

'What happened to the family?'

'Mrs Spencer and the boys are still there, and as I said, the boys go to BC. I used to see her around town. She had a hunted look, poor woman, but I suppose she's no option but to keep going.'

Rona said tentatively, 'Were there any rumours circulating about that time?'

Catherine gave a brief laugh. 'My dear, Buckford, like most small towns, is a hotbed of rumour. What had you in mind?'

'I'm not sure. An illicit romance, I suppose.'

Catherine Bishop raised an eyebrow. 'And where did you get wind of that?'

Rona smiled shamefacedly. 'From Miss Rosebury, actually. She seems to have seen something – or thought she did.'

'Oh, if she says she saw something, you can take it that she did. She's as sharp as a pin, that one.'

'But that's just it – unfortunately she's not, just at the moment. Nuala's worried about her.'

'Oh? Why?'

'She's becoming forgetful, and when I was with her, she thought at first I was her friend, who died ten years ago.'

'Maisie Farrell? That doesn't sound good. What did she say?'

Rona hesitated. 'I felt I was there under false pretences. She was asking Maisie for advice.'

'Too late for that, I'm afraid.'

Nuala hadn't asked her not to mention the interview – and, thought Rona with a chill, someone else already knew about it. It could do no harm to repeat it to Catherine Bishop, who might well have the solution to the riddle.

'She referred to a scandal, and said she'd seen a couple together several times. Apparently she walks around the town at night.'

Catherine nodded. It seemed this was common knowledge. 'But why should a couple of unknown lovers interest you? I presume they *are* unknown?'

'Miss Rosebury knew them, but she didn't mention names. What interested me was that she thought she ought to report them to the police.'

'The *police*?'

'She said they'd appealed for information, however unimportant it might seem. But Miss Rosebury decided against it, because "his poor wife" had suffered enough, and because of "the child". I'd assumed she was referring to an illegitimate baby, but when I played it back to Nuala, she thought it might be Charlotte, since the police *had* made a television appeal after the murder of the car driver.'

Catherine said slowly, 'To have had even remote relevance, a Spencer or a Pollard must have been involved.'

'That's what I thought.'

'Well, I've no knowledge of the Pollards – they didn't live in Buckford – but it's hard to imagine either of the Spencers kicking over the traces.' Her brow creased. 'And Mr Pollard had just got divorced – it was one of the mitigating circumstances in his defence – so why should Edna or anyone else care if he was seeing someone?' She shook her head. 'I think she made the right decision; it couldn't possibly have any bearing on the case.'

'Perhaps Pollard was killed not because he ran over Charlotte, but for some other reason? Suppose he crossed someone while he was in prison – one of the other inmates, who arranged to have him killed?'

'And planted the Spencers' knife in the Spencers' garage?'

Rona lifted her shoulders, conceding the invalidity of the suggestion. She glanced at her watch and reached forward to switch off the recorder. 'Enough theorizing – I must be going. Thank you so much for all your help.'

Catherine rose with her. 'Now the interview's over, may I say how much I enjoy your biographies? I think I've read them all.'

Rona flushed with pleasure. 'That's very kind of you.'

'Have you any more on the stocks?'

'No, I – ran into some trouble with the last one, so I'm having a short break.'

'Of course – I remember now. I'm so sorry. Come inside, then, and I'll unearth those scrapbooks for you.'

Rona snapped her fingers at Gus, sleeping peacefully under the table, and he obediently came trotting after her. Catherine Bishop opened the top drawer of a Queen Anne bureau and extracted three bound volumes, one considerably thicker than the others.

'Use anything you like,' she offered, handing them to Rona. 'Or nothing, if they're not suitable. There's no hurry to return them, and if there's anything else you'd like to ask, please get in touch.'

Catherine walked to the gate with them, gave Gus a farewell pat, and waited until Rona's car had rounded the bend. A very interesting young woman, she thought, as she went back into the house.

The previous evening, Rona had found a silk scarf down the side of a chair, and recognized it as Dinah's. Instead of phoning her, she decided to drop in to *Chiltern Life*, update Barnie on her progress, and enquire after Melissa.

Accordingly after her interview with Catherine Bishop, she deposited the books safely in her study, put the car away and set off with Gus along Dean's Crescent.

A strange girl was behind Polly's desk, so Rona had no choice but to take Gus, tightly leashed, up the stairs with her. Receiving only a grunt in response to her knock, she opened the door to find Barnie sitting at his desk, his head in his hands. He looked up sharply, ready to bark at whoever entered, but his face softened when he saw Rona.

'Hi,' he said dully.

'Barnie, what's wrong?' Anxiety sharpened her voice, and Gus raised his head to look at her.

'More complications with Mel,' he answered heavily. 'Dinah flew out yesterday.'

'I'm so sorry. Is there anything I can do?'

'Nothing anybody can do. That's the trouble.'

'For you, I meant.'

He gave her a tired smile. 'Thanks, honey, but no. The work will keep me going.'

She opened her bag and took out the vibrant silk scarf. 'Dinah left this last Friday. I've been away, so I've only just found it.'

He nodded his thanks as she laid it on his desk. 'Been making a start on your project?'

'Yes. I don't think there'll be any shortage of material.'

'That's good.' But his tone was abstracted, and Rona decided against going into any details. Gus, however, was not yet ready to leave, and, pushing round the corner of the desk, laid his head on Barnie's lap and regarded him soulfully.

Barnie scratched his ears, a smile touching his mouth. 'Hi, ole fellow. How are things?'

'He's not forgiven me for leaving him with Max,' Rona told him, glad to lighten the atmosphere. 'He's been shadowing me ever since I came back. Seriously, Barnie, if you'd like a meal, or even a drink and a chat—'

'Bless you, but Dinah left me a freezer full of one-portion

meals. She'll skin me if I don't get through them.'

'Right. Well, love to her and Mel when she phones.'

'Sure. I'll be in touch.'

Rona tugged gently on Gus's lead and they left Barnie to his worries. As he'd said, there was nothing they could do.

Lindsey phoned that evening. 'I don't like it when you're away,' she complained.

'I'm still at the end of a phone.'

'It's not the same.'

'Lunch tomorrow, then?'

'Can't, I'm tied up with a client. And I'm leaving straight from work to drive to Stokely for the weekend.'

'Hugh-avoidance tactics?'

'Got it in one.'

'Have you heard from him?'

'No, but it's only been five days. This weekend will be the crux: will he or won't he come up as usual?'

'If you're not here, you'll never find out.'

'That's the drawback; I need to know if he's still intent on moving back here.'

'Who are you seeing in Stokely?'

'Keith and Patsy. I've a standing invitation, and never taken them up on it. Are you swanning up to Buckford again next week?'

''Fraid so, but we could meet on Thursday.'

'Right, I'll hold you to that. Perhaps there'll be some news on the Hugh front by then.'

The next phone call was from Tom. 'I was wondering how you got on with Mrs Bishop?' he asked diffidently.

'Fine, she was most helpful. Thanks so much for fixing it, Pops. She's lent me three scrapbooks she's done on schools up there.'

'Sounds useful. And what did you think of her?'

'That she wasn't as unassuming as you'd led me to suppose!'

He laughed. 'She didn't come over all school-marmy, I hope?'

'No, no, nothing like that. I liked her; we got on really well.'

'Good. I'm glad she could help. And how was the frozen north?'

'As hot as the sunny south. Unbearably so, in fact.' She paused. 'We're not expected for Sunday lunch, are we?'

'Not as far as I know.'

'Right. No offence, but with being away half the week, I've masses of things to do.'

'That's fine, we quite understand. See you soon, love.'

'What do we "quite understand"?' Avril asked sourly, coming into the room as he put down the phone.

'That Rona's busy this weekend.'

Avril sniffed. 'She's always busy. Seeing her parents is obviously low on her list of priorities.'

'It's just that with being up in Buckford she has things to catch up on,' Tom said placatingly.

'Nevertheless, I think we're due a bit of consideration, after all we've done for her – and Lindsey too, for that matter. I invited her for this Sunday, since for once Hugh's not coming up, but no, she's dashing off to see friends in Stokely.'

'It might help if you were more welcoming.'

Immediately he'd spoken, he realized his mistake and braced himself for the inevitable. It was not long in coming.

'And exactly what do you mean by that?'

Tom juggled with the need to explain himself without causing further upset. 'Well, these days you seem to spend more time criticizing the girls for not coming often enough, than being glad to see them when they do.'

'I might know it's my fault.'

'I'm not saying that, love, but they have their own lives to lead. Surely it's better that they should come because they want to, rather than from a sense of duty?'

'Oh, you! You're always making excuses for them,' Avril retorted, and slammed out of the room.

With a sigh, Tom picked up his newspaper.

* * *

The next morning Rona carried Catherine Bishop's books outside, laid them on the patio table and, shaded by the umbrella, seated herself beside them. The scent of herbs reached her from the trough near the door; a fall of campanula cloaked the far wall in purple, and the low murmur of bees sounded among the riot of flowers in the containers. She could hardly ask for a more perfect work place, she thought contentedly.

Her mood was broken by the sound of a sash window being thrown up in the house next door. From where she sat, Rona could see none of her neighbours, nor they her. If, however, she walked to the end of the patio – some twenty-five feet away – she could look up at the back walls of the houses on either side.

She and Max barely knew their neighbours. The house on their right was owned by a family with three teenaged children, while that on their left belonged to a couple who spent most of their time abroad, and was therefore occupied by a succession of relatively short-term tenants. It was from this last that she'd heard the window raised, and a minute later a woman's voice called down to someone presumably in their garden.

'I've ordered the taxi for two o'clock,' she said.

'Right,' answered a nearer male voice, just beyond Rona's wall. 'Are the bags all packed?'

'I'm just finishing the last one. Have you confirmed the time of the flight?'

'No, I'll come and do it now.'

There came the sound of the back door being opened and closed, and a minute later the window came down.

Off on their holidays, Rona thought. Or perhaps leaving for good. And she still hadn't the faintest idea what they looked like. Smiling to herself at this omission, she reached for the book on St Stephen's and settled down to read it.

An hour or so later, she had learned, among other things, that the school had been founded in 1871, on its present site and under the auspices of the nearby church. What really interested her, though, was the imaginative way in which its history was recounted. At the beginning of the book the children had pasted in a series of pictures of Victorian classrooms – rather blurred in this photocopied edition, but she could make out little boys in wing collars and girls in pinafores, while on the facing pages were brief accounts, in copperplate, of what was happening in the larger world – the passing of the Trade Union Act, the publication of George Eliot's *Middlemarch*, the foundation of the Rugby Union – a layout that was maintained throughout the book. Poems, laboriously copied out in childish hands, recounted events that had taken place over the years, providing not only a history of the school but of the times through which it had existed.

There were sepia photographs of school groups, even harder to distinguish, members of staff in voluminous sleeves seated stiffly on chairs while the children knelt on the grass in front of them. The grass might have gone, but the outline of the building behind them was recognizable as that which Rona had glimpsed across Market Square. There were also sections on recreation, home life, hobbies and fashion. Newspaper cuttings, yellow even in reproduction, advertised a variety of objects from carpet sweepers to leghorn hats, and a Ladies' Help Agency offered parlour maids of the highest diligence and respectability.

Rona flicked through the decades, full of admiration for the research that had gone into this record. There was, of course, far more detail than she could make use of, but she'd extract a snippet here and there to illustrate the school's place in the history of the town.

It wasn't until after eleven that she remembered Max had warned her they were out of bread and milk. Reluctantly she closed the scrapbook, and with Gus at her side, set off to replenish supplies.

Rona had just completed her purchases when she heard her name called, and turned to see Magda Ridgeway hurrying towards her.

'Rona – hi! Have you time for a coffee? I was hoping for a word with you.'

'Yes, of course. Nice to see you.'

They went together up the spiral staircase leading to the walkway above the shops and turned into the doorway of the Gallery Café. From here, since it straddled the street corner, there were grandstand views of both Guild Street and Fullers Walk.

'Did you hear about the break-in?' Magda demanded, as they seated themselves at a window table.

'No?'

'The Buckford boutique. They got away with thousands of pounds' worth of stock.'

Rona regarded her in horror. 'Magda! I'd no idea – how awful.'

'I thought you might have heard, since you were up there. It seems quite a mini crime wave has broken out.'

'Oh, that I do know,' Rona said feelingly; 'I was on the receiving end myself.'

'Good God! What happened?'

She shook her head dismissively. 'No, I'm exaggerating, but it was a bit unnerving. I must have dropped one of my cassettes as I got into the car. It had several interviews on it, and later someone left a note on my car implying that he'd listened to it.'

'What an odd thing to do. Did he give it back?'

'No, but fortunately I'd transcribed everything. What upset me, though, was someone unauthorized listening to it, specially since he made a reference to my landlady's aunt, a frail old lady who'd been rambling a bit.'

'What kind of reference?'

'Oh – had I any idea what she meant – that kind of thing. She'd been telling me about a couple meeting secretly and wondered whether she should inform the police.'

Magda lifted an eyebrow. 'Not a criminal offence, is it?'

'No, but – oh, it's a long story. But to get back to the break-in: you were fully insured, I hope?'

'Yes, but that's hardly the point. All our new autumn stock has gone. We'll have to plunder the other shops to make up the shortfall. But enough of my troubles. Apart from the cassette business, how was your trip?'

'Quite successful, actually. My first article's on education through the centuries, so I did the rounds of one or two schools, Buckford College among them.'

Magda leaned to one side as the waitress put down their coffee. 'The head's wife is one of our customers,' she remarked.

'Mrs Maddox? Really?'

'Why the surprise? Did you meet her?'

'No, I saw her in the town, but I didn't know who she was till later. I must say she's a good advertisement for you – very chic.'

'I met her years ago, before she married Richard, though I've never known her well.'

'How did you meet?' Rona asked curiously.

'She came into the Chilswood shop. One of my friends who was there knew her, and she introduced us. Helena was giving her son piano lessons.'

'I didn't realize she taught, as well.'

'She only takes a handful of pupils these days.' Magda stirred her coffee. 'I don't know why, but I've always felt rather sorry for her.'

'Was she married before?'

'No, there'd been a long-term relationship that didn't work out. She was terribly cut up when it ended, and had some sort of breakdown, apparently. She's still highly strung – goes with the musical temperament, perhaps. Anyway, in due course Richard came along, a handsome, eligible widower, and when he asked her to marry him, she jumped at it. According to Briony she desperately wanted children, and he needed a wife before he could apply to Buckford. They're quite strict about that.'

'A marriage of convenience, then.'

'Oh, I'm not saying there's no love there – I hope there is – though Richard seems a pretty cold fish, and the longed-for children never materialized. I might be wronging him, but his own sons were already in their teens and I doubt if he'd have wanted any more.'

Magda gave a brief laugh. 'Why are we discussing Helena Maddox? What I wanted to ask you was if you'd have lunch with me next week? I have to go to Buckford to sort some things out, and it occurred to me you'll be there. We've just opened a little café at the back of the shop – at least that's still intact, thank God – and I wanted an honest opinion of it. You know, atmosphere, choice of food, décor, prices – things like that.'

'From one who's an expert on all things culinary?'

Magda smiled. 'From one who enjoys eating.'

'I'd love to, thanks. It'll provide a bit of light relief; I'm hoping to concentrate on churches next week. I'm even having supper with the vicar on Monday, so I'll probably be ready to let my hair down!'

'Great.' Magda finished her coffee. 'Let's make it Tuesday then, about twelve thirty? Now I really must dash – I've a buyer arriving any minute. See you.'

'I'll look forward to it.'

Rona finished her own coffee more slowly, turning over in her mind what she'd learned about Helena Maddox. How little you could tell from the persona people presented to the world, she thought. She had written Mrs Maddox off as a rich, lovely woman with a penchant for complaining, knowing nothing of her unsatisfied longing for children or her gift for music. As a writer, she should be more cautious in labelling people, she upbraided herself, and resolved to be less hasty in future.

Eight

It was not until Sunday evening that Rona checked her mobile for messages, and saw to her astonishment there were over a dozen. The explanation soon became clear; Lew Grayson had kept his word and run another snippet in Friday's *Courier*. She retired to her study and, with pen poised, started to play through them.

As was to be expected, they were a mixed bag. A group of boys kept interrupting each other as they spun a lurid story about a vampire stalking the town, to the accompaniment of hysterical giggles in the background; an elderly lady stated that her grandmother had been housemaid to what was then known as 'the gentry', and had some tales to tell. More scandals, Rona thought with wry amusement, but since the caller had left neither name nor number, they were lost to her. There were a couple of obscene calls, then one that startled her into full attention.

'How's the old girl?' came a strident voice, loud in the quiet room. 'Told you who the lovers are yet?'

She'd been right, then, the thief was a man, though something in the timbre of the voice suggested it was disguised. Why? Did he think she might recognize his normal one? The thought made her uneasy, as did the fact that he hadn't, as she'd hoped, considered it a game, forgotten once the note was written. Perhaps, after all, she should warn those featured on the tape.

Determinedly she continued with the messages. Several claimed to have material of interest, and left contact numbers

111

without being any more specific. They might well be a waste of time, but since they'd taken the trouble to phone, she would have to call them back.

'Are you coming down for a drink?' Max called from the foot of the stairs.

'I've nearly finished; just a couple more to go.'

And it was the next call that made up for all the time-wasters. 'Miss Parish,' said a hesitant voice, 'my name is Beth Spencer and my husband's in prison convicted of murder. I know beyond shadow of a doubt that he's inno-cent, and I wonder if you can help me prove it? You're prob-ably my last hope. I'd be so grateful if you'd contact me. My number is—'

Rona switched off the phone and sat staring into space, her heart hammering. One thing was certain, there was no way she could tell Max about this call. But nor, she accepted, was there any way she could ignore it. God, she should have known the Harvey affair would haunt her. People seemed to have got it into their heads that she could solve problems that defeated the police, which was plainly ludicrous; she wasn't even an investigative journalist. Furthermore, in this case the police had not been defeated: they had brought to trial a man whose daughter had been killed by the victim, and who had concealed a knife stained with his blood on his own premises.

Should she go and see Beth Spencer? Or should she phone back and tell her gently that it wasn't part of her remit to reopen criminal files? She closed her notepad and went back downstairs. By the time she reached the kitchen, she knew which option she would take.

Beth Spencer worked as a dental receptionist, and since she preferred Rona not to come to the house when the boys were home, she suggested a lunchtime meeting. It was arranged that they would meet at St Stephen's Coffee Shop at one o'clock.

As she drove to Buckford the next morning, Rona agonized over whether to tell Nuala about the missing cassette. She'd not seen her to talk to since she'd found the note, should she admit the loss, or would it simply add to Nuala's worries? She was already concerned about her aunt, and the raised voices that had greeted Rona's unexpectedly early return last Wednesday hinted at further problems.

Over the weekend she had reread the transcript of the missing tape, and convinced herself there was nothing on it to compromise anyone. The mention of the errant lovers was the only item remotely capable of causing trouble, and since they hadn't been named, any damage it could do was limited. Surely, then, for everyone's peace of mind, it was better to say nothing.

As the previous week, Rona parked her car, grateful for the vacant space, and carried her case into the house. Nuala appeared at the top of the stairs. 'Hello – had a good weekend?'

'Yes, thanks.' Rona went up the stairs towards her. 'Not at work today?'

'No; I'm in the office at Samuel's department store for the next three weeks, and they're closed on Mondays.'

'Nice way to start the week! How's your aunt?'

'Not good.' Nuala followed her as far as the bedroom door. 'I've slept over there the last few nights to make sure she doesn't go walkabout, but as you can imagine it wasn't well received, and she still refuses to see the doctor. She insists she's perfectly all right, and she was certainly compos mentis all weekend.'

'Perhaps it was just a hiccup then,' Rona said, putting her case on the bed. The window was open and there was a small vase of flowers on the dressing-table. She sniffed at them appreciatively. 'Thank you for these; they're lovely.'

'From the garden.' Nuala's mind was still on her aunt. 'I did ask her about the couple,' she continued, 'but she swore she didn't know what I was talking about. She's obviously decided to clam up.'

'She might have forgotten,' Rona suggested, but Nuala shook her head.

'No, I could tell she knew. Still, it doesn't look as though we'll get anything out of her.' She turned to go, then glanced back. 'You did say you wouldn't be in for supper tonight?'

'That's right, I'm going to the vicarage. I'll be back about five as usual, though, to type up my notes and have a wash and change.' She wondered fleetingly whether to ask if she might return earlier, but decided against it. Jack Stanton might not care to have comings and goings during the day.

'Fine,' Nuala replied. 'We might not be home, but you have your key.'

After she'd gone downstairs, Rona hung up the dress she intended to wear that evening, then glanced at her watch. Still nearly two hours before her lunch appointment. Since this was officially her ecclesiastical week and she'd be seeing the vicar this evening, she could do worse than make a start on St Giles's, just over the wall.

This time a church welcomer was on duty, a pleasant, middle-aged woman waiting just inside the door. Several other people were wandering around farther up the aisle, and one or two were reading the bronze memorial plates on the walls.

Feeling it would be unethical to present herself as a tourist, Rona identified herself and explained what she was hoping to do.

'Oh yes, Miss Parish, Mr Breen said you might be in. Is there anything I can help you with, or would you prefer to walk round by yourself? There are several pamphlets, which might help.'

'Thanks, I'll take one.' She remembered now that she had one from her last visit, but had foolishly left it at home. 'Perhaps I should look round first, and ask you for further information afterwards?'

The church was as lovely as she remembered, and she

walked slowly round, referring to the informative little booklet. The font, she learned, was thirteenth century and the tower had been erected in 1400. One of the memorial plates commemorated those killed during the Civil War, two of whom had died in that very building under Roundhead fire. She and Max had seen the cannonball on their previous visit.

Several chapels dedicated to various saints lay off the side aisles, and two of them had early wall paintings that had been uncovered some twenty years previously. The paten, Rona read, had been made for Jane Seymour, to celebrate the birth of her son. It had passed into Queen Elizabeth's possession, and she had later given it to one of her favourites who lived nearby, who in turn had presented it to the church.

The sun slanting through the stained glass, the smell of beeswax mingling with perfume from the flowers massed in the chancel and the organ playing quietly in the background combined to make Rona linger, and with a start she realized she must hurry to keep her appointment. She thanked the woman at the door, promising to return later, and set off quickly down Clement's Lane.

There was no market in progress today, and the square had reverted to its normal appearance. Rona turned into the coffee shop, identifying the woman sitting alone at the same moment as she hesitantly raised a hand.

She rose as Rona approached. 'Miss Parish? Beth Spencer. Thank you so much for seeing me.'

'As I warned you,' Rona reminded her, 'I really don't see how I can help.'

Beth Spencer was small and neat, with short blonde hair curling close to her scalp. She was wearing a white blouse and blue denim skirt, possibly her receptionist uniform. Her face was endearingly freckled and she had earnest green eyes that she kept fixed on Rona.

'I don't know how much you've heard about my husband?' she began at once.

'Not a great deal,' Rona confessed. 'I read a brief account of the case when I was researching newspaper archives.'

'But since you've been here, people have spoken of him?'

'He seems to have some local support,' Rona answered obliquely.

There was a pause while, prompted by the waitress, they chose what they'd like to eat. As she moved away, Beth leaned across the table, her hands clasped. 'I hoped they might have said they thought he was innocent. Obviously, as his wife I believe it, but I'm not alone, I promise you.'

Rona remembered Catherine Bishop's words – positively the last man she'd have expected to commit murder. 'Suppose you tell me what happened, from the beginning?' she invited.

'Well of course it all started when Lottie was killed.' Beth's hands tightened their clasp but her face remained impassive. Rona wondered how many times she'd had to go through this account.

'It was a Saturday afternoon, and Alan – my husband – was taking her to a birthday party. The house wasn't far away, and they were almost there when this car came screeching round the corner, lost control and mounted the pavement. Lottie had run on ahead, and caught the full impact. She was – pinned against the wall.' Beth closed her eyes briefly. 'There was nothing anyone could do.'

'Your husband witnessed it?'

'Yes. He ran over and started clawing at the car, as though he could move it away from her. According to passers-by, he was screaming at the driver to reverse, to back off, but the man was in total shock, just staring straight ahead. Not that it would have made any difference,' she finished quietly. 'The impact crushed her to death.'

Rona moistened her lips, glad of the diversion as their spritzers were brought to the table.

'Anyway,' Beth resumed tonelessly, 'Alan finally wrenched the car door open, leant across the driver, and threw it into reverse himself. As the car jerked back, someone caught Lottie and laid her down on the pavement. It was clear she was already dead, though Alan refused to accept it. The – the police had to prise her out of his arms.'

Rona averted her eyes from the raw anguish on her face, unable to think of anything to say.

'The driver was arrested – over the limit, of course, after a lunchtime session, though only slightly. I know nothing would bring Lottie back, but it might have helped if he'd had to pay for what he did. He *killed* her, for God's sake! He should have got at least ten years. But he was apparently "of good character" –' her voice was savage – 'and he'd been drinking because he'd received his divorce papers. The upshot was he was sentenced to *eighteen months*, and as if that wasn't insult enough, they released him after *nine*! Can you *believe* it?'

'How did your husband react?' Rona asked quietly.

'He was out of his mind with grief – we all were.'

'I meant, what did he think of the light sentence?'

Beth Spencer thought for a minute. 'He wasn't as angry as I was – I'm not sure he even took it in; he was too busy blaming himself, because he'd not been holding Lottie's hand. He kept saying if he'd kept her back with him, the car would have missed her. But Lottie always danced ahead. That's how she was, and she knew to wait at the kerb.' The irony of that blurred her eyes, and it was a minute before she continued.

'He thought I blamed him too. Perhaps I did, in a way.' She shuddered. 'It was a nightmare existence for all of us. Alan lost about two stone in weight and neither of us were sleeping. Then we stopped talking about it. There was nothing new to say, and it was just too painful, so we shut it away and did our grieving privately. In any case, we had to keep things as normal as possible for the boys. Harry had just joined Josh at Buckford College, and I must say the staff there were absolutely wonderful.'

Their food was brought and they began to eat, each busy with her thoughts.

'And then Mr Pollard was released,' Rona said.

'Yes. We were officially informed of the date, but we didn't discuss it. We didn't discuss anything; instead of being drawn together by it all, we'd tended to drift apart – no longer knew what to say to each other.' She looked up, meeting Rona's eyes. 'So I've no first-hand knowledge of what happened next. I can only repeat what he told me, though I must stress I believe him utterly.'

She pushed the untouched food to the side of her plate and laid down her knife and fork. 'He received a letter,' she said. 'It was typed, local postmark, and it said Pollard still felt an overwhelming sense of guilt, and if Alan wouldn't meet him and accept his apology, he didn't want to go on living. Practically begged him, Alan said, to meet him outside the Cat and Fiddle in Sunningdean. Sunningdean,' Beth added flatly, 'was where Pollard lived; it's about ten miles away, on the Chilswood road. Well, he screwed it up and threw it away. Which, with hindsight, was a big mistake. Then he began to have second thoughts, wondered if he should accept the apology and perhaps prevent the man from doing something desperate. And the outcome was he decided he'd have no peace unless he went to Sunningdean.

'He still didn't tell me, and that, too, went against him at the trial. He said he didn't want to upset me, so he told me he was meeting some friends from work and might be late back.'

She took a long drink, emptying her glass. 'And that's when the second nightmare began. Since he'd said he'd be late, I went to bed, and was woken by the phone. I was half asleep and couldn't make out at first what he was saying, specially since I thought he was with friends. But he told me he'd gone to this pub to meet someone and stumbled across a man lying on the pavement. It turned out to be Barry Pollard, and he was dead. Well, he had to go to the police station and make a statement, and when the police asked why he was out at Sunningdean, the story of the anonymous letter sounded incredibly thin. By that time, of course, they'd realized who he was, and promptly arrested him on suspicion of murder. Admittedly he had blood on him, because he'd turned Pollard over, thinking he was drunk and trying to help him up. But it was Alan who *called* the police, dammit! If he'd been the killer, surely he'd have fled; added to which, there was no sign of the weapon. Then.'

The waitress materialized beside them, asking if they'd like a pudding. In the circumstances, it seemed a particularly mundane query. They shook their heads, but Rona ordered coffee for two.

Beth went on with her account. 'What's more, they wouldn't even release him while enquiries were made. Do you know, he had to spend a year in prison before he even came to trial? And that bastard Pollard, who really *had* killed someone, was at liberty from the day he was arrested until his trial six months later. How's that for British justice?'

The coffee arrived and Rona poured it.

'Then the police turned up,' Beth continued, 'and conducted a search of the house and grounds. And – I'll never understand this – they came across one of our kitchen knives hidden in the garage. God only knows how it got there. It had been wiped clean, but forensics found traces of blood and were able to match it to Pollard's. And that was that.'

'How did they account for it being there, when your husband had been in custody all the time?'

Beth snorted. 'They were convinced he'd hidden it near the scene, then rung me before dialling nine-nine-nine and told me where it was.' She looked down at her clenched hands. 'I was given the third degree, I can tell you, but eventually they had to give up because I obviously hadn't a clue.'

'And you still haven't?'

She shook her head. 'I've wracked my brains over it ever since, but I can't come up with an answer.'

'Was the garage kept locked?'

'Yes, always. That was another damning fact.'

They sipped their coffee in silence for a minute, then Rona said, 'Do you think it was Barry Pollard who sent the letter?'

Beth looked surprised. 'It must have been. He'd have been waiting for Alan, but someone got there first.'

When Rona didn't reply, Beth looked at her sharply. 'What are you thinking?'

'It seems a bit of a coincidence, that's all, unless it was a random killing. How would anyone but your husband know Pollard would be there at precisely that time? Did the police check if anyone else wanted him dead?' She wished, too late, she could bite back the word 'else', but Beth didn't appear to have noticed.

'Oh yes, to give them their due, they checked. When he first went to prison there'd been a lot of hostility – about the light sentence and everything – but that was eighteen months earlier and it had all died down. People forget.'

'Perhaps not everyone. Suppose someone else was after him, and it was nothing to do with Charlotte? This person might have been biding his time till he came out, and had the brainwave of framing your husband – an obvious suspect – for the murder.'

Beth was staring at her wide-eyed. Obviously this hadn't occurred to her. 'You mean the *murderer* sent the letter?'

'I'm only saying it's a possibility.'

Beth slammed her hand on the table, making Rona jump. 'Oh, *why* didn't he keep it? They could have tested the envelope or the stamp for DNA, and perhaps traced the real killer.'

They were silent for a minute, regretting lost opportunities. Then Beth said in a low voice, 'I'm worried about Alan. Not just because he's locked up, but because he seems to have given up hope. It's as though he thinks he deserves to be there, not for killing Pollard but for allowing Lottie to die.

The boys and I go to see him regularly, and I can tell he's making an effort for us, but every time we go he's a bit thinner and more haggard-looking.'

Suddenly she leant forward and gripped Rona's hand, her eyes alight. 'I've had an idea: would you go and see him yourself? In prison?'

Rona stared at her, her mind spinning. 'Would it be allowed?'

'As long as he's agreeable. Oh, please say yes!'

Briefly, Rona pictured Max's reaction to her becoming involved in another murder case; but excitement was beginning to stir. 'I shouldn't want to give him any false hope,' she prevaricated.

'Leave it to me; I'll explain everything, say I talked you into it and you can't promise anything. After all, what harm can it do? He might be more open with you, and at the very least it would be a fresh perspective on things.'

Still Rona hesitated. 'What exactly would be involved?'

'He'd have to send you a visiting order. Then you phone the prison to book your visit.'

That would be an article in itself, Rona thought, an exclusive interview with Buckford's most famous murderer. And if the police had doubted the very existence of the letter, they mightn't have gone to great lengths to discover who sent it.

'Miss Parish? Will you?'

Rona looked at her pleading face. 'All right, provided he agrees.'

'Oh thank you, thank you! I'll phone him this afternoon and ask him to send you an order. What's your address?'

'Two Parsonage Place, but I'm only here three days a week.'

'That's fine – Wednesday's one of the visiting days, and if you phone tomorrow, you'd be giving the necessary twenty-four hours' notice. Visiting's from three to four. I'll leave a message on your mobile when I've spoken to him – and I can't tell you how grateful I am.'

She insisted on paying for the meal and they parted on the pavement, with Beth promising to phone as soon as she had news. Rona walked slowly across to the library, settled at her usual table and took out her laptop. It had not been possible to record their conversation – the noise level in the café was too high, and the meeting in any case too informal. Now, she attempted to write down everything that had been said over the meal, and by the time she had done so, was already regretting having agreed to see Alan Spencer. What on earth could she say to him? The police weren't fools; they must have had a pretty good case against him, and the court had agreed with them. She wondered if she could find out who'd been handling his defence, but it was doubtful if any barrister would see her after so long and with nothing new to suggest.

When her notes were up to date, Rona searched the shelves for volumes on the town's history. On the whole, the books didn't make for interesting reading, though she was able to extract figures showing the growth in population, and the date when the market charter was granted by King John. For the most part, though, they were simply more detailed accounts of what she'd already extracted from the archives in Marsborough.

At five o'clock she collected her things together and walked back through the warm streets to Parsonage Place. The pubs would be another interesting angle to follow, she thought as she passed the King's Head. Many of them were almost as old as the town itself.

There was no sign of the family when she let herself into the house. She went up to her room, and, sitting at the little table, checked her mobile, which had been switched off during lunch and her session at the library. There was another sheaf of messages, and she played them through, but found nothing promising. Since she had time in hand, she rang back everyone who'd left a number, leaving messages for those who didn't reply and thanking those who did, and telling them she'd be in touch in due course. Too bad she couldn't screen them in advance, but she daren't write any of them off; it had, after all, been as a result of giving Lew Grayson her number that Beth Spencer had contacted her, though she was reserving judgement on whether that had been a good or a bad thing.

Since the house was still quiet, she then had a bath and washed her hair before changing for her supper engagement. The sleeveless lemon-yellow dress felt cool and fresh, and accentuated the tan she'd acquired from walking in the sunshine. She picked up her bag and the potted plant she'd bought for Lois, and had started down the stairs when she heard a key in the front door. A moment later it opened, and she came to a sudden stop. Because it wasn't either Nuala or Will who was walking into the hall, but a man she didn't know. He caught sight of her at the same moment and halted in his turn, and as their eyes met, Rona recognized him. It was the man who'd been watching her last week in Market Square.

'Well,' he said softly, 'the paying guest, I presume?'

She slowly continued down the stairs. 'Rona Parish,' she said coolly. 'And you are?'

'Clive Banks, Nuala's husband. How do you do?'

She was taken by surprise, having been under the impression firstly that they were divorced and secondly no longer in touch. Wrong on both counts, it seemed. At any rate, he still had a key to the house.

'I don't think anyone's in, and I'm about to go out myself.'

'And very nice you look, too. Walking sunshine.' His eyes moved approvingly over her, and to her annoyance she felt herself flush. He was slightly built, barely her own height and with narrow shoulders, and was dressed in cords and an open-necked shirt. His hair and eyes were dark, and he had a small moustache. The old-fashioned word 'spiv' came to Rona's mind. What had Nuala seen in this man? Yet, she admitted unwillingly, there was a certain virility about him.

He did not move aside to let her pass, which necessitated her brushing against him to reach the door.

'Nice perfume,' he commented. 'None of your African Violets; it must have cost a pretty penny.'

By now she had the door open. 'Good evening, Mr Banks,' she said, and walked quickly down the path and out of sight along the road.

Lois Breen opened the door to her.

'My dear, how charming you look! Do come in. Gordon's not back from evensong yet, but he won't be long. Come and have a drink on the terrace.'

The house was large, rambling and untidy in an acceptable, homely way. There was a selection of coats, anoraks and macs hung on top of each other on the hall stand, and an assortment of shoes and boots beneath it. Lois received Rona's offering with delight, and led her through an over-furnished sitting room to the terrace.

'Far too many chairs,' she said over her shoulder, as though reading Rona's thoughts. 'We have to cater for study groups, Mothers' Union meetings and goodness knows what else. When we're alone, Gordon and I curl up in the den. One thing about a house this size, you've plenty of rooms to choose from. Obviously the clergy used to have large families.'

'Have you any?' Rona ventured, taking the seat indicated, a sagging deckchair.

'Two married daughters, one living in Devon and one in Scotland. Very inconsiderate of them! Couldn't be farther apart if they tried. Now, I've made a jug of Pimm's; is that all right?'

'Wonderful!'

Ahead of them stretched the long garden with the oddly shaped wooden building she'd seen from her window – and, in fact, she could see the window itself, open as she had left it, beyond the far wall. As she looked, she thought she caught a flicker of movement behind it, and felt a touch of alarm. She had left Clive Banks alone in the house; had he gone to her room, and if so, why? To snoop among her things? She tried to remember what she'd left out on her table, but brought herself up short. She was being silly, she told herself; Nuala was sure to be back by this time. *If* anyone was up there, and she was by no means certain, there would be a perfectly obvious solution, such as clean towels or a topping up of the little flower vase.

Lois had returned with a jug of Pimm's smelling deliciously of mint and cucumber, some of which sloshed into Rona's glass as she poured.

'Sorry,' Lois apologized. 'Drink round it, if you can.'

The sound of the front door reached them, followed by approaching footsteps.

'You'll never guess who I saw in town,' came Gordon Breen's voice. 'Clive Banks! No doubt that means trouble.'

His words had brought him to the glass doors, where he caught sight of Rona and looked slightly taken aback. 'Sorry; I saw Lois out here but I didn't realize you'd arrived. Me and my big mouth!'

'He came to the house just before I left,' Rona said, her apprehension returning. 'Nuala wasn't in, and I left him there. I hope that's all right.'

Lois shrugged. 'Not much else you could have done. Pimm's, darling?'

'Please. Work's over for the day, and I can now relax.' He sat down heavily in another of the deckchairs and turned to Rona. 'Sorry, I was speaking out of turn. Obviously, my words were meant for my wife's ears only.'

'I thought they were divorced?' Rona said.

'No, he just walked out,' Lois answered, ignoring the warning glance her husband sent her. 'I wondered how long it would be before he turned up like a bad penny.'

'I really think we should change the subject,' Gordon said firmly. 'And my apologies for introducing it in the first place.

Now.' He turned to Rona. 'How's the research going? Doesn't your husband mind your coming up here every week?'

'Apart from the dog, he doesn't notice the difference,' Rona answered unthinkingly, her mind still on Banks. Then, seeing the surprise on their faces, she laughed. 'Sorry, I'd better explain: Max is an artist who can only work with music playing at full volume. As a writer, I need complete silence. Therefore he has a cottage ten minutes' walk away, and on three nights a week, when he has evening classes and I'm working all hours, he quite often spends the nights there. But he comes home on Wednesdays, and I'm also back by then, which is what I meant by there being no difference.'

'I must say you have an unusual marriage,' Lois commented mildly. 'You told me earlier that you haven't taken his name.'

'Only when it would be embarrassing not to!' Rona confirmed with a smile. She nodded in the direction of the wooden hut. 'Is that a summer house?'

'No, it's my workshop,' Lois said surprisingly. 'I'm a sculptor, for my sins.'

'How fascinating! May I have a look, or isn't that allowed?'

'It's certainly allowed, but I'd strongly advise you to wait until you haven't got your glad rags on. The air's thick with dust in there and it gets everywhere.'

'What kinds of things do you sculpt?'

'Anything that takes my fancy – busts, animals, figurines. Don't expect marble statues, though; I limit myself to wood.'

'She exhibits in London,' Gordon put in proudly. 'I'll show you one of her catalogues when we go inside.'

Lois laughed. 'Meet my publicity agent! Speaking of going in, supper's almost ready, if you are.'

The dining room, at the front of the house, was dark and grew darker as the meal progressed and the light began to fade outside. There were candles on the table in old, tarnished candelabra, and their flickering light emphasized rather than alleviated the encroaching darkness. The first course was a tangy gazpacho served with olive bread, and was followed by a huge dish of lasagne and a Greek salad. Dessert was fresh figs, and the coffee was dark and bitter, served in small cups. Not standard vicarage fare, Rona thought, but this was no standard vicarage.

A few large moths had blundered through the open windows, drawn by the candles, which Lois quickly blew out and switched on the light. 'Can't have them cremating themselves,' she said lightly, 'it's bad for business!'

Throughout the meal they had talked easily on a variety of subjects but Rona, who'd intended to bring up the subject of Alan Spencer, decided against it. Gordon had been embarrassed earlier in the evening, and was unlikely to welcome any other contentious subjects. He did, however, regale her over coffee with some amusing stories about past incumbents, and Rona wished she'd had her recorder with her. Before she finished up here, she must interview him properly.

The clock on the shadowed mantelpiece chimed two quarters, and Rona, surprised to find it was ten thirty, rose to go. 'Thank you so much,' she said. 'It's been such an interesting evening, and the food was delicious.'

'I'll walk you back,' Gordon said, rising with her.

'No, I wouldn't hear of it! It's only round the corner.'

'No arguments; at the moment, this isn't the place to be out after dark.'

This was the second time she'd been warned, Rona remembered uneasily. So they strolled together down the cobbled alleyway and along the length of Parsonage Place to number two.

'Thanks again,' Rona said at the gate.

'I'll wait till you're safely inside.'

At the door she turned, gave him a wave, which he returned, and let herself into the house. Was Clive Banks still here? she wondered. And was it his raised voice she'd heard last week? The house was quiet, only the hall light left burning to see her safely in. Behind his closed door, she could hear Jack Stanton's gentle, rhythmic snores.

Her mind full of the day's events, Rona switched off the light and went upstairs to bed.

Nine

At first, the ringing and banging invaded her dreams in a re-enactment of past fear: once again she was alone in the house, waking to the cacophony with Gus barking hysterically in the hall. Then, opening heavy eyes, she became aware of her surroundings and the fact that although no dog barked, the ringing and banging were continuing. Rona sat up, fumbled for the light, and, blinking in the sudden brilliance, looked at her bedside clock. It was two fifteen.

The noise stopped abruptly and voices sounded below her in the hall. Alarm spread through her like wildfire. Sliding her legs off the bed, she reached for her dressing gown and, padding out on to the landing, looked over the banister. Two uniformed police officers, one man and one woman, were standing in the hall, talking to Nuala who was shivering in her nightdress. As she watched, still disorientated and half asleep, Jack Stanton's door opened and the old man, leaning on his Zimmer, appeared in the doorway in striped pyjamas.

Rona's first coherent thought was that Clive Banks was in some way involved, especially when she saw Nuala cover her face with her hands. As she watched, Nuala nodded in reply to something and, turning, came running up the stairs, tears streaming down her face.

Rona said tentatively, 'Nuala? Whatever is it?'

Nuala paused, threw her a distracted glance. 'It's Aunt Edna. She's been found lying in the street. I – I have to go and identify her.'

'She's *dead*?' Horror flooded over Rona and she added impulsively, 'Would you like me to come with you?'

'Oh Rona, would you?'

'Of course. I'll get dressed.'

Her fingers were stiff and unwieldy as she struggled with the fastening on her bra, the zip on her jeans, but she had time to splash cold water on her face and brush her hair before Nuala emerged from her own room.

'It's awfully good of you,' she said through chattering teeth. 'I could do with some moral support, and Dad has to stay here with Will.'

They went together down the stairs, where the solemn-faced officers awaited them. Nuala introduced Rona as a guest who was staying with her, and gave her father a quick, reassuring kiss. Then they were going down the path and into the police car waiting at the gate. Across the low wall, bathed in moonlight, lay the sleeping shape of the vicarage. Only a few hours ago, Rona thought, she had been there, sitting on the terrace. It seemed a different time frame.

The police constables could not answer any of Nuala's questions. Having broken the bad news, their orders were simply to escort her to the hospital mortuary, where other officers would fill in the details.

At the hospital, Rona accompanied Nuala to the small room with its window giving on to the mortuary, and waited at the door while Nuala went forward to gaze on the waxen face of her aunt. She gave a brief, confirming nod and turned away, choking back a sob. Rona put an arm round her and they were led into another room where, to Rona's surprise, two plain-clothes officers awaited them.

Introductions were made and the four of them sat down.

'Please tell me what happened,' Nuala said shakily.

DI Barrett tapped his pen on the table for a minute before replying. He was a lean, loosely jointed man with fairish hair, a long nose and a set mouth. Rona had the impression he did not care for being called out in the early hours of the morning.

'Miss Rosebury was found soon after midnight,' he began, not looking at either of them. 'The officer—'

'Midnight?' Nuala interrupted. 'But I wasn't informed till after two o'clock.'

Barrett frowned. 'Firstly, madam, the officer who found her had no means of establishing her identity, and secondly, the fact that her handbag was missing led him to suspect her death might not have been accidental.'

Nuala drew a sharp breath. 'But she never took her bag when she went out at night, just slipped the front-door key in her pocket.'

The inspector's frown deepened. 'She made a habit of walking the streets at night?'

He made her sound like a prostitute, Rona thought, her dislike of him mounting.

'Yes, she has done for years. She's never come to any harm before.'

'Then she's been lucky,' Barrett said shortly. 'As I was saying, since it seemed likely it was a suspicious death, scenes of crime and the coroner's officer were informed and the area taped off. The – your aunt wasn't removed until all the usual measures had been taken. It was only when she arrived at the hospital that one of the nurses recognized her, and gave us your address.'

'And what was the cause of death?' Rona asked.

The inspector eyed her speculatively. 'That won't be established until after the post mortem.'

'But there were no signs that she'd been – attacked?'

'No obvious signs, no, but it can't be ruled out. Unfortunately there have been several muggings lately, and it was only a question of time before one of them had serious consequences.'

'But she wasn't mugged,' Rona pointed out. 'She hadn't anything with her.'

'As I explained,' Barrett went on heavily, 'we weren't to know that, and neither, come to that, would a mugger. Ladies, particularly old ladies, usually carry handbags. There was no handbag, therefore the obvious conclusion was that she'd been robbed.'

Nuala, sensing the rising animosity, changed the subject. 'You said it was a policeman who found her?'

'Yes; in view of the present situation we've increased the number of officers on the beat.'

Rona bit back the comment that it had been of little help. 'Where was she found?'

'In Greenwood Lane, at the corner of King Street.'

'And she was just – lying there?' Nuala whispered.

He nodded, his face softening as he belatedly registered her distress. 'Don't upset yourself, Mrs Banks. After what you've told us, it seems probable it was a natural death after all – heart, possibly. Apart from robbery, there's no reason to attack an old lady like that.'

Rona went suddenly cold. 'There just might have been,' she said from a dry mouth.

Nuala's head spun round. 'What do you mean?' she demanded.

'I'm sorry, Nuala. I didn't want to worry you.'

Barrett had straightened as his attention switched to Rona. 'There's something you haven't told us?'

Aware of his eyes boring into her and Nuala motionless at her side, she explained as succinctly as she could her current project, the fact that she'd interviewed Edna, later lost the cassette, and found the note on her windscreen.

'I see.' Barrett's voice was clipped. 'And did anything Miss Rosebury told you pose a threat to anyone?'

'It's possible; she was talking about a clandestine love affair, though she didn't mention any names. She'd – seen them during her night walks.'

'A love affair?' Barrett repeated with raised eyebrow.

'And that's not quite all,' Rona admitted in a low voice, avoiding Nuala's accusing gaze. 'There was a message on my mobile, asking if I'd found out who they were.'

'You should have told me!' Nuala said ringingly.

'With hindsight, yes; I thought you'd enough to worry about.'

'But if I'd known, I'd have stayed over last night too, and this wouldn't have happened!'

Surprisingly, Barrett came to Rona's defence. 'That doesn't follow at all, Mrs Banks. If, as now seems likely, death was due to natural causes, it could have no connection with Miss – Parish, is it? – and her recording.'

But his eyes were still suspicious as he turned back to Rona. 'How did this caller know your mobile number?'

Damn! Rona thought. 'It was in the local paper.'

. 'Why, exactly?'

'So people could contact me if they'd anything of interest for my articles.'

'Oh yes, your articles. I was forgetting you're a journalist.' He managed to instil a measure of scorn into the word. 'Have you a transcript of the interview?'

'I have, yes.'

'I'd be grateful if you'd drop it into the station tomorrow morning. It would be as well for us to go over it. Anything else you've omitted to mention?'

Rona flushed and her chin lifted as she met his eyes squarely. 'No.'

He held her gaze for a moment, then scraped back his chair and stood up. 'I won't keep you any longer, ladies. Sergeant Tyson here will show you out and there's a car waiting to take you home. I'm sorry about your loss, Mrs Banks. My condolences.'

He had turned away before Nuala had a chance to reply.

'Better late than never,' Rona said as they reached the corridor, uncaring that the sergeant was within hearing. 'What an odious man.'

Tyson reddened but made no comment, conducting them in silence to the main entrance of the hospital and handing them over to the uniformed constable waiting there. Still in silence, they were driven home.

Mr Stanton was waiting up for them, his door ajar, and Nuala went in to bring him up to date.

'I'll make us all a hot drink,' Rona volunteered, going on to the kitchen. As she was setting out the mugs, Nuala joined her. 'Dad doesn't want anything; he made himself a drink half an hour ago.'

Rona said awkwardly, 'I'm sorry I didn't tell you about losing the cassette, Nuala.'

'It's all right.' She pulled out a chair and sat down. 'I know you meant it for the best, and as the inspector said, I don't suppose it would have made any difference.'

Rona set the mugs of hot chocolate on the table and seated herself opposite. 'I still can't believe it. What a horrible thing to have happened.'

'Yes; I suppose we'd all prefer to die in our beds.'

'She'd had a long and useful life, though,' Rona added, aware even as she said it that it was a cliché and as such probably not much comfort.

They drank their chocolate in silence for several minutes before, to distract Nuala from her grief, she said lightly, 'I met your husband last night. Did he tell you?'

Nuala's head jerked up and she flushed. 'He mentioned it, yes.'

'I wasn't sure if you were expecting him.'

'No, I wasn't.' Her eyes dropped away. 'He phoned out of the blue a couple of weeks ago; that was the first we'd heard of him since he left. I thought we'd settled things, but he appeared on the doorstep last Wednesday. You – might have heard us arguing. The trouble is we're not divorced and there's no restraining order, so technically he can come and go as he pleases. If he'd stopped to think, though, he'd have realized we'd be out yesterday; Dad has his exercise class on Monday evenings, and Will goes to one of his school-friends for tea. We're never back before eight. We only missed last week because it was your first night.'

It seemed that was all she was going to say. Rona would have liked to know more about the elusive Clive, but probing was out of the question. They finished their chocolate, rinsed the mugs, and went wearily back up the stairs. It was four o'clock and dawn would soon be breaking.

'I shall have to get up as usual,' Nuala said, stifling a yawn. 'I have to get Will to school and myself to work, but there's no reason why you and Dad shouldn't sleep in.'

'I think I will,' Rona said. 'I hope you manage to get at least some sleep yourself.'

Exhausted though she was, it was a while before she dropped off. Her mind kept replaying the visit to the hospital and the inspector's supercilious stare, and she prayed fervently that Edna Rosebury's death would prove to have no connection to the recording she had made.

The room was full of sunshine when Rona finally stirred, and she stretched luxuriously. Then the events of the previous night flooded back and she sat up, amazed to find it was already ten o'clock. Fifteen minutes later, showered and dressed, she went downstairs and paused outside Jack Stanton's door. She could hear his radio playing softly, so she tapped on the panel.

'Mr Stanton? It's Rona. I was wondering if you'd like any breakfast?'

There was a pause, then his voice called, 'Come in, come in.'

She'd not been in his room before, and her first impression was of relief. It resembled a pleasant bedsitter rather than the sickroom she'd anticipated. Jack, tidily dressed as always, was seated in an armchair doing the crossword, and beside him on a low table were his glasses case, a telephone, a dictionary and a library book. The radio was within easy reach, and he switched it off as she came in. Across the room a television straddled one corner, and there were some well-stocked book shelves. The neatly made bed against the wall, piled with cushions and with no headboard, had the appearance of a divan.

He smiled shyly at her, and she thought again that the centre parting in his grey hair gave him a curiously old-fashioned look. Pain had cut grooves in his cheeks and around his mouth, but he was still a handsome man. 'Breakfast, did you say? That sounds tempting.'

'Would you like eggs and bacon? There are some in the fridge.'

'Now you really are spoiling me. They're usually reserved for Sundays.'

'Let's pretend it's Sunday, then. I'll bring it through when it's ready.'

'No, I'll come and have it at the kitchen table, if you've no objection.'

'I'd be delighted. Give me ten minutes – I'll have to find where things are.'

This, Rona realized, frying the eggs, would be the first proper conversation she'd had with the old man. When Nuala was present, he always stayed quietly in the background. The sound of his Zimmer reached her as she tipped the eggs on to a plate, and he manoeuvred himself into a chair.

'I hope you don't mind if I restrict myself to toast,' she apologized, setting a coffee pot on the table. 'I'm meeting a friend for lunch in a couple of hours.'

'You shouldn't have gone to this trouble just for me,' he demurred. But she saw, to her pleasure, that he was tucking into his meal with gusto.

'Dreadful business about Edna,' he said suddenly.

Rona nodded cautiously.

'They think it was a heart attack, Nuala says.'

'That's right.' Please God.

'She was a great case when she was young. Helped bring up the younger ones, and was like a mother to Nuala when

136

Florence died. Sunday tea times won't be the same.' He shook his head sadly. 'Still, I suppose we all have to go sometime.'

He wiped a piece of toast round the last remaining egg yolk, touched his napkin to his mouth, and abruptly changed the subject. 'I hear you met Clive last night?'

Rona met his sharp, interested gaze. 'Yes.'

'What did you think of him?'

'We only exchanged a couple of words. I was on my way out to the vicarage.'

'Always one for the easy buck,' Jack continued, gazing into a past she could not see. 'Edna and I saw through him from the first, but Nuala wouldn't listen. She can be self-willed when she wants.'

'What had you against him?' Rona asked, topping up his coffee cup.

'Never did an honest day's work in his life,' Jack said bluntly. 'Always full of hair-brained schemes only just this side of the law. Then one time it caught up with him; he crossed the dividing line and ended up inside. We hoped it would serve as a lesson, but no, he had to get in with the wrong crowd, didn't he?'

Rona, remembering the foxy face, could well believe it. 'Do you think he wants to come back?'

Jack shook his head decidedly. 'Not on your life; can't take the responsibility. To tell you the truth I thought we'd seen the last of him, until he surfaced again a couple of weeks ago. Nuala was shaken, I could tell, even said something about starting proceedings, but I doubt if she's done anything about it. Jonty Welles at the bank is sweet on her, and he'd soon make a move if the coast was clear. Perhaps Clive actually coming here will spur her on.'

He took another piece of toast, buttered it lavishly and spread marmalade on top. Rona wondered guiltily if butter was also reserved for Sundays; there had been low-fat spreads in the fridge.

'Don't let me keep you,' he said suddenly. 'You must have

things to do before your lunch engagement. Thank you for feeding me so well.'

'It was a pleasure. If you really don't mind, I will make a move. I – have to drop something in at the police station. Where is it, by the way?'

'Granton Street. Runs along one side of the mall.'

Close to the boutique, then. That was fortunate.

'Thanks.' She stood up and carried her plate and cup to the sink.

'Never mind that. I'm used to tidying up.'

She nodded her thanks, knowing he valued such independence as he had. 'See you this evening, then,' she said.

Lindsey closed her office door with a sigh of relief. It had been a long and difficult morning, and she decided to treat herself to lunch at Dino's. Too bad Ro wasn't here to join her. She emerged on to Guild Street and was almost at the corner of Dean's Crescent when she heard her name called, and turned to see a woman smilingly hurrying up to her.

'I'm so glad I caught you, Miss Parish,' she was saying, 'I was going to telephone.'

Lindsey regarded her blankly and the woman's smile faltered as her eyes moved over her face.

'I'm sorry,' she said hesitantly, 'you *are* Miss Parish, aren't you?'

'I'm Lindsey Parish, yes,' Lindsey acknowledged. 'Perhaps you thought I was my sister? People often mistake us.'

'I do beg your pardon. Now I look more closely I can see the difference, but you're incredibly alike. Twins, I take it?'

'That's right.'

The woman smiled and held out her hand. 'How remiss of me – I've not introduced myself. Catherine Bishop.'

The name sounded faintly familiar, but Lindsey couldn't place it.

'Your sister came to see me about her articles on Buckford,' Mrs Bishop continued. 'I used to teach there.'

Of course! Pops's client, whom Rona had wanted to interview. 'I've heard her mention you, and my father, too. I'm sorry I can't help; Ro's in Buckford until tomorrow evening.'

'Yes, I should have realized that. It was just seeing you ahead of me . . .' Her voice trailed off. 'Anyway, I'm glad to have met you. Don't trouble your sister, it was nothing important. We'll catch up with each other some time.' And with a smile and a nod, she continued on her way, feeling foolish and vaguely disappointed.

She'd been pleased when she thought she recognized Rona, even wondering if she could spare the time for lunch. Her sister was amazingly like her; not quite as tall, perhaps, and her hair was longer – well below her shoulders. But the main difference lay in their personalities. She had exchanged only a few words with Lindsey, but the empathy that had been instantaneous with Rona was lacking. A nice enough young woman, no doubt, but she hadn't Rona's warmth.

With a small, suppressed sigh, Catherine went to her solitary lunch.

Since she had no way of knowing if or when the police would return her transcript, Rona decided to take the precaution of having it photocopied before parting with it, and was relieved to come across a shop offering the service. She purchased a large envelope, slipped the original inside with a brief note, and addressed it to DI Barrett.

Then, following directions, she walked alongside the mall until she saw the squat building of the police station on the opposite side of the road. In front of it was a forecourt with a somewhat desultory fountain playing in the centre and several parked panda cars. Rona went through the swing doors into the foyer, keeping a weather eye open for Barrett. To her relief, there was no sign of him. She handed the packet to the sergeant at the desk, and thankfully made her escape.

It was now twelve twenty, and time to track down Magda's boutique. She crossed the road again, and entered the mall by one of its side doors. Surprisingly enough, it was the first time she'd been inside the vast, glass-covered structure, and she could well understand the town's pride in it. She found herself in a short passage lined on both sides by open-fronted shops selling a variety of goods, from mobile phones and exotic flowers to baby-wear. The passage ended in a T-junction with the main concourse, and opposite her was an enormous, two-storeys-high fountain with lights playing on it, that put the police effort to shame. On either side of the fountain, vast stretches of marble flooring led away into the distance, lined with a bewildering array of stores and coffee bars, all filled with a moving, talking, laughing throng of shoppers. At intervals, escalators gave access to the upper floor, which was also heavily populated.

To Rona's relief, a stand at her side displayed leaflets showing the layout of the mall. She took one and ran her eye down it till she came to *Magdalena*, and, judging by the number of the store alongside her, guessed it must be some twenty yards down to her right.

In fact, she recognized it even before checking its name; all Magda's boutiques looked the same, and in this instance she'd achieved that effect even without a frontage. Rona would have expected nothing less.

A notice on a stand just inside apologized to customers for the temporary paucity of choice following the break-in, though to Rona's eyes the rails seemed remarkably well stocked. No doubt Magda had arrived that morning with a fresh input, plundered from her other outlets. The interior stretched back quite a way, and at the far end Rona could see the layout of the new café.

She threaded her way towards it between browsing customers, and at once caught sight of Magda at a corner table. She had started towards her when a girl at the entrance smilingly barred her way, asking if she'd booked a table. Must be doing well already, Rona thought, and certainly all the tables seemed occupied.

'I'm meeting Magda,' she explained. 'Don't worry – I can see her.'

The girl checked a list. 'Ms Parish?'

'That's right.'

'If you'd like to go in, then.'

It was only as she approached the table that Rona registered Magda was not alone; she was talking to a woman who had her back to Rona, a woman with auburn hair. As she drew level, Magda looked up and smiled, and her companion turned. It was Helena Maddox.

'I'm so glad you could come,' Magda said, jumping up to kiss Rona. 'I don't think you two have met: Helena Maddox – Rona Parish.'

'I do hope you'll forgive my gate-crashing,' Helena said. 'I came in on the spur of the moment, and as there was no free table, Magda kindly invited me to join you.' She spoke quickly, while her fingers continued to crumble a roll on her side plate.

'I'm delighted to meet you,' Rona replied, taking a seat. It was true: Helena Maddox had interested her from the first, and she was looking equally elegant today, in a short-sleeved suit in rust and cream silk – possibly from *Magdalena*.

'I hear you're planning to write about Buckford for the celebrations?' Helena continued.

'That's right; part of my research involved being shown round the college.'

'So Magda was saying. What did you think of it?'

'Very impressive. Do you live on the premises?'

'Yes, we've a flat on the top floor. Where are you staying while you're here?'

'With Nuala Banks, in Parsonage Place. It's ideal, since it's both comfortable and central.'

As they talked, Rona took stock of her. She was certainly attractive; her skin, unusually for a redhead, was tanned to a pale gold, and her almost navy-blue eyes were fringed with black lashes – doubtless mascara'd, but still stunning. Close to, though, there was a sense of strain about her, apparent in the nervous flicker of her eyes, the constant movement of her hands. Anyone who lived with Richard Maddox, Rona thought uncharitably, had a right to be stressed.

Magda passed the menu to Rona. 'You're here to work, remember! What do you think of the selection?'

Rona quickly read it through. 'Very innovative. Normally I'd have been spoilt for choice, but I'm afraid I shan't want much today; it's only a couple of hours since I had breakfast.'

Magda looked at her in disbelief. 'Well, a lot of help you're turning out to be! What were you thinking of, having a late breakfast when we'd arranged lunch?'

She shouldn't have volunteered that information, Rona realized. She'd no wish to discuss Edna's death in front of a virtual stranger.

'I only had a slice of toast,' she prevaricated.

'But why so late?' She should have known Magda wouldn't let it rest.

'We had a disturbed night.' Rona paused, but had no alternative but to continue. 'It was all very upsetting, actually; Nuala's elderly aunt was found dead in the street.'

Both her companions exclaimed at once.

Helena, her face filled with sudden horror, cried, 'Not Miss Rosebury?'

And Magda: 'The old lady you interviewed?'

Rona nodded in reply to both. 'Nuala had to go to the mortuary to identify her, and I went along for company. Then we had to talk to the police.'

'Why the police?' Magda demanded sharply.

'They – thought she might have been attacked.'

'But – God – that's terrible!' Helena this time. 'What gave them that idea?'

'There was no sign of her handbag. When Nuala said she never took one at night, they seemed to revise their opinion.'

'Never . . . ? She made a habit of going out after dark?'

'Apparently she sometimes went for a walk.'

'Dangerous, I'd have thought.'

Magda clapped a hand to her mouth. 'God, Rona! The cassette! Do you think there's any connection?'

Rona, seeing Helena forming another question, said quickly, 'No, I'm sure not. Look, I really don't want to go into it again, if you don't mind. I had enough of that last night.'

She was helped in her request by the need to give their orders, and opted for artichoke hearts in a special dressing. That settled, she turned back to Magda.

'Were any other shops broken into? I'd have thought the mall would have security guards.'

'It has,' Magda said gloomily, 'but the thieves got in at the back, where we take deliveries. The guards only became aware of them as they were driving off – but don't get me started on that. Yes, they got away with some jewellery from next door, as well. That, not unnaturally, is what the police are concentrating on.'

Rona wondered fleetingly if DI Barrett was involved. Perhaps that was why he'd resented being distracted by Edna's case. 'Well, I certainly wouldn't have known from the rails that you'd had a robbery,' she said rallyingly.

They started talking about the autumn collection, and Rona relaxed a little. To rectify her shortcomings, she ordered a dessert from the well-stocked trolley, and pronounced it excellent, as was the coffee that followed.

'I'm glad you think so,' Magda said. 'This is by way of an experiment. If it proves a success, I'm hoping to introduce cafés into some of the other shops. While I remember, Rona, Gavin was asking when you're coming to dinner. Are you free any evening next week?'

'That would be nice, but it would have to be Friday or Saturday. Max has classes on Thursdays.'

Magda shook her head. 'Friday and Saturday are both booked next week, and Gavin's away on a course the week after.' She hesitated. 'Would Max mind if you came solo on Thursday?'

143

Rona smiled. 'I shouldn't think so.' Magda and Gavin were more her friends than his.

'It's a date, then.'

Rona and Helena left soon after, both insisting, despite Magda's protests, that they pay for their own lunches.

'You'll never make a profit if you treat all your friends,' Rona told her.

'We must meet again,' Helena said as they separated at the mall's entrance, 'and if you'd like any more details about College, do let me know.'

Rona looked after her as she set off along the pavement, trying to sum up her impressions. Helena had seemed charming, intelligent, at times preoccupied, but there was an overall sense of vulnerability about her that Rona found oddly touching. Yes, she would like to meet her again.

She'd decided to devote the afternoon to more church-visiting, and was crossing the road towards the Church of the Holy Cross when her mobile rang. Safely on the pavement, she moved out of people's way and flicked it open.

'Rona Parish.'

'Oh, Miss Parish!' Beth Spencer's voice, and she sounded close to tears.

'Hello, Mrs Spencer.'

'He won't see you,' Beth said in a rush. 'I phoned him last night and argued till I was blue in the face, but he wouldn't give way. I *told* him it might be his last chance, but he just wasn't interested.'

Despite her earlier misgivings, Rona was aware of disappointment. 'That seems to be that, then.'

'I shan't give up!' Beth assured her. 'I'll keep on at him till he changes his mind.'

'I really don't think that would do any good,' Rona put in gently. 'It's no use my seeing him under duress, he has to want to.'

'When he's had time to think about it, he'll change his

mind. I was trying to rush him, so we could fit it in this week, but the more I pressed, the more he dug his heels in. Now it'll have to be next week at the earliest.'

'Well, I'll be here then and the week after,' Rona soothed her. 'But as I said all along, I doubt I can do much good.'

Beth rang off, still convinced of eventual success, and Rona walked out of the bright sunshine into the candlelit gloom of the Catholic church.

It wasn't until she was setting off for home the following afternoon that she saw the note, again wedged behind the windscreen wipers, and her heart seemed to stop. With shaking fingers she extracted it and smoothed it open.

WHY DON'T YOU GO HOME AND STOP POKING YOUR NOSE INTO WHAT DOESN'T CONCERN YOU? YOU'RE NOT WANTED HERE.

It seemed that, his scare tactics not having worked, her anonymous persecutor was increasing the pressure. Rona glanced at the house behind her, wondering whether to go back and tell Nuala of the latest development. She'd been in trouble for keeping quiet before. But this was a more personal attack, and nothing further could harm Edna Rosebury. She decided to compromise: she'd tell Nuala when she came back on Monday. About one thing, however, she was in no doubt. She would not tell Max.

Ten

Max said, 'What bad luck, to be caught up in it.'
'The fact that I'd met her made it worse,' Rona admitted, sipping a much-needed vodka. She'd told Max briefly of Edna's death when he'd phoned the previous evening, and had just finished a more detailed account, though the omission of any reference to the missing cassette or the two notes screamed in her head.

'She sounds a dotty old bird, to go wandering the streets at night.'

Rona rushed to Edna's defence. 'Why? She'd lived in the town all her life, and everyone knew her. If she couldn't sleep, why shouldn't she go for a walk?'

Max raised both hands in mock submission. 'All right, all right. But weren't you saying there have been several muggings recently?'

'Yes, but she wasn't mugged,' Rona said stubbornly.

'Then she was lucky.'

'You sound like that odious policeman.'

'Thanks!'

They glared at each other, then both smiled shamefacedly. Rona said more calmly, 'Anyway, since she died of a heart attack, it could just as easily have happened at home.'

'Except that you don't know what brought it on. Something or someone might have frightened her.'

Rona went cold. That was a point she'd not considered. Should she have done? Had Edna in fact been frightened to death? If so, there would have been nothing to show for it.

'I wish you hadn't said that,' she told him.

Max shrugged, finishing his drink. 'Since we'll never know, there's no point in losing sleep over it. She was old, and her time had come, that's all.'

'So if she *was* frightened to death, it doesn't really matter?'

Max's mouth tightened. 'You're twisting my words, and you know it.'

There was a short silence. They were in danger of quarrelling, and Rona, taking a deep breath, opted for safer ground. 'As you say, what's done is done. So, what's been happening here this week?'

He poured himself another drink. 'Not much.' He stared into his glass for a minute, then added, 'Actually, there is something. I'm a bit worried about this new student.'

'The watercolourist? Why?'

'I told you she was pale and quiet, didn't I? After today's class, I suspect there's rather more to it. She has some nasty bruises on her arm.'

Rona raised an eyebrow.

'It was hot in the studio,' he continued, 'and she was the only one wearing long sleeves. I noticed that last week, too. At one point, when she reached for something, they rode up, and she went bright pink and pulled them quickly down again. But not before I'd seen the bruises.'

Rona regarded him over the rim of her glass. 'You think she's a battered wife?'

He looked at her quickly, then away. 'I don't know what to think. She certainly seems withdrawn and – nervous.'

'Well, there's not much you can do about it, is there?'

'The trouble is, she doesn't know anyone. They've only just moved here, and by a stroke of coincidence, they live in Fairhaven.'

Which was Lindsey's road. 'What's her name?'

'Adele Yarborough.'

'Any children?'

'I've no idea.'

'Well, you know what it's like when you move house. She probably banged herself heaving boxes around.'

'I was wondering—' He broke off.

'What?'

'If you'd meet her. Let me know what you think.'

Rona stared at him. 'Meet her how? For God's sake, Max, I'm not a social worker.'

'You could get Lindsey to be a good neighbour and invite her for coffee.'

'And how exactly would that help?'

He looked up, and she was surprised by the genuine concern in his eyes. 'I don't know, love, but I feel I should do *something*. I might be the only one who suspects anything.'

'I'm sure you are,' she said dryly.

He said flatly, 'So you won't help?'

She shrugged, irritated at being made to feel guilty.

'Fair enough. Well, her phone number's on the pad, in case you change your mind.'

'I'll think about it,' she said ungraciously. 'Now –' she pushed herself away from the counter she'd been leaning against – 'what's on the menu this evening?'

For a minute longer Max remained deep in thought. Then he looked up. 'Cheese soufflé and salad,' he said.

Tom Parish walked across the tarmac to his car, opened the door and stood back to let the furnace-like blast of hot air escape. It was a humid, thundery evening, overcast despite the hazy sunshine. He loosened his tie and flung it on the back seat, opening the neck of his shirt. Avril had gone with the bridge club on their annual outing to a West End theatre, and wouldn't be home till after midnight. The evening stretched ahead of him to do with as he chose, and he intended to go home and change, do a bit of gardening, and then go to the Jolly Wagoner for a bite to eat.

The interior of the car now being bearable, he climbed in and drove slowly out of the car park. The traffic lights were against him as usual, and as he sat waiting, he caught sight of Catherine Bishop at the bus stop diagonally across from him. The lights changed and he turned right into Alban Road, drew up alongside and wound down his window.

'Mrs Bishop? Can I give you a lift?'

She looked round in surprise. 'Oh – Mr Parish. That's very kind of you.'

He leant over to open the passenger door, taking her parcels from her as she got in.

'Car playing up?' he asked.

'Yes, I've been having a bit of trouble with it. It's in for a service and won't be ready till tomorrow. This really is very good of you. With that number of people ahead of me, I shouldn't have got on the first bus, and there's quite a walk at the other end.'

'I don't know where you live, so you'll have to direct me.'

'We turn off in about a mile, at Barrington Road, and drive past the park. Then it's first right into Talbot Road and first left into Willow Crescent – number twenty-three.'

'Sounds simple enough.'

She laughed. 'My son wouldn't agree with you, though admittedly he comes from the other direction.'

The development off Barrington Road, Tom saw, consisted mainly of bungalows. Following her directions, he drew up at one of them, distinguishable from its neighbours only by the riot of colour in its small garden.

'Are you the gardener?' he asked her.

'Yes, but as I was saying to your daughter, I'm restraining myself until I know what comes up of its own accord.'

He helped her out of the car and opened the gate for her.

'Would you like to come in for a cup of tea? Or a glass of something, if you'd prefer?'

He hesitated, and she said, 'Please. It's the least I can do, after bringing you out of your way like this.'

'Then thank you. Tea would be very welcome.'

She showed him into the sitting room, opened the patio

doors for some fresh air, and excused herself to put the kettle on. Tom went to study the photographs on the mantelpiece. One was a head and shoulders portrait of a young man in slightly dated clothes – her dead husband, presumably – and the other a wedding photograph of a tall young man and a pretty blonde girl. The groom, Tom thought, had quite a look of his father.

He turned as she came into the room. 'I've been admiring your photos.'

She smiled. 'The entire extent of my family.'

'Your son lives in Cricklehurst, you said?'

'That's right.' She poured his tea and handed it to him. 'His wife's expecting their first baby, and she's having a difficult pregnancy. We're a bit worried about her.'

'This is my week for seeing the Parishes,' she went on quickly, as though anxious to change the subject. 'I met your other daughter yesterday. I didn't realize you had twins.'

'And you took her for Rona? A lot of people do.'

'I was one of them, but of course there are differences, and I suppose they're more noticeable when you see both girls together.'

'Rona was very grateful for the time you gave her.'

'It was a pleasure. I thought her charming. Would you tell her I found something else that might interest her? I was going to phone, but there's no urgency.'

Tom sat back in his chair, feeling pleasantly relaxed. It was an attractive room, welcoming and restful, and the Impressionist prints reminded him of her weekend away.

'How was Paris?' he asked.

'Wonderful, as always.'

'You saw the exhibition?'

'Fancy your remembering. Yes, I did. It was fantastic.'

'I enjoy looking round galleries myself, but—' He broke off, unwilling to say that Avril had no interest in art.

'It's hard to find the time,' Catherine supplied, and he nodded gratefully.

'I brought back some catalogues, if you'd like to see them?'

'Oh, I would,' he said eagerly.

She opened a bureau drawer and brought a pile of them over, settling herself next to him on the sofa. 'This is from the Matisse exhibition. They'd arranged the paintings very cleverly.'

She went on to explain the layout of the gallery, pointing out juxtapositions and contrasts which Tom knew would have completely passed him by. He found himself thinking how pleasant it would be to walk round a gallery with this quiet, knowledgeable woman at his side.

Going through the catalogues took some time since she kept stopping to discuss individual paintings, and they were both surprised when the mantel clock chimed seven.

'How inconsiderate of me to keep you so long!' she exclaimed. 'Your wife will be wondering where you are.'

'No, she's not home and won't be back till late,' Tom assured her. 'They've gone on a coach trip to London.'

'Then let me at least offer you a sherry before you go. Or a whisky, if you'd prefer?'

Before he could answer, the phone rang in the hall and she went out to answer it. He heard her voice change, become anxious.

'But what exactly happened? Are you sure? Oh, darling, I'm so sorry . . . Yes, of course I will. Oh God, Daniel, I've just remembered – the car's at the garage. Never mind, I'll get a taxi. . . . Yes, of course I'll come.'

Tom walked quickly to the door, and she turned a worried face to him.

'Can I help?' he asked.

'Just a minute, darling.' She put a hand over the phone. 'My daughter-in-law has been rushed into hospital with a threatened miscarriage. Obviously I shall have to go to them. I was just saying—'

'I'll drive you there,' Tom said quickly.

'Oh – oh no, I couldn't possibly—'

'Where is she? Stokely?'

Catherine nodded.

'A taxi would cost the earth. Of course I'll take you. As I said, no one's expecting me home.'

'Then – thank you.' She turned back to the phone, explained the position swiftly to her son, and within five minutes they were in his car again, her overnight bag on the back seat.

'I do so hope it'll be all right,' Catherine said tightly. 'They've been trying for a baby for some time. It would be too bad if she lost it.'

'They can do wonders these days,' Tom assured her. 'At least she's in the best place now.'

'It's Stokely General, maternity wing. Do you know where it is?'

'I've a rough idea. Don't worry, we'll find it.'

From the corner of his eye, he saw that her fingers were gripping her handbag. 'Try to relax,' he said gently. 'We'll be there in under an hour.'

'It's what we find when we get there that worries me,' she said in a low voice. 'Daniel sounded distraught; he's turning to me now like he did when Neil died. I pulled out all the stops to be strong for him then; suppose I can't do it again? I'm so terrified of letting him down.'

Tom put a hand quickly over hers. 'You'll find the strength,' he said.

She gave a shaky laugh. 'Just as well you didn't know what you were letting yourself in for when you drew up at the bus stop! It's really too bad, expecting you to play knight errant twice in one evening.'

'I'm just glad I can help.'

She was right, of course: he'd had no way of knowing what his impulsive offer of a lift would lead to. All he knew was that he didn't for one moment regret it.

They had come off the Marsborough bypass and were now on the main Stokely road. The evening had clouded over, a thin rain was misting the windscreen, and the banking clouds ahead of them seemed to presage a thunderstorm.

'I hope you brought an umbrella, Mrs Bishop; it looks as though we're in for a downpour.'

She smiled. 'I think, in the circumstances, we might dispense with "Mrs Bishop", don't you? Not many people call me Catherine these days; I'd like you to be one of them.'

Taken by surprise, Tom could only murmur, 'Thank you.'

'So, Mr T. E. Parish—?' she prompted.

'Tom. It's Tom.'

'Thank you, Tom. That's settled, then.'

They drove in silence while the rain intensified and the evening grew darker. It was just on eight o'clock when they came to the outskirts of Stokely, and Tom prayed that his recollection of the hospital's location would prove to be correct. He was beginning to wonder if he should stop to ask directions when he saw it looming up on their left, and turned thankfully into the gateway signposted to the visitors' car park. The nearest space was a long way from the hospital entrance, and Catherine had not in fact thought to bring an umbrella.

Tom took her case out of the car, and with it in one hand and the other under her elbow, they ran, heads down, over the shining, slippery tarmac as the first peals of thunder broke overhead. By the time they reached the maternity wing, they were both soaked.

Daniel, white as a sheet, was waiting in the corridor. He strode forward, caught Catherine in his arms and held her tightly against him while Tom stood awkwardly to one side.

'She's lost the baby,' Daniel said unsteadily, 'but that wasn't even the worst of it. For a long time they couldn't stop the bleeding. God, Ma, I thought I was going to lose her too. It's been a nightmare.'

Catherine's face over his shoulder was as white as his, and her eyes were tightly closed. Tom, his throat tight, knew what this was costing her.

After a minute she put her son gently from her and said, her voice calm, 'She's out of danger now?'

'Yes, thank God. But Ma, she's heartbroken – we both are. If ever a baby was wanted—'

'I know, my love, I know, and of course you're both grieving for it. But the main thing is that Jenny's safe, and in time there'll be other babies.' She became aware of Tom, silent against the wall.

'Daniel, this is a friend of mine, Tom Parish. He very kindly drove me over here. My son Daniel, Tom.'

The young man seemed to register Tom for the first time, and came forward with his hand out. 'I can't tell you how grateful we are, sir. Thank you.'

'I'm only sorry we've not arrived to better news.'

Daniel nodded distractedly and turned back to his mother. 'Could you possibly stay the night? They're keeping Jenny in, of course, and I'd be glad of the company. Her parents will be down tomorrow to look after her.'

His eyes fell to the holdall Tom was carrying, and he gave a bleak smile. 'I should have known you'd think of everything.'

Tom said tentatively, 'If there's nothing else I can do, I think I'll be getting back.'

'Just a minute.' Catherine turned to her son. 'Are we able to see Jenny?'

'Not at the moment; they've given her something and she's asleep.'

'Then I think we should all have something to eat. Tom and I haven't had supper, and I'm quite sure neither have you. No, don't tell me you're not hungry; nor am I, but we can't function on empty stomachs and we both need our strength. No doubt there's a hospital canteen?'

Tom said quickly, 'Look, don't worry about me – I'll find something down the road. You don't want me around at a time like this.'

'Of course you must join us,' Daniel said firmly. 'Ma's

right, we all need to eat. The canteen's down that corridor.'

He relieved Tom of the overnight bag, took Catherine's arm, and started off down one of the long passages radiating from the lobby, and Tom, his mind buffeted by conflicting emotions, fell into step behind them.

Avril was surprised to find him downstairs when she arrived home.

'You didn't need to wait up,' she told him, walking into the sitting room, where he was watching a late-night film. 'I told you I'd be late.'

'I wasn't tired,' he said.

'But it's nearly one o'clock! The play overran, then some people had gone to the loo and we had to wait for them, so we finished up setting off even later than we'd expected.'

'Did you enjoy the show?'

'It was all right. A musical. Always seems a bit unnatural to me, the way they burst into song in the middle of a conversation. I prefer a straight play.'

His eyes had gone back to the screen and she watched him for a moment. He seemed somehow different, though she couldn't have said why.

'What did you do with yourself all evening?'

'I went to see a client,' he said.

She made a sound of impatience. 'I don't know why you dance attendance on them like that. Why can't they see you in office hours?'

'I wouldn't have gone if you'd been home,' he said levelly. 'Since you weren't, it didn't matter.'

'Suit yourself.'

She went out into the kitchen and he heard her running the tap to fill the kettle. Whatever time Avril went to bed, she had to have a hot drink. Tom never did; it would have led to his getting up in the night, and he prided himself on never having to do so.

His thoughts went back, as they'd been doing all evening,

to the hospital in Stokely. He didn't know how far the pregnancy had progressed, but it must be traumatic to lose a baby at any stage. He couldn't imagine not having the girls.

And Catherine. He smiled a little, savouring the name. She'd introduced him to her son as a friend, not her bank manager. Was that how she thought of him?

The clock on the mantelpiece chimed one. By this time, surely, she'd be asleep. It had been a strain on her, and he was glad she'd be coming home the next day – today, now – when Jenny's parents took over. Would it, he wondered, be in order for him to phone in a day or two, to ask after her daughter-in-law? Or would their 'friendship', accelerated by the unusual circumstances, simply sink back into a manager/client relationship?

'Are you going to sit there all night?' Avril's voice asked from the doorway. Resignedly he switched off the television. He'd not really been watching it, anyway.

'Just coming,' he said.

The overnight rain had lasted into the morning, and Rona, up in her study, settled down with Catherine Bishop's records. The format of those for the grammar school and college were, she saw, necessarily different; their compiler had not been on the staff of either school and there was no pupil participation. Certainly that for the college, despite its Speech Day programmes and team photographs, had an altogether more serious slant – doubtless a nod in the direction of the academic Mr Maddox.

She opened a notebook and began to jot down such facts as she might, with permission, make use of, trying to work out as she did so how many thousand words she could allow for each school. It would, she thought, be an exercise in précis-writing.

The phone interrupted her, and Lindsey's voice said, 'Still OK for lunch?'

'Yep. Where do you want to go?'

'There's a new wine bar in Market Street. We could try that.'

'OK by me. See you there about twelve thirty?'

'Right. By the way, I met your Mrs Bishop the other day. She accosted me in the street, thinking I was you.'

'What did she want?'

'I don't know. Nothing urgent, she said. Not much to look at, is she?'

'She grows on you,' Rona said. 'Any news about Hugh?'

'No; it's beginning to get to me, Ro. Every time the phone rings I wonder if it's him, and every time I come out of the flat or the office, I expect him to be waiting for me.'

'And you're disappointed when he's not?'

Lindsey paused. 'To be honest, I don't know,' she said.

When they met a couple of hours later, Lindsey continued from where she'd left off. 'Why did it have to change?' she asked plaintively. 'It was working perfectly well, with him coming up at weekends and then going back again. I don't want him here all the time, but I'm finding that doesn't mean I don't want to see him at all.'

'It sounds to me as though he's playing a very clever game,' Rona said. She paused. 'To change the subject completely, how do you feel about playing the Good Samaritan?'

'Which involves what, exactly?'

'Simply asking a new neighbour of yours to coffee. She doesn't know anybody.'

'A neighbour of mine?'

'Yes; she's joined Max's Wednesday class, and he's convinced himself she's a battered wife.'

'Ye gods!'

'So he wants me to vet her and tell him what I think. Though what qualifies me to recognize a battered wife when I see one, I can't imagine.'

'Me neither,' agreed Lindsey ungrammatically.

'Have you got a Neighbourhood Watch scheme or anything?'

'Not as far as I know. If we have, they were pretty useless back in March.'

The two of them had been in Lindsey's flat when a double-murderer broke in, and only Hugh's timely arrival had saved them.

'What number is she?' Lindsey added.

'One, according to the note Max pointedly left out.'

'That's on the corner of the main road.' Fairhaven was a cul-de-sac with four detached houses of varying styles on either side. The one where Lindsey lived had been built as two flats, and she occupied the upper one. 'I didn't know the Baxters had moved out, but I wasn't particularly friendly with them.'

'Look, I'm no keener to get involved than you are,' Rona admitted, 'I'm just trying to keep peace in the marital home. So would you be an angel? Have her to coffee, and I'll just happen to drop in.'

'But when? I'm at work all week, and if I ask her at the weekend, the bruiser would have to come too.'

Rona smiled. 'Then knock off early one afternoon, and invite her for tea. Come to think of it, could you possibly make it tomorrow? Otherwise, it'll be another week before I'm available.'

'The things I do for you,' Lindsey said resignedly.

'Or, in this instance, for Max.' Rona pushed across the slip of paper giving the phone number.

'Whatever. OK, I'll give it a go, and let you know how I get on.'

Intent on her thoughts, Rona did not notice the young man approaching her up Dean's Crescent until he spoke her name.

'Hello, Mrs Allerdyce. And – Gus, isn't it?'

Looking up, she recognized Max's ex-student and her own ex-shadow, Dave Lampeter. 'Hi, Dave. How are things?'

'Not brilliant, to be honest.'

'Max told me you haven't managed to find a job yet. I'm sorry.'

'Yes, stacking shelves wasn't quite what I had in mind when I graduated.' He paused. 'I hear you're writing again. That's good news.'

'I've got something on the go, yes.'

'Excellent. Well, nice to see you. Any time you want a bodyguard, let me know!'

'Hang on!' Rona exclaimed as he started to move away. 'Funny you should say that. Come to think of it, I just might.'

He stared at her. 'You're not serious?'

'I could be. Look, can you spare me a few minutes?'

'Sure, I'm on shift work. Off now till the store closes, then I start refilling the shelves.'

'So you've time to come back for a coffee?'

'All the time in the world.'

Back at the house, they went down to the kitchen, where Dave prowled about admiring things while Rona made the coffee and took it over to the table by the patio doors. As she pulled them open, the scent of warm wet earth reached them.

'So,' Dave invited, seating himself and pulling a mug towards him. 'What's the problem? Not another murdered author?'

She shook her head, not looking at him as she stirred her coffee. 'You'll think we're a very odd family,' she began. 'Max originally hired you to keep watch on me without my knowing. Now, I want you to do the same again, but without telling him. Would you be prepared to do that?'

'Suppose you fill me in.'

So Rona told him about the Buckford project, about her interview with Miss Rosebury, the lost cassette, the phone call and the two notes.

'He seems to be stepping up the pressure,' she ended, 'and I'm getting a bit jittery.'

'I'm not surprised. You do land yourself in it, don't you?'
Rona nodded ruefully.

'How much of this have you told Max?'

She flushed. 'Very little.'

'Could I ask why?'

'Oh Dave, you know how he was last time. If he thinks
I'm in any danger, he'll start laying down the law and
demanding I drop the whole thing.'

A smile twitched at his mouth. 'I can't see you complying.'

'No, but it makes for unpleasantness. Anyway, so far I've
been writing it off as a joke that's got a bit out of hand. Now,
I'm not so sure, especially since, on top of everything, old
Miss Rosebury was found dead in the street.' She went on
to recount their visit to the mortuary and the police interview. 'I'm just praying it had nothing to do with the
cassette.'

'And this landlady of yours – the old lady's niece: she's
no idea who her aunt saw?'

'None whatever.' Rona hesitated. 'I might as well tell you
the rest. You're not going to like this, but a murderer *is*
involved, though this time he's already locked up. At least,
I think he is.' And she told him about Alan Spencer and
Beth's account of what had happened.

'I presume Max doesn't know this, either?'

She shook her head.

'He'd blow his top if he found out, and I can't say I'd
blame him.'

'I don't want to put any pressure on you,' Rona said.

'What's more, I'd come in for my own share of the fallout.
Probably a large share.'

'On the other hand, if you don't agree, and something
happens to me, and he finds out I asked you for help . . .'

'Oh, no pressure at all!' said Dave with a wry grin. 'As
far as I can see, though,' he went on slowly, 'there's nothing
whatever to connect this couple with the man in prison. Or
have I missed something?'

'No, you're right; on the face of it, there isn't.'

'But you think there *is* a connection?'

'I honestly don't know.'

'Suppose I agree to all this: what would you require me to do?'

'Well, I've only got two more visits up there, next week and the week after. Ideally, I'd like you to go up when I do, keep me in sight during the day to see if anyone's following me, and check me safely back into the house at night. I'm sure you could get a room at the pub, which is only minutes from the house. Naturally, I'll pay all expenses, together with a retainer.' She glanced at him. 'What about your job, though? Even if you don't like it, I don't want to be responsible for your losing it.'

He made a dismissive gesture. 'That wouldn't be a problem; I've some holiday due to me.'

'Well then?'

There was a brief pause. 'I'd be much happier if Max was in on this.'

'No deal.'

Another pause. 'Only two visits, you said? Four days in all?'

'More or less; mid-morning Monday to Wednesday afternoon, both weeks.'

He sighed. 'I might well regret this, but I'll do it.'

Rona breathed a sigh of relief and leant back in her chair. 'Thanks, Dave. I'll sleep a lot easier now.'

Eleven

'All fixed for tomorrow,' said Lindsey's voice, as Rona lifted the phone.

It took her a moment to decipher the message. 'Oh, the damsel in distress. What did she say?'

'She sounded surprised, but said she'd come.'

'How did she seem?'

'Not jittery or anything, if that's what you mean.'

'And you didn't mention Max or me?'

'Nary a word.'

'Bless you, Linz, that's great. What time's she coming?'

'Three thirty. I'm taking the afternoon off.'

'So if I drop in about four?'

'Fine. God knows what we'll talk about till you get here.'

'You'll manage,' Rona said.

When Max phoned an hour or two later, Rona relayed the arrangements.

'Oh, that's wonderful, love. Thanks so much for fixing it.'

'I'm not sure what you want me to do?'

'Look for bruises, if you can without being obvious. Otherwise, just take note of her manner, whether or not you think she's on edge. If you can get her to talk about her husband, so much the better. God, I don't know – use your imagination. I'm just uneasy about her, that's all.'

'Shall I mention you?'

'Better not, unless you can't avoid it. I certainly don't want her thinking we've discussed her.'

'OK, I'll see what I can do, and report back.'

'You're a gem,' he said.

Max had described Adele Yarborough as pale and quiet. He had neglected to say she was also extremely pretty. She had a small, pointed face, large eyes of an indeterminate slatey colour, and ash-blonde hair cut very short in a gamine style. Mascara and lipstick seemed to be the extent of her make-up, but the luminous quality of her skin made anything else superfluous. Her dress was long-sleeved, Rona noted, and its colour – rose-pink – added to a general impression of fragility. Her only jewellery was a watch and her wedding ring.

All this Rona took in in the first, lightning glance. Adele had looked up as she came into the room, and now gave her a shy smile. 'My goodness!' she said. 'Am I seeing double?'

'My twin sister, Rona,' Lindsey introduced. 'Ro, this is Adele Yarborough. She and her husband have just moved in across the road.'

Adele stood to greet her. She was petite in build – not much over five foot, so that Rona and Lindsey towered over her – and the hand she held out was small and firm.

Rona smiled back. 'Nice to meet you. Sorry to drop in unannounced,' she added to Lindsey. 'I came across that book you lent me, and thought I'd better return it.' And she put the book down on the coffee table. It was, in fact, one of her own.

'I'm glad you came,' Lindsey said. 'I was apologizing to Adele for not inviting some other neighbours, but it was all rather short notice.' She turned to her guest. 'Have you spoken to any of them yet?'

'No; with being on the corner, I don't pass anyone else's house, and they all drive past mine.'

Her voice was quiet, and Rona noticed she had not looked directly at Lindsey, either when she was being addressed or when she replied. Instead, her gaze seemed to flutter like a distracted butterfly from a point just over Lindsey's shoulder to her own lap.

'Well, we'll have to rectify that,' Lindsey said brightly. 'If you'll excuse me, I'll go and make a fresh pot of tea.' Rona saw there was a plate of home-made scones on the tray, and blessed her sister for the trouble she'd taken.

'Where were you living before?' she asked Adele, as Lindsey left the room and they both seated themselves.

'In Suffolk.' Again the downcast eyes. 'My family comes from there.'

'So you won't know anyone in Marsborough?'

'Quite honestly, I've been too busy getting the house straight. However –' the smile again, tilting the corners of her mouth – 'I've followed the time-honoured advice and joined a club. Or at least, an art class.'

Rona bit her lip. No help now but to admit to Max. 'Really? What a coincidence. My husband teaches art.'

The slatey eyes, taken unaware, flew to her face. 'Not – he's not Mr Allerdyce?'

'The same.'

'Well, that really is a coincidence.' There was a pause as her eyes fell away. Then she added, 'He's been very encouraging.'

Rona just stopped herself from passing on Max's opinion of her talents. As Lindsey came back with the teapot, she exclaimed, 'You'll never guess, Linz, but Adele has joined Max's class.'

Lindsey expressed suitable surprise.

'Have you been to art classes before?' Rona asked.

'Before I was married. I enjoyed it, but somehow or other it just lapsed.'

'What does your husband do?' Lindsey asked artlessly, pouring Rona's tea.

'He's the sales director at Netherby's.' Netherby's was the town's premier department store, with a prime position on Guild Street. 'He's just been promoted from their Ipswich branch.'

'I hope he gets staff discounts!' Lindsey said. 'Have you any family?'

Rona, afraid she was overdoing the interrogation, gave her a warning glance, but Adele was answering, 'Yes, a boy and a girl. They're staying with my parents during the week, so they can finish the term at their present school. I miss them a lot.'

Taking Rona's hint, Lindsey abandoned personal questioning, instead giving Adele a thumbnail sketch of her neighbours. 'The guys in the flat below me are gay,' she told her. 'They're a great pair, always ready to help with any jobs I can't manage myself. The man directly opposite is a doctor, but his surgery's in town. His wife's a theatre nurse at the General.'

Rona let the conversation drift over her. So far, there was nothing positive she could report to Max. Adele's arms remained hidden, and no bruises were visible. As to whether or not she was on edge, it was hard to tell, not knowing how she behaved normally. She was obviously unwilling to meet their eyes, but that might have been due to shyness. All she'd volunteered about her husband was where he worked, but Rona didn't see how they could probe further. Reckoning she'd done all that could be expected of her, she made general contributions to the conversation until, just after four thirty, Adele rose to go.

'It was so kind of you to invite me over,' she said to the wall behind Lindsey. 'We're having some decorating done, but when the house is less of a shambles, you must come to me. You, too,' she added in Rona's direction. 'It was good to meet you both.'

'Well?' Lindsey demanded, when she returned from seeing her out.

'You were a trooper,' Rona told her. 'Scones and all. Thanks, Sis.'

'Are you any the wiser?'

Rona shrugged. 'What did you think of her?'

'I'm not sure. Whether I like her, I mean.'

'Oh?'

'I wasn't quite convinced by all that diffidence. Perhaps it's just that she's not my type. Anyway, thanks to you I've done my neighbourly duty. I shall now rest on my laurels.'

'You'll be rewarded in heaven,' Rona said.

The front door slammed and Max's voice called, 'Hello?'

'In the kitchen!' Rona called back, and he came clattering down the stairs. Gus pattered over to greet him, tail waving, as she lifted her face for his kiss.

'To coin a phrase, thank God it's Friday,' Max commented, bending down to rub the dog's ears.

'Likewise,' Rona agreed.

He picked up the pile of mail lying on the counter and flicked through it. 'How did the tea party go?'

'No bruises in evidence.'

'I didn't think there would be. I presume she was wearing long sleeves?'

Rona nodded. 'She knows who I am, by the way. She mentioned the class, so I'd no option but to come clean. She thinks my dropping in was a coincidence, though.'

'So what was your impression of her?'

'Hard to say, after one meeting.'

His eyes narrowed. 'But?'

'Well, I wasn't quite sure that it wasn't an act.'

He frowned. 'What wasn't?'

'Not daring to look you in the eye – all fluttering eyelashes and so on. Is she like that in class?'

He said shortly, 'She's shy. I told you that.'

'No need to snap; I'm only telling you my impression, as requested.'

'I wasn't snapping, I just think you're being rather hard on her. No doubt you discussed her with Lindsey?'

'Well, of course.'

'And decided she wasn't your type, right?'

166

That was too close to the truth, and Rona didn't answer.

'Well, of course she isn't!' he said forcefully. 'She's the exact opposite of you – shy, vulnerable and unsure of herself.'

Rona's temper rose to meet his. 'Oh, really? Since when did you become a psychologist? You can't possibly form a judgement like that on the strength of two art classes.'

'You're forgetting the bruises.'

'No, I'm *not* forgetting the bloody bruises – you don't give me a chance to forget them! Look, I don't know why you're getting so hot under the collar: it was you who wanted me to meet her, and Lindsey went to considerable trouble to arrange it, taking time off work, baking scones, etc. I don't see why we should now both be castigated because we're not prepared to go along with your opinion of her.'

There was a long silence. Then he said stiffly, 'I'm grateful.'

'So you should be. From now on you can do your own analysing – you seem to be a dab hand at it.' She walked quickly across the room and out of the patio doors, coming to a halt in the middle of the little garden and staring unseeingly at a pot of petunias. After a minute she heard him come after her, and felt his hand on her shoulder.

'I'm sorry,' he said quietly. 'I was out of order. Of course I'm grateful, both to you and Lindsey. It's just that with Adele being one of my students I feel somehow responsible for her, which of course I'm not. Or at least, not her private life.'

He turned her gently round to face him. 'Apology accepted?'

She stared for a minute into his face, then smiled reluctantly. 'Apology accepted,' she said.

Adele's name was not mentioned again, and the altercation faded into the background. They walked in the park with Gus, had dinner at Dino's on the Saturday, and made love. Harmony was restored, and Rona was duly grateful.

* * *

It was Sunday evening before she checked her mobile for messages, and found one from Beth Spencer, asking her to call back. Rona did so.

'Oh Miss Parish, thanks for getting back to me.' Beth's voice was excited. 'Great news! Alan's changed his mind, as I thought he might, and agreed to see you. The visiting order will be waiting for you at Parsonage Place.'

Rona felt a jolt of alarm. Her last meeting with a murderer had not gone too well. 'That's – great,' she said. 'So what do I do?'

'When you get it, phone the prison and make an appointment. They require twenty-four hours' notice so Tuesday might be pushing it, but Wednesday should be fine. It's from three to four.'

Which meant she could still leave for home at the usual time, Rona reflected.

'And a word of warning,' Beth continued. 'You'll have to go through security and you'll need photographic identification – driving licence or something. Oh, and Alan says don't let them know you're a journalist, or they mightn't let you in.'

No recorder, then, but she'd never seriously considered it.

'All right, Mrs Spencer, I'll do what I can, but please remember I can't make any promises.'

'Just seeing him will convince you he's innocent,' said Alan Spencer's wife.

Another of the messages was from Dave Lampeter. He'd booked a room at the King's Head for Monday and Tuesday nights, and would be in Buckford ahead of her, ready to begin his surveillance. If she intended to deviate from the agreed schedule for Monday, would she please leave a message on his mobile. He'd be checking it regularly.

Now that she'd be seeing Alan Spencer, Rona was even more glad she'd enlisted Dave's help. If Alan were indeed guilty there'd be no danger; but if, as various people surmised, he'd been wrongly imprisoned, then the real murderer might learn of her visit, with unpredictable results.

Closing her mind on the possibilities, she went down for supper with Max.

As Rona was getting out of the car in Parsonage Place, she could see Lois Breen digging in her garden. She raised a hand in greeting and Lois dropped the spade and came over, leaning her elbows on the warm stone of the wall.

'I met Beth Spencer in Tesco's,' she said, after they'd exchanged the usual pleasantries. 'She tells me you're going to see Alan.'

'That's right, yes.'

'With what purpose, exactly?'

Rona met her steady gaze. 'Not sensation-seeking, I assure you. In fact, she talked me into it against my better judgement.'

'But what are you hoping to achieve?'

'I don't know,' Rona said frankly. 'She's so convinced of his innocence, and various other people obviously have doubts.'

'But even if you find you agree with them, what could you do?'

Rona hesitated. 'If I could discover some other motive for killing Pollard, the police might reopen the case.'

'Then surely the obvious person to speak to is Barry's widow, not his supposed killer.'

'Yes, but—' Rona stopped, reinterpreting the expression in Lois's eyes. 'Do you know her?'

'I do, as it happens. Our last parish was in Sunningdean, though we'd left by the time of the murder. Gordon used to visit Barry in prison; he said he was in a terrible state, and it took months before he'd even begin to look forward to his release as a new beginning. Then, within ten days of it . . . It was an appalling shock, especially since we'd always liked Alan, too.'

'And you're still in touch with Mrs Pollard?'

'She's Mrs Bryson now, but yes, I still see her occasionally.'

Rona moistened her lips. 'Do you think she'd speak to me?'

'She might, if I asked her. If they *have* the wrong man, presumably she'd want to know.'

'Lois, I—'

'I'll ask her here to meet you. That would be less awkward, provided you don't mind my sitting in on the discussion. Tomorrow morning suit you?'

'It's very good of you; yes, any time at all.'

'I'll see if I can arrange it, then. If you don't hear from me, come over at eleven.'

'Thank you. I really am grateful.'

Rona was turning away when Lois added dryly, 'And to forestall any unguarded comments, I should tell you her second marriage broke up, too. Ironic, isn't it?'

Nuala emerged from the kitchen as Rona, having left her case in her room, came downstairs. She was pale and there were black circles under her eyes. These were not easy times for her.

Rona laid an instinctive hand on her arm. 'How are you?' she asked.

'Bearing up. The funeral's been arranged; I'll be glad when that's over.'

'When is it?'

'Thursday morning. I – suppose you'll have gone back?'

Rona rapidly reviewed her plans for the week. Max would object to missing his mid-week visit home, but she felt an obligation towards Miss Rosebury. 'I'd like to be there,' she said tentatively. 'Could I possibly stay over Wednesday night? Obviously, I'd pay you the extra.'

'You'd do nothing of the kind,' Nuala contradicted, her eyes filling with tears. 'I really would appreciate it, Rona.'

'That's settled, then.' She hesitated. 'Nothing further came out at the post mortem?'

'No, it was natural causes, thank God. A massive coronary, which considering the condition of her heart, could have happened at any time.'

'That's a relief, anyway.'

'You do remember supper will be late this evening, after Dad's exercises?'

'Don't worry about me; I'll give the local hostelry a try.'

'Well, if you're sure. Oh, and there's a letter for you.' Nuala handed over the envelope.

The visiting order. Rona avoided her eyes. 'Thank you,' she said.

Tom reached absent-mindedly for the ringing phone, his eyes still on the balance sheet.

'Yes?'

'Mrs Bishop for you, Mr Parish.'

A wave of heat washed over him and he automatically straightened. 'Put her through.'

'Hello, Tom,' said a quiet voice in his ear.

'Catherine! I was going to ring you today. How's your daughter-in-law?'

'Slowly recovering, poor lamb. Her parents are still with her; Daniel says they'll stay as long as necessary.'

'He ran you home?'

'Yes, the following evening. And I now have my car back, thank goodness. I wanted to thank you again for all your kindness. I don't know what we'd have done without you.'

'I just happened to be there at the right time,' he said.

'I – wonder if you'd accept a small token of our gratitude?'

'Oh, now Catherine—'

'Wait – it's nothing really, but I have two tickets for *Pissarro in London* at the National Gallery. I'd booked them for Daniel and Jenny – it's their anniversary on Wednesday

– but obviously they won't be able to make use of them. I wondered if you and your wife might like to go?'

Tom's mind spun as various possibilities presented themselves, evaporating before he could clutch at them.

'It's very generous of you,' he began stumblingly. 'I'd have enjoyed it very much, but I'm afraid it wouldn't appeal to my wife. Art galleries aren't really her scene.'

There was a pause. Catherine said, 'So you never go, either?'

No use saying it's no fun by yourself; Catherine had flown to Paris expressly for that purpose, and presumably she'd gone alone. The sudden doubt alarmed him.

As he sought for a reply, she asked, 'Would you like to?'

'Well, yes; of course. But—'

'Then why not come as my guest? I'd intended going myself later, but if your wife doesn't want the ticket, it's a shame to waste it. Do you think she'd have any objection?'

'I'm sure she wouldn't,' he lied.

'It's short notice, that's the trouble: the day after tomorrow. Would that be a problem?'

'No, I think I can rearrange my diary.' He'd make damn sure he did.

'I'll look forward to it, then. I usually catch the ten forty; that gives time for a light lunch first. Shall we meet at the station?'

'I'll be there,' Tom said.

She rang off, but it was some time before he returned to his balance sheet.

Catherine stood stock-still, suddenly appalled by what she had done. What must he think of her, calmly suggesting they spend the day together? Certainly she'd had no intention of doing so; it was his assumption that since his wife wasn't interested in art, he must also miss out that had goaded her to action.

Yet, if she were truthful, she knew she'd welcome a day

in Tom Parish's company. He'd been in her thoughts frequently, a solid, comforting presence behind the family traumas. It was, she told herself, because he'd been there when she was at her most vulnerable; no more and no less than that.

And she liked him; why pretend otherwise? His slow smile, his steady brown eyes and his innate kindness appealed to something deep within her and made her want to know him better. This was, she recognized, a new experience for her; since Neil had died, fourteen long years ago, her associations with men had been minimal, the few who'd shown interest having been gently but firmly pushed away. Tom, though, was in a totally different category, and there was no reason that she could see why she shouldn't enjoy his company. When all was said and done, everything was entirely above board.

Having satisfied herself on that point, she dismissed him from her mind and went out to do some gardening.

Rona spent the afternoon being shown round the town hall and having an interview with the mayor. He was a fussy little man, very conscious of the fact that his term of office would spill over into Jubilee Year. However, his knowledge of the history of the town was extensive, and she acquired some welcome new material.

She had arranged to have supper with Dave, and since she might be recognized at the King's Head and his cover blown, they'd agreed to meet in the White Horse off Market Square. There were, however, a couple of hours in hand, and, confident he would be shadowing her, Rona decided to continue her exploration of the town.

Once or twice during the day she had glanced over her shoulder, trying to spot him in the crowds, but had never managed to. That was a great thing in his favour, she reflected; though pleasant enough to look at, he was completely unmemorable. Of medium height, he had mid-brown hair and the kind of face that didn't attract notice. If he dressed in a different style, wore glasses, or parted his hair on the opposite side, to the casual observer he'd be totally unrecognizable.

Rona took out her map and studied it. Miss Rosebury's mention of Witch's Pond had stuck in her mind, and she felt it would be worth a look. Behind the almshouses, she had said. But where were the almshouses? In the end, Rona had to ask directions, and eventually located both the houses – a terrace of quaint, thatched cottages – and the pond behind them.

Edna had said children fed ducks there, but that afternoon there were neither children nor ducks, and since the day had clouded over, an almost sinister air hung over the dark water. Rona approached it and stood staring down at her wavering reflection, imagining the terror of the women subjected to the ducking and the gloating cruelty of the onlookers. *If they drowned, they were innocent; if they floated, they were guilty and were hauled out to be burned at the stake.*

At one end of the pond were ancient wooden stocks, another indication of suffering in this area. She walked round to have a look at them. A plaque gave the date 1690. An age of cruelty: but was ours any better?

Suddenly she'd had enough of the foreboding atmosphere, and wished Dave would manifest himself. However, since they'd agreed early on that he would only do so in an emergency, she walked quickly away from the deserted area, only realizing she'd been holding her breath when she rounded the corner alongside the almshouses.

He was at the White Horse ahead of her, and raised a hand to attract her attention as she hesitated in the doorway. Today, he looked like himself. He half rose in his chair and pulled one out for her.

'Were you watching me just now?' she challenged him as she sat down.

'By the pond? Of course.'

'I didn't see you.'

'I thought that was the idea. What can I get you?'

'I'll have a shandy, thanks.'

'So?' she asked as he returned and set down her glass. 'Anything to report?'

'No; I enjoyed the tour of the town hall, even if I wasn't privy to the Mayor's Parlour!'

'And there was no one following me?'

'I'm willing to bet on it.'

She smiled, sipping her shandy. 'Perhaps I'm just being paranoid and you're here on a wild-goose chase.'

'Better safe than sorry. What's on the agenda for tomorrow?'

'Coffee at the vicarage at eleven.'

'You should be safe enough there!'

'I'm meeting the widow of the victim.'

'Oh-ho.'

'And that's not all; on Wednesday afternoon, I've an interview with Alan Spencer.'

'In prison? Good God!'

'What worries me is that his wife seems to be spreading the news. She certainly told the vicar's wife, and as it was in the supermarket, God only knows how many others heard. And some might be less than happy about it.'

'Especially if they'd thought they'd got away with it themselves. Frankly, Mrs Allerdyce, I can't help hoping this man *is* guilty. At least we know he's behind bars.'

'Do call me Rona,' she said. 'Every time you say "Mrs Allerdyce", I look round for Max's mother.'

Dave grinned. 'OK, Rona, but it doesn't alter what I said.'

'I know. Don't think that hasn't occurred to me.'

'Any more news on the old lady?'

'Natural causes, thank goodness.'

'Well, that's one less thing to worry about.'

Except, as Max had said, they didn't know what precipitated the attack.

'And that reminds me,' Rona added, ' there's been a change of plan: I'll be staying over Wednesday night this week, to attend the funeral on Thursday.'

'Want me to stay, too?'

'If you wouldn't mind.'

'No problem. So – the vicarage tomorrow morning. What else?'

'This is the week I'd earmarked for civic matters, hence the town hall. I'd like to see the old Counting House, and possibly the courts, if I have time.'

'And the police station?'

'No,' she answered shortly. 'I saw the lobby last week, and that was enough. I've no firm plans as yet – I'll let you know as I go along – but I tend to go to the library in the afternoons and transcribe what I've done that day. It's a pain, really, having to be out of the house between nine and five, but at least it means I get most of my work finished, leaving the evenings free.'

'And what do you do with your free evenings?'

Rona smiled ruefully. 'Nothing wildly exciting, to be honest. I went to the cinema once, had dinner at the vicarage, which was good, spent two reading in my room, and this one with you. So – what's the bar menu like?'

The evening passed pleasantly and by unspoken agreement they kept off the topic of the business between them. Rona learned that Dave came from the West Country, but after being at university in Buckfordshire, had decided he'd like to stay on there.

'Though if I don't come up with a job soon, I might have to look farther afield,' he said gloomily.

At ten o'clock they prepared to leave.

'I'll follow at a discreet distance,' Dave told her. 'Will you be going anywhere before the vicarage in the morning?'

'Probably the library again. It's quiet there, which is conducive to thought, and I need to work out exactly what to ask this woman.' She bent to retrieve her handbag. 'To be honest, though, I'm finding there's a lot of time to fill in. On reflection, it would have been better to have left a gap between visits; I need to write up the info I have, before I can tell what else I need. Still, I booked four weeks' worth, and that's what I'm stuck with.'

'It must have been hard to judge,' he agreed. 'Never mind, only one more to go. Come on, I'll see you home, and that'll be another day you can cross off.'

The out-of-town supermarket was on Lindsey's way home, and as usual she stopped there to replenish her supplies. She'd invite the parents to supper, she decided. It was a week or two since she'd seen them, and it might cheer Mum up. Come to that, she could do with cheering herself; life seemed to be pretty static these days. She'd give them a ring when she got home, see if she could fix one evening this week.

She pushed her trolley down one aisle and up another, dropping in items from her list and vaguely looking for ideas for the proposed dinner. In her abstraction, she didn't at first pay attention to the figure at the end of the aisle, and it took several seconds for her to realize it was Hugh. She stopped suddenly, causing the woman behind to bump into her, and stared at him unbelievingly. He looked so *right* standing there, so familiar. On his weekend visits they had often called in, scouring the aisles together in search of the evening's meal, and for an instant's time-freeze it almost seemed this was such an occasion. But why was he here now? How could he be, when he hadn't contacted her? Had he, perhaps, been hoping they'd meet?

She started down the aisle towards him, and at the same moment he turned and caught sight of her. She saw him stiffen and glance briefly over his shoulder, as though seeking escape. The tumult he always aroused in her rose in a wave, threatening to suffocate her, and she was glad of the trolley for support. His expression didn't change as she reached him; he simply stood waiting.

She stopped, a tentative smile on her lips. 'Hugh! What are you doing here?'

He raised an eyebrow. 'Much the same as you, I imagine,' he said coldly.

'I mean, why are you in Marsborough?'

'I work here,' he said. 'I told you I was coming back at the end of the month. This is the end of the month.'

'But – where are you living?' she stammered.

'Forgive me, Lindsey, but I don't think that's any of your business.'

She opened her mouth to protest, but a young woman had come quickly round the corner, bearing a packet of asparagus tips.

'I found them!' she said triumphantly. 'They'd been moved from their usual place.' She stopped, looking from Hugh's still figure to Lindsey's stricken face. 'I'm sorry, is—?'

Hugh took her arm and turned her back in the direction from which she'd come. 'Well done. Now all we need is the Parmesan.'

As they rounded the corner, Lindsey heard the girl say something in a low voice, and Hugh's reply reached her clearly: 'No, it was nothing – just someone I used to know.'

With a supreme effort, Lindsey, the rest of her list forgotten, propelled her leaden feet towards the checkout, blindly handed over her credit card and signed where indicated. Then, scooping her purchases into her carrier bag, she fled to the car, threw the bag inside, and, climbing in after it, burst into tears.

Tom frowned at the telephone. 'Are you getting a cold, love?'

At the other end of the line, Lindsey surveyed her swollen eyes in the hall mirror. 'No,' she said thickly, 'it's just a touch of hay fever.'

'I didn't know you were prone to that.'

'I must be, mustn't I? Anyway, which evening would be best, do you think? It makes no difference as far as I'm concerned.' Her voice shook a little, and she coughed to cover it.

'Sounds more like a cold to me,' her father said.

'Stop fussing, Pops! Thursday or Friday, perhaps?'

'Friday would suit me better, I think, but I'll see what your mother says.'

Avril, run to earth in the kitchen, had no preference. 'Conscience getting the better of her,' she sniffed. 'I can't remember when we were last over there.'

Tom turned away. 'Friday would be fine, darling,' he said. 'Thanks for the invitation.'

'She must be at a loose end,' Avril said, as he put down the phone. 'That's the only time she thinks of us.'

'For God's sake!' he burst out angrily. 'Do you have to be so ungracious all the time? Why not accept the invitation in the spirit it's offered? No wonder we don't get many!'

Avril stared at him in surprise. Her mild-mannered husband wasn't given to such outbursts. 'Who rattled your cage?' she asked sourly, turning back to the potatoes, and Tom, already ashamed of his temper, returned to the sitting room.

In her Fairhaven flat, Lindsey felt the tears welling again. She longed above all to speak to Rona, to analyse every word with her, see what she made of it. But she knew the minute she started to speak of the encounter she'd begin crying again, and little would be achieved. Better to wait till tomorrow, when she'd absorbed the first shock. She couldn't, in any case, explain why she'd been so upset; it was she who'd sent Hugh away, she who'd wanted rid of him. He had arranged his transfer to be with her, but, having accepted she didn't want him, he appeared to have found someone who did. She had no reason for complaint.

Having reached that conclusion, Lindsey ran into the bedroom and threw herself across the bed in a renewed storm of tears.

Twelve

Sally Bryson had a fringe of jet black hair and was slightly overweight. She remained solidly seated when Rona was introduced, her black eyes wary. It was clear she'd agreed to come only because Lois had arranged it.

Rona said pleasantly, 'It's good of you to see me, Mrs Bryson. I do appreciate it.'

'A waste of time, in my opinion,' Sally replied, a Welsh intonation in her voice. 'God knows, the police went over everything with a fine-tooth comb.'

'I'm sure, but I'm trying to look at it from a different angle.'

'To get Spencer off the hook, you mean. Going to see him, aren't you?'

'At the request of his wife, yes.'

'Much good it'll do you. He did it all right. Stands to reason, with the kid's death eating away at him, all the time Barry was inside. Barry's blood was on him, and the knife found at his home. Seems cut and dried to me.'

'Perhaps a little *too* cut and dried?' Rona suggested. 'As you point out, he was the obvious suspect; the police set their sights on him from the word go, he was charged within days, and I doubt if they bothered even looking for anyone else.'

'With the murder weapon in their hands,' Sally retorted, 'who was there to look for?'

'I don't know,' Rona confessed, 'but I've been asking myself if anyone else could have had a motive for killing

180

your husband.' She paused. 'For instance, did his firm keep his job open for him while he was in prison?'

Sally Bryson's eyebrows shot up, disappearing under the fringe. 'To the best of my knowledge,' she said after a minute, 'but I wasn't around by then. What possible bearing could that have?'

'I wondered if it might have caused resentment; someone perhaps who'd been filling in for him, and felt he shouldn't have to step aside when your husband came back?'

'He wasn't my husband by then; call him Barry, for pity's sake. And it would have to be a damn sight more than "resentment" for someone to stick a knife in him.'

Rona admitted she had a point. She tried another tack. 'Had he any women friends, do you know?'

'I do know, and he hadn't. I was the one who kicked over the traces.' She held Rona's eye defiantly. 'I went through a bad time too, you know. Got a lot of hate mail after the accident; people saying if I hadn't run out on my husband, he'd never have got drunk and killed the kid.'

'That must have been hard,' Rona said quietly.

Sally shot her a glance, perhaps surprised by her sympathy, and when she spoke her voice was less belligerent. 'I knew how cut up he'd be,' she said. 'He loved kids, and we never had any of our own. I wanted to go and see him in prison, but Kevin wouldn't let me. I did write, but he never replied.'

Rona took a biscuit from the plate Lois silently offered. She had almost forgotten she was there. 'Did anyone ever have a grudge against him?' she asked.

Sally shook her head. 'I'm sure not. Always popular, was Barry. Got on with everyone. That's what stood him in such good stead at his trial.'

'How long after his release was he killed?'

'Ten days.' Her eyes brimmed with tears, which she impatiently brushed away. 'A mere taste of freedom, then it was snatched away again – for good, this time.'

Rona said gently, 'Did you have any contact with him during those ten days?'

'No; I saw in the local paper that he was out, and sent a card wishing him luck. If I'm honest, I was already regretting leaving him. I hoped he might get in touch, but he didn't.'

There was a silence while everyone reflected on what had been said. Rona wasn't sure what she'd hoped to achieve from this interview, but it seemed to have been, as Sally had predicted, a waste of time. She could, she supposed, find out who Barry's employers were and go and see them, though what more they could add, she'd no idea. She was beginning to suspect Spencer was guilty after all, in which case her visit tomorrow would also be a waste of time – except, of course, that it was grist for the mill of her article. She needed to remind herself that that was, after all, the object of the exercise.

Seeing the two women had talked themselves out, Lois gently broached another topic, and a less fraught discussion ended the visit.

'Thank you,' Rona said at the door. 'It was good of you to arrange this.'

Lois shrugged slightly and pulled a face. 'Good luck tomorrow.'

Rona nodded. 'I might well need it.'

'Hugh's back in town,' Rona told Max on the phone that evening. 'Lindsey's just phoned in quite a state about it.'

'Well, I have to say she brought it on herself,' Max replied crisply. 'She's been dangling him like a fish for the last three months.'

'She says he was with another woman.'

'Is the phrase significant?'

'How should I know?' Rona snapped. 'A woman was with him, is that better?'

'Makes little difference to me, either way. Is this prickliness on Lindsey's behalf, or your own?'

Rona drew a breath. 'Sorry,' she said contritely. 'I've a lot to think about at the moment, and to be honest I could have done without a hysterical sister bending my ear for twenty minutes. She's convinced that from now on, she'll see him every time she leaves the house.'

'What did she expect, when she's been supplying him with creature comforts every weekend?'

There was a pause, then Rona said, 'Is it too late to take back my apology?'

He laughed. 'Pax! So tell me, what's on your mind to the extent that you grudge your sister twenty minutes of your time?'

The wife of a murder victim I had coffee with this morning. Tomorrow's appointment with the murderer himself.

'Oh,' she hedged, 'nothing specific. Everyone's upset about the old lady, and the funeral's hanging over us.'

'I'm still not sure why you're staying for it, since you only met her the once.'

Rona crossed her fingers. 'It's to support Nuala, really,' she said ambivalently. 'People will be coming back here afterwards, so I offered to help.' She hesitated. 'I'm sorry about not seeing you tomorrow, love.'

'Doubtless I'll survive,' he said.

As the prison was at the far end of town, Rona took the car. It was impossible to park anywhere near the high walls, and it took her over ten minutes to find a space in a multi-storey. Alan Spencer would think she'd chickened out.

The security check was as thorough as Beth had warned, added to which a sniffer dog was led past the visitors, no doubt checking for what the authorities called illegal substances. They were then directed to sliding electronic gates giving access to stairs that led up to the Visits Hall, while CCTV cameras covered every inch of their progress.

At the entrance to the hall a prison officer asked for her name and whom she'd come to see, and directed her to table five. The hall was fairly large and furnished with some thirty bench-like tables, each with three yellow chairs on one side and a green one, on which the cameras were fixed, on the other. The prisoners, already waiting on their green chairs, wore orange tabards over jeans and blue and white striped shirts.

Alan Spencer didn't raise his head as Rona sat down opposite him, but his eyes flicked up, raking her face. His own was gaunt and hollow-cheeked, his hazel eyes seeming to have sunk into his skull. Rona could appreciate his wife's anxiety.

'Mr Spencer? I'm Rona Parish. Thank you for agreeing to see me.'

He straightened then, meeting her eyes squarely. 'Let me say at once that I've only done so to placate Beth. I've nothing new to tell you. I apologize for wasting your time, but you're free to go now.'

He had a singularly pleasant speaking voice, though its tone was bitter.

Rona leaned forward, then, seeing a passing prison officer pause, hastily sat back again. 'Your wife told you I'm writing some articles?'

'You'll be hard pressed to find anything new to say about me. I was a seven-day wonder at the time.'

'I mean that I'm not here as an undercover lawyer, or an investigator into rough justice.'

'So don't get my hopes up?'

She saw to her surprise that he was smiling, if wryly.

'That's about it. Having said which, quite a few people still believe you're innocent.'

'They'll have a job proving it.'

'*Did* you kill Barry Pollard, Mr Spencer?'

She saw she'd startled him, and the half-smile faded. He held her eyes for a minute, then said quietly, 'No, I did not. Oh –' he made an impatient gesture with his hand – 'I wanted to, all right, when Charlotte died. I could have strangled him

184

with my bare hands.' The words were all the more shocking for being delivered in so calm and measured a tone. 'But good God, by the time his trial had come up and he'd served his time, it was getting on for two years. You can't keep anger at white heat for that long. The grieving goes on, heaven knows, but by that time we were resigned to it.'

'Then have you any idea who might have done it?'

'Obviously not, or I'd have shouted it from the rooftops.'

'Tell me why you went to Sunningdean that evening.'

He sighed, leaning back in his chair. 'Didn't Beth explain? I received this letter, allegedly from Pollard. We'd been told he was being released, but I'd refused to let it get to me. The letter came as a shock though, I can tell you. It said something about Lottie still being on his conscience and he'd like to apologize in person.'

He ran a hand over his red-brown hair. 'Well, I'd no intention of stirring all that up again, so I chucked it. But it lodged in the back of my mind. By all accounts Pollard was a decent enough chap, and much had been made of his grief and remorse. Also, he'd hinted at doing something stupid if I wouldn't see him.

'So I thought, why the hell not, if it helps him? It might even help me, too, forgiveness being good for the soul. I did wonder why he'd not made it earlier in the evening, but I didn't attach any significance to it. Beth didn't know about the letter – I knew it would upset her, so I told her some lads from work were going for a drink and I'd be late back. Sunningdean's a twenty-minute drive away.'

He stared down at his hands, folded on the table in front of him, and Rona wondered what grim scene he was reliving. 'I didn't see him at first; he was huddled against the wall, midway between two lamp posts, so the light was dim. I didn't even know it *was* him; I just thought some drunk had fallen over. So I said something like, 'Need a hand, mate?' and bent down to help him up. But he was a dead weight – literally – and then, of course, I saw the blood. All over my sleeve, in fact. There was a phone box on the corner, so I hared over and dialled nine-nine-nine. And the rest,' he added ironically, 'is history.'

There was a brief silence while Rona processed the information, lining it up with what Beth had told her. There were no significant differences. She said, 'It wasn't Pollard who sent the letter, was it?'

'No. Someone wanted me at the scene.'

'Then he'd have had a letter too, supposedly from you?'

Spencer shook his head. 'It wouldn't have been necessary; it came out at the trial that he'd been drinking at that pub every night since his release. Furthermore, he always left at ten twenty, to catch the bus home.'

'What about that night?'

'On the dot, as usual.'

Rona said slowly, 'So the murderer, who knew his timetable, would have time to dispose of him before you arrived on cue.'

'Exactly. How come you can see that, when the authorities couldn't?'

'And this selfsame murderer,' Rona continued, 'was someone who was able to gain access to your kitchen without arousing suspicion, remove a knife, and later, having wiped it more or less clean, hide it in your garage, where it was bound to be found.'

'Beggars belief, doesn't it?'

'There's nobody at all that you can think of?

'Nobody.'

Rona looked at him consideringly. 'Could I ask you a very personal question?'

He gave a snort of laughter. 'You've already asked if I'm a murderer. You can't get much more personal than that.'

'A confidential one, then, strictly between you and me?'

His eyes narrowed. 'Go on.'

She said carefully, 'Were you by any chance having an affair around that time?'

It was clear the question came as a shock. His eyes went momentarily blank and his face stiffened, but the flush that stained his cheeks was her answer.

After a tense minute, he said levelly, 'What makes you think that?'

'I'm not thinking, so much as asking.'

'Then what made you ask?'

'It's – possible that you were seen.'

He gave a deep sigh. 'All right, if we're playing the truth game and it's going no further, I was, as it happens. Can you tell me why it's any of your business?'

'She was married, too?'

'Yes; still is.'

'Could her husband have found out?'

He gave a shout of laughter, and those at the next table turned to stare at him. 'Sorry, but you're way off track there. No, he did not find out; I'd stake my life on it.'

'You may have already done so,' Rona said.

He stared at her for a moment. 'Look, even if he did – and I know he didn't – why go after poor old Pollard? Mine was the throat to cut, which would have been much simpler all round.'

Rona shook her head. 'I can't help you on that one.' She paused. 'Still confidentially, are you prepared to tell me who you were involved with?'

'Positively, absolutely and definitely, no. Anyway, it had been over for some time by then. Look,' he went on, his voice changing, 'I know it would be a scoop for you to prove my innocence, but – and I'm serious now – I don't want you even to try. You could be putting yourself in danger, and as far as I'm concerned, I've accepted my lot. I'm a model prisoner; with luck, my sentence will be reduced. I can sit it out.'

There wasn't much more to say, and Rona reluctantly rose to her feet. 'I'm so sorry,' she said.

He nodded. 'Goodbye, Ms Parish. Take care.'

* * *

There was a man sitting on the bench at the bus stop, reading a newspaper. Rona, her mind still on Alan Spencer, had almost passed him when she stopped and looked more closely.

'Hello, chameleon,' she said, sitting down beside him.

He grinned, removed his spectacles and folded the paper.

'Why all the disguises?' she asked curiously. 'Anyone would think you were on the run.'

'If someone did happen to be following you,' Dave pointed out, 'he sure as hell would notice if the same bloke was always in the vicinity. So – how did it go?' He nodded towards the prison across the road.

'He didn't do it, Dave.'

'You know that for a fact, do you?'

'Yes,' she said seriously. 'He couldn't have; I'm sure of it.'

'Well, even if you're right, there's not much you can do about it.'

She thought for a moment. 'No, but there's something you could do for me. I shan't be going out this evening so you'd officially be off-duty, but I'd be awfully grateful if you could drive out to the Cat and Fiddle at Sunningdean and see what you can suss out.'

'I can, sure, but won't the trail be a bit cold by now?'

'Yes, but it was a major event for the pub regulars. If you say something like, "Didn't a murder take place around here?" I bet they'll be more than willing to give you their two-penn'orth.'

'OK; no skin off my nose which pub I drink at.'

She looked at her watch. 'Normally, I'd be setting off for home about now.'

'What time's the funeral?'

'Eleven. Nuala's inviting people back to the house, so I said I'd give her a hand. Miss Rosebury was well known and respected; I think there'll be a large turnout.'

'Well, watch yourself. I'll be at the church, see you back to the house, and then hang around till you leave for home.'

Rona nodded absently. 'I just wish I knew for certain that the interview didn't lead to her death,' she said.

Her mobile rang just as she turned into her parking place, and she flipped it open. It was Beth Spencer.

'Miss Parish? You saw him?'

'I did, yes.'

'And what do you think?'

Rona hesitated. 'Mrs Spencer, it doesn't make much difference what I think, but for what it's worth I'm sure he didn't do it.'

'Thank you.'

'There really is nothing I can do, you know.'

'Couldn't you make a few general enquiries? No one would think anything of it – you're a journalist, after all.'

Briefly, she considered telling Beth of her proposed enquiries at the pub, but decided against it. It might give her false hope.

'I'll do what I can,' she promised.

As she rang off, Rona reflected on Spencer's admission to an affair. Beth wouldn't learn of it from her, but would she be irreparably hurt if she did find out? Rona thought not; it was in the past, after all, and Beth admitted their marriage had been under a strain. At least his time in prison seemed to have strengthened it, and as Spencer had implied, the affair could have no relevance to the murder: had it led to any consequences, Spencer himself would have been the victim.

Thank God this murderer's safely behind bars, Max had said, right at the start. But it was beginning to look as though he mightn't be, after all.

Tom lay next to his wife in the large double bed, but he had never felt farther away from her. Though wide awake, he barely heard the rhythmic little puffs she emitted, prelude to the soft snores that had punctuated his nights for the last forty years. For he was pleasurably engaged in recycling his day with Catherine – her smile, her laugh, the things they'd talked about.

They'd been relaxed with each other from the start, able to let silences develop without the need to fill them. Frequently, they'd started to say the same thing, and broken off with a laugh. Her knowledge of art had reawakened his own love of it, dormant now for many years, and to his delight brought back remembered snippets that were new to her. During the whole magical day, they'd said nothing that her son and his daughters could not have heard, but he was acutely aware of a growing attraction. Whether or not she'd registered it, he had no idea. Either way, these could be dangerous waters, but for the moment he didn't care; he felt rejuvenated, invigorated, revitalized – just when he'd thought he was about to be thrown on the scrap heap.

Another startling fact had emerged: he'd realized for the first time that his marriage hadn't been happy for years, and the knowledge came as a shock. The creeping disenchantment had been so gradual that he'd accepted it as normal, but it was a long time indeed since he'd looked forward to seeing his wife, enjoyed her company, even – apart from the twice-daily peck on the cheek – kissed her. He had grown used to her discontented grumbles and her criticism of their daughters, always trying, for the sake of peace, to smooth them over, lighten her mood. It was this, he now saw, that, more than lack of male companionship or empty, stretching days, had led to his dreading retirement. Only when he compared the way he felt with Catherine did he appreciate how dull and pointless his existence had become.

They had parted at Marsborough station, where they'd both left their cars.

'Thank you so much for today,' he had said. 'I hope we can do it again some time.'

She'd smiled at him. 'I hope so, too,' she'd said.

Was that standard politeness, or had she meant it? He intended to find out, and soon.

Rona was suddenly, totally, awake, every nerve stretched taut as a wire. She lay motionless, eyes straining into the darkness. Something had woken her. What was it?

And into the thick, throbbing silence it came again, a faint rattle and a squeak, this time followed by a draught of air that passed over her face. She lay unmoving, scarcely breathing, deafened by her heartbeats. Her bedroom door was opening. *Someone was coming into the room.*

The board that always creaked when she stood on it creaked now, pinpointing his position, though her sleep-dimmed eyes could make out only a shadowy shape. Rapidly she ran through the objects to hand should he approach the bed. They were not of much comfort: her clock, a glass of water, her library book. With luck, the water might shock him long enough for her to make a run for it.

But, to her untold relief, he was not approaching the bed. Instead, he'd moved to the far side of the room and she temporarily lost his outline, till she realized he'd knelt down behind the table where, she remembered, a small door some three feet high led to the roof space.

The darkness paled slightly – the shielded beam of a torch, she deduced – then came the unmistakable sound of the wooden door being lifted aside. A faint shuffling followed, a gentle thud and then another. Then a scraping of wood against wood as the door was fitted back into place. The shadowy figure rose, became man-sized again, and moved soundlessly back towards the door.

As he pulled it open and the blackness leached into grey, Rona could see he was now carrying something, presumably retrieved from his hidey-hole. In one lightning movement, her arm snaked out for the light switch and the room flooded with brilliance, temporarily blinding both her and the intruder, who froze in the doorway. As her vision cleared, she found herself staring across the room at the startled face of Clive Banks. He was holding a small, cheap suitcase in each hand.

'What the hell do you think you're doing?' she demanded ringingly, emboldened by the light.

Everything happened at once. After an instant's paralysis, he turned and hurled himself towards the stairs. In the same moment Rona flung herself out of bed and caught up her dressing gown, shouting, 'Nuala! Nuala! Stop him!' There was a clatter of feet on the stairs, an oath, and then a series of thumps as Clive lost his footing and went hurtling down the remainder of the steps, the suitcases tumbling after him and flying open to send a hoard of silver, jewellery and bank notes cascading over the hall carpet.

Rona went after him, conscious of Nuala at her heels and Jack Stanton flinging open his door on the scene. Clive, making no further attempt at escape, sat nursing an injured ankle and glaring up at Rona.

'Why the devil are you here on a Wednesday night?' he demanded.

Ridiculously, she answered him. 'I stayed over for the funeral.'

'My God!' he said, shaking his head. 'What timing!'

Jack took up the interrogation. 'More to the point, what are *you* doing here, tonight or any other night?'

'Only reclaiming my property, that's all.' Clive was still prepared to bluster.

Jack looked scathingly at the cache on the carpet. 'Possibly the suitcases are yours; I'm quite sure nothing else is. Nuala, you'd better call the police.'

'No – wait.' Clive made an attempt to get up, and grimaced with pain. 'Look, you can't grass me up – I'm family.'

'Not for much longer,' Jack said grimly.

'It's her fault,' Clive continued in an aggrieved tone, his eyes going back to Rona. 'All I wanted was to stash the cases – they had to be got out of the flat. But Nuala said no, her ladyship was coming. I did my best to shift her, but she wouldn't be shifted.'

Rona said sharply, '*How* did you try to shift me?'

His eyes slid away.

'Answer her!' Jack commanded.

'Can't we go into the kitchen?' Nuala broke in, speaking for the first time. 'We'll wake Will if we go on talking here.'

She came down the last few steps, held out her hand to Clive, and with her help he pulled himself upright, favouring his left foot. Together, the incongruous little group moved into the kitchen.

Clive and Jack lowered themselves into chairs, Rona and Nuala leant against the counters.

'How did you try to shift me?' Rona repeated.

Clive looked at her sullenly, then his eyes fell away. 'Well, I decided to check if Nuala really had someone coming or was just making an excuse. So I came over, but I'd not even got out of the car when you came running out of the house, as large as life. I saw you drop your bag, pick up what fell out of it, and drive off, leaving the cassette lying there.'

'*You* took it?' Nuala exclaimed, at the same time as Jack asked in bewilderment, 'What cassette?'

Clive ignored them both. 'Well, I retrieved it and listened to it on the cassette player in the car. Boring lot of stuff with the schoolmarms, then the bit with old Aunt Edna, which opened possibilities. It was obvious that while you were ensconced here Nuala wouldn't budge, so I decided to scare you off.'

'By leaving notes on my windscreen.'

''Fraid so,' said Clive, not sounding in the least repentant.

'And a message on my mobile?'

'Guilty as charged.'

Rona leaned intently towards him. 'Tell me this: did you go to Miss Rosebury and ask her who she'd seen?'

Jack said querulously, 'What *is* all this?' but Nuala silenced him with a lifted hand.

Anthea Fraser

Clive was frowning. 'Go to old Edna? Not likely, she'd have torn me off a strip. Never did have any time for me, the old bag.'

'And you didn't see her in the street, the night she died?'

'Do me a favour! I've better things to do at night than put the frighteners on old ladies.'

'Did you see her that night?'

He answered her with equal emphasis. *'No, I did not.'*

Rona felt tears of relief come to her eyes. She already blamed herself for a death during her last project; she could not have borne another laid at her door.

Nuala's mind had moved on. 'I suppose this means you've been behind the recent burglaries?'

'Only some of them,' Clive muttered. 'I certainly wasn't a one-man show.'

'Clive, you *promised* you'd go straight when you came out of prison!'

'And I meant to, babe. But I lost a packet on the gee-gees, and a pal of mine offered to cut me in.'

'You brought the cases over the night I saw you,' Rona said. 'That's when you hid them, isn't it?'

She'd thought she'd seen a movement from the vicarage garden.

'Got it in one. The house should have been empty at that time on a Monday. It hadn't occurred to me you'd be hanging about here on your own.'

'I seem to have continually thwarted your plans, don't I?' Rona said coolly.

'Too right. I'd asked around and learned you were only here two nights a week. Then you go and land me in it again.'

Jack said, 'What's this cassette you were talking about?'

'I'll explain later, Dad. What we have to do now is decide about Clive.'

'As I see it, we've no option but to report him. If we don't, we become accessories after the fact.'

194

'Give us a break, Jack,' Clive pleaded. 'I will go straight, I promise.'

'We've heard that before.'

'If I go back in, it'll be for a long stretch. Look, it's obvious I'm not cut out to be a villain – this is the second time I've been rumbled. I won't risk a third.'

'Then turn yourself in,' Nuala urged. 'If you hand back what you've taken, they'll be lenient with you.'

'There's only the stuff in the hall,' he said sullenly. 'The rest has been disposed of.'

'Then own up to what you did, at least. That'll save the police some legwork.'

'I'm not grassing on Joe and the others.'

'We're not asking you to. Just admit to your own jobs. Will you?'

'Looks like I've no choice. If I don't, you'll shop me anyway.'

'And there's one other thing. Now I know where you'll be for the next few months, I'll be filing for divorce.'

He looked at her for a moment, then slowly nodded. 'I suppose I saw that coming.'

'All right,' Jack said briskly. 'This is what I suggest. We move all the goods from the hall into my room for the night and Clive can bed down on the sitting-room sofa. Then, first thing in the morning, Nuala drives him to the police station with the suitcases, and waits till he goes inside. Agreed?'

They all nodded.

'And that's more than enough for tonight. We've a long and difficult day ahead of us, so let's not waste any more time.'

In the hall they collected the valuables together, piled them back into the cases and put them in Jack's room for safe keeping. Then Nuala bandaged Clive's ankle, and, closing the sitting-room door on him, they went wearily back to bed.

Thirteen

Rona phoned Dave before eight the next morning and put him in the picture.

'So it seems I don't really need you after all,' she ended. 'At least I wasn't being neurotic; someone *was* hassling me, but not for any sinister reason.'

'Don't you want to know how I got on at the Cat and Fiddle?'

'Sorry, I'd forgotten about that. Anything new?'

'I now have at least a dozen accounts of that evening, all slightly different, but I suppose that's to be expected. One thing came up, though I don't know if it's significant: Pollard told them that although he'd received a lot of hate mail when he was first sentenced, it tailed off within a few weeks except for one letter-writer, who continued to bombard him until he was released. He said what upset him most was that this writer – he didn't know if it was male or female – had obviously known the dead kid really well. Do you think it could have been one of her parents?'

'I doubt it. I've met them both, and neither strikes me as an anonymous letter-writer.'

'Any other relative, then?'

'I could ask around. You're thinking whoever it was could have been waiting for him when he got out? But why drag Alan Spencer into it? Hadn't he suffered enough?'

'Search me, I'm just reporting what I was told. There was one other thing: the letters that kept coming were all written in red ink.'

'Symbolic, you think?'

'Could be. On the other hand, a lot of people use red ink, and they're not all homicidal maniacs.'

Rona laughed. 'That's a relief.'

'Look,' Dave said, 'I'm not trying to screw you for more money, but I think it would be as well if I stuck with it. It's only till next Wednesday, after all, and if Spencer *is* innocent, and the killer hears you've been to see him, you could still be in danger. Not that I want to worry you, of course,' he ended hastily.

'Of course not,' Rona responded drily. 'OK, we'll leave it as it stands.'

'Where's Banks now?'

'Nuala's just driven him to the police station. They're welcome to him. As soon as she comes back, we're going to rearrange the sitting room for the wake and then start on the sandwiches and canapés.'

'Perhaps I'll look in after all!' he said.

Several of Nuala's friends had arrived to help with the food, and between them they'd provided a suitable spread for some forty people. Now, looking at the packed church, Rona hoped only about a third of the congregation would return to partake of it.

She took a seat near the back, partly because she'd been Edna's most recent acquaintance and partly to keep an eye on everyone. Over the last two and a half weeks she'd met several members of the congregation; the mayor was present, wearing his chain, and there were representatives from all the schools, joined by a contingent of children from the Sunday school and a group of Brownies and Cubs. She could see Mr and Mrs Maddox up near the front, and Beth Spencer was seated a few pews ahead of her, between her two sons. It seemed that local schools had closed for the duration of the service, to allow pupils and teachers to attend.

Gordon Breen gave the eulogy, stressing Edna's lifelong

association with children and the good work she had done in the parish. The hymns chosen were from the Sunday school hymnal, 'All Things Bright and Beautiful' and 'Jesus Wants me for a Sunbeam', and Rona's eyes pricked at the preponderance of young voices raised in song.

When the service was over, Nuala, Jack and Will went with the vicar to attend the interment while Rona, as arranged, returned with the other helpers to open up the house, and by the time the rest of the mourners arrived, kettles were boiling and cling film had been removed from the cakes and sandwiches.

It appeared that people had travelled from all over the country to attend, having been in Edna's classes up to twenty or even thirty years ago. In all the scraps of conversation Rona caught, the same warm affection was being expressed.

Beth Spencer approached her and introduced her sons, Josh and Harry, smart in Buckford College uniform.

'It's the end of an era,' Beth said sadly. 'I was in Miss Rosebury's class at Sunday school. She was a real character; Buckford won't be the same without her.' She hesitated. 'Miss Parish, I wonder if I could ask you another favour?'

'Do please call me Rona. I have to confess I think of you as Beth.'

Beth smiled warmly. 'Then I will, thank you. What I was going to ask might be of interest to you, too. At least, I hope so. Next Monday is Middle School Sports Day at the college.' She lowered her voice, but the boys had caught sight of Will, just returned from the graveside, and moved away.

'To be honest, I hate going without Alan; all the other parents are in couples – or at least, that's how it feels – but I have to support the boys, especially since they're both running in races this year.' She hesitated. 'I was wondering if you'd come with me?'

'Oh!' Rona was momentarily taken aback. 'That's very kind of you.'

'It's not wholly altruistic, as I explained.'

'But it would be useful for me to see more of the college,' Rona said, with growing enthusiasm. 'Thank you, I'd love to come.'

'That's great; I'll phone you over the weekend and let you know the arrangements.'

She moved away in search of her sons, and Rona felt someone touch her sleeve. It was Helena Maddox.

'Rona, hello. I'd forgotten you were staying here.'

Today, she was a vision in navy-blue silk that exactly matched her eyes. Rona wondered a little impatiently why Helena's clothes always made such an impact on her. Richard Maddox had joined them, and nodded as Rona glanced at him.

'I think you've met my husband?' Helena said.

'Briefly,' Rona acknowledged with a smile, taking his hand.

'I hope we were able to provide you with all the information you needed?' he asked with a grave smile.

'Thank you, yes. In fact, I'll be paying a return visit; Mrs Spencer has just invited me to your Sports Day next week.'

'Oh? I didn't realize you knew each other.'

Beth, her plate laden with asparagus rolls and smoked salmon, had overheard the exchange.

'Yes,' she confirmed, 'Rona's interested in Alan's case, and as a journalist she has lots of contacts. She went to see him yesterday.'

'Really?' Helena raised an eyebrow. 'And how was he?'

Rona flashed Beth an apprehensive look. 'He seemed a bit drawn, I thought.'

'I suppose,' Richard put in smoothly, 'you'll be featuring the case in one of your articles? It seems a pity to rake it all up again.'

Beth flushed. 'Not when they've got the wrong man,' she protested, adding defiantly, 'And I'm not alone in believing that; Rona, for one, agrees with me.'

'My dear, we all do,' Helena assured her.

To her discomfort, Rona noticed that several heads had turned in their direction, and was relieved to see Nuala signalling her from across the room. Excusing herself, she went quickly to replenish the emptying plates.

It was after two before the last of the guests left, and Rona's feet were aching.

'Bless you for staying,' Nuala said, giving her a hug. 'Please don't worry about clearing up; as you can see, I've a willing band of helpers, and you've a long drive ahead of you.'

'Thanks, then I'll make a move.' It would be good, Rona thought, to be home, and able to put all this behind her for a few days. She'd have a bath and spend a relaxing evening in her dressing gown, with supper on a tray.

It was only as she was approaching Marsborough that she remembered her dinner date with Magda and Gavin.

Tom sat in his car outside Catherine's bungalow and fought an inward battle.

There had been a row with Avril over breakfast. That is to say, she had made some disparaging remark that in all fairness was no different from her usual comments, but this time he'd reacted to it. It was as though he'd lost a layer of skin over the last couple of weeks, leaving his emotions nearer the surface and more volatile. A month ago he would have smiled, shrugged, glossed it over, as he'd been doing for God knew how many years when she was in one of her moods. Today, he'd snapped, and the result had been raised voices on both sides. For the first time in their married life, he'd left for work without the kiss on the cheek. He doubted, anyway, if she'd have accepted it.

The episode had put him off-key for the whole day. It was the second time in as many days that he'd criticized her, and he guessed she'd have been waiting for a phoned apology, or, failing that, a conciliatory bunch of flowers when he arrived home. She would receive neither. The worm, he told himself with a wry smile, had finally turned, and he knew all too well what had caused the turning. It was simply the realization that other women – one other woman in partic-ular – could appreciate him and enjoy his company without writing him off as a fuddy-duddy. So why couldn't his wife? He'd had enough of it, and if he didn't put his foot down now, his retirement would be nothing short of purgatory.

At the end of the working day he had gone as usual to his car, where the realization hit him that he didn't want to go home. The row, smouldering in their minds all day, would reignite the minute he entered the house, and he had not the stomach for it. Almost without thinking, he'd driven to Willow Crescent and, having arrived there, cursed himself for his stupidity. What the hell would Catherine think of him, turning up unannounced on her doorstep? He'd better either grit his teeth and drive home, or go somewhere else to sort himself out.

Catherine had, in fact, already seen him, and her quick spurt of pleasure turned to uncertainty as, making no attempt to get out of the car, he continued to sit staring straight ahead. If he wanted to see her, why not come to the door? And it was odd, surely, that he hadn't phoned in advance? She stood for a moment undecided, remembering last night's resolution.

After all these years alone, it hadn't occurred to her that she could be attracted to another man, and she'd looked forward to the day in London as a pleasurable occasion in the company of someone she liked. Last night, though, thinking back over it, she'd been forced to accept it had been more than that. There was a deepening friendship between them that was just possibly teetering on the brink of some-thing more dangerous, and, alarmed, she'd resolved that if he did indeed contact her again – though in the cold light of day he'd probably think better of it – she would make some excuse. Far be it from her to take any step that might endanger a marriage – and, on the other side of the coin, she'd no intention of being hurt again herself.

And now there he was, outside. Better, she told herself, to pretend she hadn't seen him; it looked as though he was about to drive off again. Yet there was something in the set of his shoulders, his bowed head, that gave the impression of unhappiness. Suddenly making up her mind, she hurried outside.

'So far and no farther?' queried a voice at his side, and Tom spun from his contemplation of the steering wheel to see Catherine at the open car window.

Feeling a complete fool, his colour rose. A hundred excuses for his presence jostled for precedence and he abandoned them all and said simply, 'I don't want to go home.'

'Let's go for a walk, then,' she said, as though it was the most natural thing in the world, and went back to lock the front door.

The evening was cloudy and close, and the day's heat rose from the pavements as they walked. Neither of them spoke, each content in the other's company.

Eventually, as they rounded the corner into Talbot Road, he asked, 'Any news of Jenny?'

'She's gradually getting over it. Her parents are still there, but they're going home at the weekend. She doesn't need nursing any more, and she's determined to go back to work. I think that might be the best thing.'

'What does she do?'

'She manages a little florist shop in Stokely.'

Barrington Park was now on their left, a green oasis in the built-up area. Catherine opened the gate and they went in. The grass was cool and comforting, and the sprinklers circled endlessly, sending arcs of sparkling water cascading to the ground.

'I've had a row with my wife,' Tom said baldly. 'I think it's the first ever.'

'My goodness, that must be a record.'

'It takes two, doesn't it?'

'And you've never risen to the bait before?'

'I suppose not.'

'Why did you this time?'

He didn't answer, and she glanced at his averted face. 'She didn't object to yesterday?' she asked anxiously.

'I didn't tell her.'

'Look, Tom, I don't want to be the cause of—'

'It's nothing to do with you,' he cut in harshly. Then, seeing her face, laid a hand quickly on her arm. 'I'm sorry, that didn't come out as I intended. What I meant was that this has been building for some time and I've refused to face it. But I'm due to retire later in the year, and the thought of the kind of life we'll be living frankly terrifies me.' He glanced at her miserably. 'And now I feel disloyal and mean and altogether despicable for talking about it.'

'It sounds to me as if the talking's overdue, though it ought to be with your wife.' She paused. 'What's her name?'

'Avril.'

'Can't you talk to her?'

'I suppose I'll have to try.'

'Perhaps not this evening, though,' she suggested. 'You need time to sort things out in your mind.' She looked at him with a smile. 'Ready to go home yet?'

He smiled back. 'No.'

'Then how about coming back with me for supper? You can ring – Avril – and say you've been delayed.'

'I don't want to put you to any trouble—'

'No trouble at all. It will be good to have company.'

Having traversed the small park, they'd arrived at the gate giving on to Barrington Road and, emerging through it, started back along the pavement. As they reached the corner of Talbot Road, Tom came to a sudden stop.

'Oh, my God!' he said.

'What is it? What's wrong?'

He was staring down the road ahead of them. 'That car that just passed us,' he said. 'It was Rona's.'

Catherine went still. 'Did she see us?'

'I don't know.'

'Oh Tom, I'm sorry. Would you rather go straight home after all?'

'No,' he said grimly, 'I wouldn't. Whether she saw us or not, having supper together won't make any difference now.'

Rona had indeed seen them, and was trying in some bewilderment to make sense of it. She'd been under the impression that Pops and Catherine Bishop barely knew each other, yet there they were, strolling companionably along as though they'd known each other for years. If they were friends, why hadn't either of them said so? A possible answer occurred to her and was instantly quashed. This was her *father*, she reminded herself.

But she'd no time to probe further. The Ridgeways' house lay ahead of her, and she drew into the kerb, pushing all speculation out of her head until she'd time to examine it in detail.

'No Gus?' Magda asked, kissing Rona's cheek as she went into the hall.

'No; I'm only just back from Buckford, so Max is keeping him till tomorrow.'

'I thought you came home on Wednesdays?'

'I do normally, but it was Miss Rosebury's funeral this morning, so I stayed over for it. She was the old lady I told you about.'

'Oh yes. What happened to the missing cassette, did you ever find out?' She turned to Gavin, who had come forward to greet Rona.

'She's up to her eyes in mystery again! Secret lovers, rambling old ladies, stolen cassettes—'

'My God,' Gavin said humorously, 'you certainly attract them, don't you? How about nailing whoever pinched Magda's collection, while you're at it?'

Could it have been Clive? Rona wondered suddenly, but

immediately discounted him. He'd said he wasn't a one-man crime wave and she believed him; he wouldn't have been sufficiently organized to pull off a coup like that.

'Still on vodka and Russchian?' Gavin was asking, as he showed her into the sitting room. It was a light, pleasant room with masses of flowers on every surface – a weakness of Magda's – and low, comfortable chairs. The French windows were open to the garden and a welcome breeze was drifting through them, bearing the scent of stocks from the bed just outside.

Rona watched Gavin as he poured the drinks, assessing his recovery. His long, rangy body remained on the thin side, and the short-sleeved blue shirt revealed arms still tanned from their holiday. It was odd to think that if she hadn't met Max when she did, it would be she rather than Magda who'd be Gavin's wife; odder still that, having waited so long to experience love, she should have fallen for two men in the space of a year.

During their teens and twenties Lindsey had fallen in and out of love as regularly as clockwork, each time convinced it was the love of her life. Rona, on the other hand, had felt nothing stronger than affection for the string of young men who courted her. Perhaps, she'd begun to think, this was as good as it would get.

Conventionally enough, it had been at Lindsey's wedding seven years ago that she'd met Gavin. Rona had been a bridesmaid, as had Hugh's sister, who was going out with him at the time. It had been love at first sight for both of them, and poor Lucy Cavendish had fallen by the wayside.

She'd been deliriously happy, Rona reflected now, intoxicated by the wonder of love after all the years it had eluded her. At the time she was still living in the flat she'd shared with Lindsey, and though Gavin didn't actually move in with her, he spent many a night there. Eventually, some eight months later, he asked her to marry him. She'd not accepted at once, pointing out humorously that one wedding in a year was enough for her father to stand, and in any event, surely they were happy as they were?

And the following week, at an art exhibition she was covering for *Chiltern Life*, she had met Max. Again, the attraction between them had been instant and mutual, but this time Rona wasn't free to succumb to it. Her emotions had see-sawed violently between the two men, not helped by the fact that they were entirely different characters, Gavin being easy-going, amusing and spontaneous, and Max introverted and reserved.

The next few weeks had been agonizing as she tried to decide between them, the hurt on Gavin's face almost more than she could bear. Seated now in his sitting room, with the ice-cold glass in her hand, Rona had a sudden memory of an evening she'd spent with Magda, endlessly discussing her dilemma. Finally, Magda had cut through her prevarications and said bluntly, 'It's Max, isn't it? You're only humming and hawing because you don't want to hurt Gavin. Well, don't worry about him. I'll look after him.'

And, Rona reflected with an inward smile, she had been as good as her word.

'So,' Gavin said, seating himself on the sofa opposite, 'what's all this mystery you've been stirring up in Buckford?'

'Solving, my love, not stirring up,' Magda corrected him. 'And what about that cassette, Ro? Did you get it back?' She explained briefly to Gavin what had happened.

'No, but I know who took it; it was my landlady's husband.'

'Why on earth would he do that? Ah – he'd have known the old lady in question, wouldn't he, since she was his wife's aunt? You've certainly got yourself involved with that family!'

'It's been sorted out now.'

'But what about the lovers she saw?' Magda persisted. 'You never did explain why she thought she should report them to the police.'

'I haven't progressed much on that front,' Rona prevaricated, reluctant to bring Alan Spencer into the conversation. She had, after all, promised confidentiality.

Dinner in the oak-panelled dining room was as elegant and delicious as always in this house. Candles glowed in antique candelabra, and the old crystal glasses were heavy in the hand. The food served was, again as always, Italian, and Rona gave herself up to the enjoyment of it.

'So have you finished these Buckford visits?' Gavin asked, as they sat over their zabaglione.

'One more to go,' Rona replied. 'And believe it or not, I'm going to the college Sports Day on Monday.'

'Did Helena invite you?' Magda asked, pouring more dessert wine into her glass.

'No, actually it was Beth Spencer.'

'Who's Beth Spencer?'

Rona hesitated, sorry, now, that she'd introduced the name. 'The mother of the little girl who was killed.'

'Oh, of course. How did you meet her?'

Rona smiled wryly. 'She wants me to prove her husband's innocence. My difficult assignments I do immediately,' she paraphrased; 'the impossible take a little longer.'

'I don't see how he *can* be innocent,' Gavin objected. 'From what I remember, the evidence against him was pretty conclusive.'

'It was a ghastly business,' Magda said sombrely. 'Helena was absolutely distraught.'

Rona frowned. 'Helena Maddox?'

'Yes; she gave the child piano lessons, didn't you know?'

'No.' Rona thought back to the meeting between the two women that morning. 'I thought they just knew each other from the boys going to the college.'

'I'm sorry for the mother,' Magda said, 'losing first her daughter and then, to all intents and purposes, her husband. It's a wonder she keeps going.'

* * *

A couple of streets away, Tom and Catherine also sat over a dinner table in the deepening dusk. On returning from their walk he'd telephoned home, and been relieved to hear the answerphone click in. He left a brief message, saying he'd be late home and offering no explanation; there was none that he could give.

'I really must make a move,' he said reluctantly. 'Thanks so much for granting me asylum.'

'Any time,' she replied. No further mention had been made of Rona's passing them, but now she said tentatively, 'What will you do about Rona?'

'Wait and see.'

'She might think—' Catherine began, and broke off, flushing.

'Indeed she might,' he agreed.

They met each other's eye and smiled. Then he pushed back his chair.

'Thanks again, Catherine, for the meal and especially for the company.'

'Remember my advice,' she said, 'and talk to Avril. I'm sure you'll sort things out.'

Which, he found to his discomfort, was not what he wanted to hear.

Rona slid into her car with a last wave at her hosts, standing together at the gate. They were happy, she thought. Thank God for that.

She knew what she must do, even though she hated herself for doing it. Instead of reversing in the drive as usual, she drove on a few yards and took the first turning on the right, which led in an arc back to Barrington Road via Willow Crescent. As she came round the curve, she saw at once that there was no car parked outside Catherine Bishop's house and a wave of thankfulness washed over her. What, she asked herself blisteringly, would she have done if there had been?

Almost light-headed with relief, she drove home, grateful

to find a parking space only a few doors down, and thankfully slipped into it. Without Gus for company, she didn't fancy the five-minute walk back from garaging the car in Charlton Road.

So, she thought, as she prepared for bed, Pops had spent at least the early part of the evening with Catherine Bishop. Was he aware that she'd spotted them? Looking into her mirror, she thought she'd seen him come to a halt on the pavement. Would he say anything to her? Expect her to say something to him? If the meeting had been innocent – and, for God's sake, what else could it be? – it would strike each of them as surprising if the other didn't mention it. So – who would go first? And where did Mum think he'd been at the time?

Shelving the questions, Rona slid into bed. It had been a long day.

The puzzle was, however, revived on the Saturday morning, by a phone call from Lindsey.

'Ro, what's going on with the parents, do you know?'

Rona felt a clutch of apprehension. 'How do you mean?'

'I had them to dinner last night, and there was an atmosphere you could have cut with a knife. I've never seen them like that before – it was horrible. God, I've enough problems of my own without this.'

'What exactly happened?' Rona asked fearfully.

'Well, nothing *happened*.' Lindsey's voice was impatient. 'It was Pops, really, more than Mum. I mean, we're used to her being difficult and everything, and Pops is usually the peace-maker. Not last night, he wasn't.' She paused, added suspiciously, 'You don't sound particularly surprised.'

Rona glanced over her shoulder, but Max had taken Gus to get the morning paper.

'I didn't know you were having them round, or I'd have warned you,' she began.

'*Warned* me?'

'I went to dinner at the Ridgeways' on Thursday, and on the way there, I saw Pops and Mrs Bishop walking along the road.'

'Mrs Bishop?'

'You know, the—'

'I know who she is, for God's sake. What was she doing walking with Pops? *Where* were they walking?'

'Near the park in Barrington Road.' Rona paused, added heavily, 'Just round the corner from her house.'

'My – God!' Lindsey said, slowly and with emphasis. Then, 'She's not even attractive.'

'Look, Linz, don't let's jump to conclusions.'

'But the conclusion's already been reached, hasn't it? I mean, your seeing him with Mrs What's-her-name is one thing, and my sensing an atmosphere between him and Mum is another. But put them together . . . God, Ro, what are we going to do?'

'I think Pops knows I saw them. I'm waiting to see if he says anything.'

'And if he doesn't?'

'I haven't worked that out yet.'

'Well, when you have, let me know,' Lindsey said, and rang off.

Rona had wondered if Max would refer to Adele Yarborough over the weekend, comment, perhaps, on how she'd seemed at the Wednesday class, and whether or not she'd mentioned meeting her.

But he didn't raise the subject, and Rona found herself unaccountably reluctant to do so. The last time they'd discussed her, they'd come perilously close to a row.

On the Sunday afternoon, when they returned from walking Gus in Furze Hill Park, the light on the answering machine was flashing, and Max flicked the switch as he passed. To Rona's dismay, Dave Lampeter's voice filled the hall.

'Hi, Rona, Dave here. Sorry, I've had a mental blip: is it tomorrow or Tuesday you're going to the Sports Day? I'd be grateful for a buzz. Thanks. Bye now.'

Max had come to a halt at the top of the basement stairs.

'What the hell was that all about?' he demanded, and, as Rona floundered helplessly, his voice grew angry. 'Dave Lampeter, was it? Since when does he have to know where you're going?'

'He's – been doing some work for me,' she said unwillingly.

'What kind of work? And why don't I know about it?'

'I was going to—'

'When, exactly?' he broke in, his voice now dangerously calm. 'How long has this been going on?'

'Max, for pity's sake! You make it sound as if we're having an affair!'

'Are you?'

She stared at him, stupefied. 'Thanks all the same, but I'm not in need of a toy boy.'

'Then what is this work he's doing?'

Gus, aware of raised voices, whined softly and Rona abstractedly reached down to him. 'It looked at one time as though I might be in a rather dodgy position.'

'Dangerous, you mean?'

'Possibly. Then I bumped into Dave in the street, and you'd told me he was at a loose end, so it seemed a good idea to ask him to – watch my back.'

'Without my knowing?'

'I didn't want you to worry.'

'Suppose I'd met him myself, would he have mentioned it?' His eyes narrowed. 'Or had you told him not to?'

'I didn't want to worry you,' she repeated. Anger suddenly came to her aid. 'Look, I don't know what you're being so high and mighty about. You did exactly the same to me, if you remember – employed him to follow me without my knowing.'

'That was different,' Max said, but his voice was calmer.

'No, it wasn't. *You* didn't tell me you'd employed a body-guard in case it worried me; *I* didn't tell you for the same reason.'

'You didn't tell me,' he said astutely, 'in case I put a spoke in your wheel.'

She gave him a tentative smile. 'Touché,' she said.

She waited, still on edge, until he returned her smile, then went quickly to him, feeling his arm enclose her. Their rows were not infrequent – storms that blew up as suddenly as this one – but they tended to be of short duration, usually ending in shamefaced laughter.

'*Were* you in danger?' he asked, his mouth on her hair.

'No, though I thought I was.'

'Suppose you come clean over a cup of tea?'

She let out her breath in a long sigh. 'It's a deal,' she said.

Fourteen

'Well, you needn't worry any more about Max knowing of our arrangement,' Rona told Dave when she returned his call the next morning. 'Your voice came over loud and clear when we played back our messages.'

'Oh God, was that your home number? Rona, I'm sorry! I must have pressed the wrong one – they're underneath each other on the menu. Did he blow his top?'

'Briefly, but as it happens, I'm glad he knows. I don't like secrets.'

'Did you tell him about the prison visit?'

'I – glossed over it a bit, but yes.'

'And I bet you also "glossed over" your doubts about Spencer's guilt?'

She laughed reluctantly. 'Right, but there was no need to go into all that; it's pure speculation, after all. Anyway, you asked about Sports Day; it's this afternoon, starting at two. Beth Spencer's collecting me at one thirty.'

'What's her car like?'

'I've no idea, but honestly, Dave, I don't think it matters any more. Clive will be in clink by now, and he wouldn't have harmed me anyway.'

'I'm being paid to protect you and that's what I'll do,' Dave said stubbornly. 'Spencer's guilt or innocence might be speculative to you, but if he's *not* the murderer, it won't be to the real one, and you *are* dabbling in murky waters. I'll wait outside Parsonage Place till she collects you, and follow you from there. If I can get on to the sports field I

213

will, if not, I'll wait till you come out again. How about this morning?'

'No doubt it'll be the library again,' she said resignedly.

As Rona lifted her case out of the car, she heard her name called, and, slamming down the boot, spied Lois Breen the other side of the wall.

'We must stop meeting like this!' Rona said with a smile, walking over to join her.

'I have to confess I was looking out for you.'

'Oh?' Rona put down her case and regarded her questioningly.

Lois hesitated. 'Are you about to dash off somewhere?'

'Only the library, *faute de mieux,* but there's no hurry.'

'This is your last visit, isn't it?' "in want of a better place"

'For the moment, yes.'

'You did say you'd be interested to see my sculpture?'

Rona brightened. 'Oh yes, I should.'

'How about coming over now?' Lois suggested, not quite meeting her eyes.

Rona had the impression that she wanted to speak to her, and the sculpture was simply a means to that end.

'Sure; I'll just leave my things and clock in with Nuala. Ten minutes?'

'Fine. I'll put the kettle on.'

'You won't forget it's late supper tonight?' Nuala reminded her, as they met in the hall.

'I won't. Is there any news of Clive?'

'He's been charged with burglary and other offences. I hope they'll be lenient, considering he gave himself up and people got their things back.'

'Only some of them,' Rona pointed out.

Nuala nodded absently, her mind elsewhere.

'How are you feeling?' Rona asked gently.

Nuala shrugged and gave her a wan smile. 'I miss Aunt

Edna,' she said simply. 'Sunday afternoons are the worst; for years she's been coming here for tea. And it's creepy, really: every time I go into the square, I automatically glance at her window, to see if she's there.' She bit her lip and added in a low voice, 'Frank Jeffries says that apart from a bequest to the Sunday school, she's left everything to me.'

She looked up, meeting Rona's sympathetic eyes. 'Thanks again for Thursday, Rona. It was good of you to help.'

'I was glad to be there. Is there anything else I can do?'

Nuala shook her head. 'I'm steeling myself to go over this afternoon, and start sorting through her things. Perhaps once that's done, I'll begin to come to terms with it.'

The vicarage was as homely and comfortably untidy as Rona remembered, and Lois herself seemed a part of it. She was wearing what appeared to be an oversized man's shirt, the sleeves rolled up to reveal brown, muscular arms, and a pair of faded corduroy trousers. Her short hair went its own way unmolested and her face, bronzed from her work in the garden, was innocent of make-up. Both she and the house seemed to be saying 'Take us as you find us', and Rona was glad to do so.

'You've something you want to say, haven't you?' Rona prompted, as the coffee was poured.

Lois smiled. 'And I thought I was being so subtle!' She handed Rona a mug. 'Yes, there is something, but it's up to you whether or not you take any notice.'

'So what is it?'

Lois seated herself and met Rona's eye. 'I'm becoming increasingly uneasy, my dear. Frankly, you seem to be stirring up things that are better left alone.'

Rona frowned. 'What kind of things?'

'Well, Beth is telling all and sundry that you're convinced Alan's innocent, and as a result people are starting to talk about the murder again.'

Rona said slowly, 'If he *is* innocent, surely that's a good thing?'

'It's raising false hopes,' Lois said simply, 'both for Beth and possibly, to a lesser degree, for Alan, too. It's even come to the ears of the police, and I gather Ed Barrett, who headed the original inquiry, is less than happy.'

'He would be,' Rona said grimly. 'He gave me short shrift over Miss Rosebury's death.'

Lois glanced at her in surprise. 'When you went with Nuala to the hospital? Why should that have annoyed him?'

Rona flushed. 'I thought she might have been murdered,' she said.

'*Edna?* For pity's sake, why?'

'I'd – had an interview with her. She made various statements that I thought might be significant, and then the tape went missing.'

'And you thought she'd been silenced?' Lois's lips twitched. 'Forgive me, my dear, but it sounds more like Chicago than sleepy old Buckford.'

'I know – it seems ridiculous now, but I was really worried at the time.'

Lois leant forward, hands clasped between her knees. 'Do you see, that's just what I mean? It's another example of your – overreacting, seeing possibilities that don't exist. Don't you think it would be better for everyone if you stepped back from this – campaign, however good a story it might make? Alan wasn't convicted by a kangaroo court, you know; he had a fair trial.'

Rona held on to her temper. 'Do *you* think he did it?' she challenged.

Lois held her eyes for a long moment, then slowly nodded. 'I wish I didn't, my dear, but to be truthful, yes, I do. So please think carefully before you get in any deeper. Remember that you'll soon be back in Marsborough, and it's we who'll be left with the unpleasant aftertaste. Now –' she sat back – 'I've said my piece and we won't mention it again;

so if you've finished your coffee, come and have a look at my studio.'

As they walked over the scorched grass, Rona was still resentful. She'd not cared for the suggestion, however tactfully phrased, that her main interest in Alan Spencer lay in making copy out of him, the more so since she wondered, in her inner heart, if there might be a germ of truth in it. But as soon as Lois unlocked the wooden door and they stepped into the studio, anger dissolved in interest.

The floor was deep in wood shavings, the scent of them sweet and clean. There were a couple of workbenches and a bewildering array of implements – planes, chisels, knives of all shapes and sizes, and other tools Rona couldn't name. Work in progress stood about in various stages of completion, and the shelves that lined the room contained dozens of finished carvings in a wide range of subjects.

'As I told you, wood's my thing,' Lois reminded her. 'No angels or cherubim, either – they're Gordon's territory. In my opinion, marble is for tombstones and statues to dead heroes; wood's a living medium, and it's the living that interests me – people, animals, flowers – you name it, I'll carve it. Mostly I work to please myself – flowers in spring, berries in autumn – but my bread and butter is models of people's pets, and the gift shop in the mall's a regular customer.'

'I think you're being modest,' Rona commented, moving along the shelves. 'Your husband said you exhibit in London, and I'm not surprised – these are really exquisite. May I touch them?'

'Of course; pick them up, stroke them, get the feel of them. That's what sculpture's all about.'

Rona lifted a slender column some eight inches high, round which had been carved a swathe of leaves and berries, each stem and vein intricately detailed.

'It feels almost warm,' she said, 'and I love its paleness. What wood is it?'

'That one's lime. Grinling Gibbons is my hero, and it's what he used. I can't always get hold of it, though.'

Rona replaced the column and, moving on, gave a sudden exclamation as she came to a model of a long-haired retriever. 'Just look at this! My dog could have modelled for it!'

'Have it!' Lois said promptly.

Rona turned to her. 'Is it for sale?'

'No, it's a gift. If you'd like it, it's yours.'

'But I couldn't possibly—'

'Nonsense!' Lois retorted briskly. 'Don't argue, just take it.'

A peace offering, perhaps, after earlier criticism? 'Then thank you – very much.'

Holding the little figure, she continued her examination of the carvings until, on the floor against the wall, she came upon a larger one, partly covered with a cloth, and turned enquiringly.

'It's Charlotte Spencer,' Lois said, adding as Rona stared at her, 'You can uncover it if you like. I'm not quite satisfied with it yet, probably because it's been done from memory.'

Almost apprehensively, Rona lifted the cloth to reveal the laughing bust of a young child, so full of joy and life that she felt tears come to her eyes. Lois had come to stand beside her. 'It's for Beth, of course, though she doesn't know anything about it.'

'It's beautiful,' Rona said in a low voice. 'I saw the newspaper photos, and you seem to have captured her exactly.'

Lois sighed and, gently taking the cloth out of Rona's hand, dropped it back over the bust. All at once, there seemed nothing left to say, and after thanking her again for the little model, Rona left the vicarage and made her belated way to the library.

Beth, who'd arranged to have the afternoon off work, arrived at Parsonage Place as agreed at one thirty. The morning cloud had dissipated and it was becoming increasingly hot.

'I wouldn't like to run far in this heat!' Rona commented, climbing into the car.

Beth nodded agreement, reversing in one of the parking places and heading back out of the end of the road. From the tail of her eye, Rona caught sight of Dave's car parked at the kerb.

'I brought a couple of sun hats,' Beth said. 'There's not much shade on the field.'

'You said this was Middle School Sports Day?'

'Yes; and thank goodness it's the only one I'll have to attend. Last year, Harry was still with the juniors.'

As they turned on to the road leading to the college, they joined a stream of other cars moving slowly in the same direction.

'How are your articles coming along?' Beth asked as they inched forward.

'Not too badly; I still have to look into the town's inhabitants through the ages – you know, merchants, builders, squires, landlords, inventors. It's the people that make the place come alive. I've already clocked up past mayors and vicars, and of course the people everyone knows about – James Cunningham, General Salter and Piers Plowright, who are always associated with Buckford.'

'We had a highwayman in the seventeenth century,' Beth volunteered, edging inside the gateway at last.

'Really? That's great! You must tell me about him.'

'Mrs Bishop included him in her scrapbook. Have you read it?'

The image of Catherine Bishop walking with her father came sharply into Rona's mind, and was instantly dismissed. 'Not thoroughly,' she admitted after a minute. 'I haven't really had time. It'll be better when I'm not coming up here every week.'

'Well, my sons will fill you in on him, gladly! They spent a whole summer holiday once, dressing up as Kit Tempest and his cohorts.'

Halfway up the drive, they were directed by senior boys to a field set aside for visitors' cars, and as they continued on foot, they could see bunting and flags in the trees and chairs lining the track, while a loudspeaker blared out its repetitious 'Testing – one, two, three, four—' Nearer to the school, two large marquees had been set up, and Beth nodded towards them.

'Tea tents,' she said. 'One for parents, the other for the pupils.'

The chairs near what would be the finishing line had already filled up, and they took their seats roughly halfway along. The sun was now burning down and Rona was grateful for the linen hat Beth handed her.

'I haven't been to a sports day since I was at school myself!' she confessed, glancing down at the programme they'd been handed. 'How long does it last?'

'Two till four, then tea. By that time, I assure you, we'll all be ready for it!'

'Which races are your sons in?'

Beth leant over and indicated them on the programme. 'There are two members from each house in every race,' she explained, 'and they compete for the house rather than individually. My two are in different houses, so my loyalty's divided.'

The chairs along the track had now filled up and people were spreading rugs on the grass. The loudspeaker blared into life with a loud Sousa march, which, after a couple of minutes, ended abruptly to give way to an announcer.

'Good afternoon, ladies and gentlemen, boys and girls. Welcome to Buckford College Sports Day. The first race will begin in five minutes, so please will those taking part assemble on the starting line?'

The races followed one another, with little to distinguish them. After a while Rona grew tired of watching wiry little bodies, none of whom she knew, dash past her, while supportive parents yelled encouragement. To Beth's delight, both the Spencer boys won their races, so family honour was vindicated here, at least. As time went on, however, Rona found herself longing for a drink and some shade, and it was with profound relief that she watched the prizes being presented and people at last collecting their belongings and making their way to the refreshment tent.

A full afternoon tea was provided. There were plates of sandwiches, scones and small iced cakes on each table, and kitchen staff wielding catering-sized teapots moved between them. At the far side of the marquee, the headmaster and his wife were circulating among their guests. Helena, cool in coffee-coloured trousers and a cream shirt, carried a large-brimmed hat which no doubt had shielded her from the heat of the afternoon.

Rona and Beth had almost finished by the time their turn came and Richard Maddox's smooth voice said, 'Good afternoon, ladies. May we join you for a few minutes?'

Without waiting for an answer, he pulled out a chair for his wife and sat down himself.

'The boys did well for their respective houses, Mrs Spencer,' he continued. 'You must be proud of them.'

'Indeed I am. I'm only sorry their father wasn't here to see it.' There was a brief, awkward silence, then she added, 'Perhaps next year, he will be.'

Richard Maddox's hand stilled on the table. 'Oh?' he said neutrally. 'Has a date been set for the appeal?'

'Not yet, but Miss Parish here has a new lead that gives a completely different slant on things. The police won't have any option but to reopen the case.'

Rona, momentarily stunned into silence, gazed at her in consternation, and was about to deny any such claim when Helena said plaintively, 'But I don't understand; what could possibly come up after all this time?'

'I heard rumours were circulating,' Richard Maddox remarked, his voice cold. 'Unsubstantiated, I don't doubt. I can't think it's very healthy to reopen old wounds like this.'

Beth said heatedly, 'The wounds are far from old, Mr

Maddox, they're raw and painful. My husband did not kill Barry Pollard, and I'm convinced the truth will clear him, once it can be unravelled.'

Maddox's nostrils were pinched, his thin lips tightly compressed. A closed face, possibly a cruel one. 'Of course we make allowances for your feelings, Mrs Spencer – only natural, after all. I simply think Miss Parish would be better employed with ancient rather than modern history. There is plenty of it, after all.'

'And talking of ancient history,' Rona put in desperately, 'Mrs Spencer tells me you had a highwayman in these parts?'

Beth, aware she'd overstepped the mark, threw her a look of apology and came to her rescue. 'That's right – we were just speaking about him.'

Richard Maddox made no reply, and it was Helena, with a quick look at his set face, who answered. 'Yes, Kit Tempest. His birthplace is only a few miles away. You ought to see it, Rona.'

Beth looked startled at the use of the first name, and Richard raised an eyebrow.

Rona said, 'Unfortunately this is my last visit for the moment. I'm not sure I'd—'

'But you really should make the effort,' Helena insisted. 'There's one of those new centres, where you walk round seeing tableaux illustrating his life. It's really very well done, and there are books for sale that you'd find useful, and show-cases of his guns and masks.'

Rona hesitated. A highwayman would certainly add colour.

'I know,' Helena said suddenly, 'why don't I drive you over, tomorrow afternoon? I haven't been for a while and there are some new exhibits. Also –' she flashed Rona a smile – 'there's a catalogue I promised to lend Magda that I haven't got round to sending. I'd be very grateful if you could take it back with you. Quid pro quo?'

Before Rona could reply, Richard Maddox intervened. 'Don't pressurize her, darling; she's already said her time is limited, and I'm sure she has more relevant things to attend to.'

Rona addressed herself to Helena. 'I'd be happy to take the catalogue, without any return favours.'

Nevertheless, Helena Maddox interested her and Richard was patently not happy with the suggestion. Perhaps an afternoon in her company might shed some light on her enigmatic husband. If *he* had had any motive for killing Barry Pollard, Rona felt sure he was capable of doing so.

'There's a good teashop there, too,' Helena wheedled, glancing at the empty cake plate.

Rona capitulated. 'That settles it! Thanks, I'd like to go.'

Richard Maddox stood up abruptly and pulled out his wife's chair. 'We must move on, dear,' he said in a clipped voice. 'We've still several people to speak to.'

'Two thirty?' Helena suggested. 'I'll pick you up at your digs.' And, with her husband's hand lightly but firmly on her arm, she moved away.

'I saw you talking to Mrs Maddox at the funeral,' Beth said later, as they waited for the boys to join them, 'but I didn't realize you knew her well.'

'I don't really; she's the friend of a friend.'

'She used to give Lottie piano lessons, did you know?' Beth flicked Rona a sideways glance. 'Sorry I dropped you in it just now, but I wanted to shake them out of their complacency. I hate the way everyone accepts Alan's guilt.'

Since he'd been convicted in Crown Court, Rona felt she could hardly blame them.

'I think you can take it their complacency was well and truly shaken,' she said.

She'd been back in her room for only five minutes when she was disconcerted by a tap on the door, and as she twisted to face it, Nuala looked in.

'Don't do that to me!' Rona exclaimed, laughing. 'I thought I had the house to myself.'

'Sorry. No, I – didn't feel up to the exercise class this evening, so a friend's taken Dad along with her father.'

Rona studied her more closely. She looked pale and tense, and, she saw, was holding some small, leather-covered volumes.

'I've been going through Auntie's things,' Nuala said rapidly, 'and I found her diaries.' A flush brought a wash of colour to her face. 'I felt really awful reading them. I wouldn't have dreamt of it, if it hadn't been for – you know – and the fact that it might be important.'

'Go on,' Rona said drily.

'Well, I found them – the entries she'd made about the lovers.'

Rona came to her feet, her heart starting to thump. 'Who were they?' she demanded urgently.

Nuala shook her head, her eyes falling to the books. 'She only wrote their initials, but Rona, it must have been going on for months. She—'

'Nuala!'

'Sorry. AS and HM. If there's a link with Lottie, as we thought there might be, then AS has to be Alan Spencer, but I can't for the life of me think of any HM.'

'Helena Maddox,' Rona supplied whitely.

Nuala frowned. 'Who . . .? You mean the headmaster's wife, up at the college? Is that her name?'

Rona sank back on to her chair without replying. Alan Spencer and Helena Maddox? It was a combination she would never have contemplated.

'But did they even know each other?' Nuala asked, clearly bewildered.

'It's possible; Mrs Maddox gave Lottie piano lessons.' Yet surely Alan would have been at work during her visits? Even if he were home, Beth would also have been there, and nothing could have been said in front of the child.

'I wonder if Mr Maddox knew?' Nuala mused, and Rona went suddenly cold. What was it she'd been thinking, only that afternoon? That if he'd had a motive, she could imagine him killing without compunction? Suppose for a moment that

Maddox had for some reason suspected *Pollard* of being his wife's lover? A completely different picture would emerge.

But, she admitted, her heartbeats steadying, she'd nothing whatever to back that theory. Even if she was right about the initials – and it was important to remember there'd be other HMs in Buckford – the stark fact remained that it was Spencer who'd been involved with Helena Maddox, and he was still alive.

All the same, it would be interesting to know where Richard Maddox had been when Pollard was stabbed. She bet it had never occurred to the police to ask – as, indeed, why should it? But if she wanted to test her hypothesis, she would have to beard Ed Barrett in his den, a prospect she did not relish.

Nuala had been watching the changing expressions on her face. 'Does it help at all?' she asked doubtfully.

'To be honest, I don't know. We're only guessing who the initials stand for – we've no proof.' Except Spencer's admission, which she'd promised not to repeat.

She glanced at the diaries in Nuala's hand. 'Is there nothing at all that gives a clearer hint of their identity? What does your aunt actually say?'

Nuala perched on the edge of the bed. 'Her first reaction was pure shock.' She met Rona's eyes defensively. 'She wasn't snooping, you know; she didn't *want* to see them – in fact, it really upset her, and she even gave up her walks for a while. She made every effort to avoid them, and whenever she did catch sight of them, she moved away at once. She didn't eavesdrop or anything.'

'Yet she knew who they were, so she must have got a fairly good look at them.'

Nuala shrugged. 'She kept going on about the danger of breaking up two families. Said she was always coming across young couples in compromising conditions, but these two were middle-aged, with family commitments.'

'And were they, too? In compromising conditions?'

Nuala flushed again. 'One time, I think.'

Rona thought for a minute. 'When was the first mention of them?'

'I thought you'd ask that. I marked the place.' Nuala picked up a diary and opened it. 'It was two weeks after Lottie was killed. That's what Auntie couldn't forgive – that he wasn't at home comforting his wife, but going after someone else's.'

'How many references in all?'

'About half a dozen, spread over a year or so. The last was a couple of months before Pollard was murdered; that's why, when Mr Spencer was arrested and the police appealed for information, she wondered if she should report it.'

'I think I'll probably have to,' Rona said thoughtfully. 'If that's all right with you?'

Nuala nodded, collected the diaries and got to her feet. 'If you think it's for the best, and provided you make it clear Auntie wasn't snooping.'

As she left the room, Rona extracted her mobile from her handbag, dialled the prison, and asked to speak to Spencer. She hadn't betrayed his trust; Nuala had arrived at his name unprompted, and though she herself had suggested Helena, it was breaking no confidences since Alan hadn't mentioned her. Now, however, it was imperative to speak of the affair.

His voice was guarded as he answered. 'Spencer here.'

'It's Rona Parish. Mr Spencer, I need a favour.'

'Go on.'

'I promised I wouldn't mention your affair to anyone.' Silence.

'I've kept my word, but I now want you to release me from it. I want – need – to tell the police.'

'No way!' he said harshly.

'Listen, I know who it was you were meeting.'

'You can't possibly.'

'Initials HM?'

She heard his intake of breath. 'I'm not having her dragged into this.'

'I know you said it was impossible,' she pressed, 'but suppose her husband had found out?'

'He couldn't have.'

'You were equally certain no one knew.'

There was a long silence. Then he said, 'As I told you before, if he *had* rumbled us and was homicidally inclined – neither of which I believe – he'd have gone for me, not Pollard.'

'All the same, I think we should know where he was at the crucial time, and only the police can find out.'

'I've just said – under no circumstances are you to go to the police with this.'

'Mr Spencer – Alan – I'm trying to help you, and they're the only ones with the authority to question Richard Maddox. Look, I've a feeling we're really getting somewhere. Please don't put a spoke in the wheel.'

Silence.

'I need your permission,' Rona persisted.

She heard him sigh. 'Well, you're playing fair, at any rate. Not every journalist would worry about keeping a promise in these circumstances.'

'Then I can tell them?'

'If you're convinced it's necessary. God knows if you can trust a cop, but try to impress on them not to shout it from the rooftops.'

'I'll do my best,' she said. 'Oh, and one more thing before you go.'

'Shoot.'

'That letter you received asking you to meet Pollard: was it written in red ink?'

'Red ink?' he repeated. 'No, why do you ask?'

'I'll explain later. Thanks again for your help.'

'Good luck,' he replied, and rang off.

Next, Rona phoned Barnie Trent at home.

'I was wondering if there's any news from America?' she asked.

227

He sighed heavily. 'They're talking of inducing the baby. It's due anyway in just over three weeks.'

'And Dinah's still there?'

'Yep; she'll stay on now till after the birth. We were planning to go over then, so I'll fly out as soon as I hear. It's all covered at this end.'

'Have you run out of freezer meals yet?'

He gave a short laugh. 'Almost. I've had enough of being on my own, I can tell you.'

'You must come over to us when I get back.'

'Back? You're not still in Buckford?'

'Yes, but this is the last trip for the moment.'

'How's the jigsaw coming along?'

'Jigsaw?' Rona echoed blankly.

'This overall picture you're hoping to fit together.'

'Oh.' She remembered the metaphor she'd given him. 'There are still a lot of pieces missing,' she said.

'I've been waiting for you to commandeer Andy and his camera.'

'I know; I was over-optimistic there, I'm afraid; it'll be a while before I'm ready for him, but I'm making mental notes as I go along of things I'd like photographed.' She paused. 'When you speak to Dinah, tell her I was at Buckford College Sports Day.'

'I will.'

'And send my love, of course, and to Melissa and Sam.'

'I will,' he said again.

'See you soon, Barnie.'

She'd been right to think of the project as a jigsaw, she reflected; sometimes she'd tried to fit a piece into the wrong place, distorting the picture, as in the case of Edna's death. And sometimes there was a piece – Pollard's killer – which, no matter which way she angled it, wouldn't fit anywhere. And until that piece was slotted into place, she hadn't a hope of getting the whole picture.

* * *

Dave was waiting for her on the corner of the road.

'I didn't see you inside the school grounds,' she greeted him.

'No, I'd have been too conspicuous, rolling up by myself and with no offspring to support. How did it go?'

'I've spent more stimulating afternoons.'

He laughed. 'I'll bet.'

'The only exciting bit was when Beth Spencer told the headmaster and his wife I had a new theory that would exonerate Alan.'

'Jeeze!'

'My own reaction precisely. There's been an interesting development, though.'

As they walked to that evening's choice of pub, she told him about the revelations in the diaries. 'So I'll have to go and see old Frosty Face tomorrow,' she finished. 'We need to know where the estimable headmaster was while murder most foul was being committed. What's more, I'm spending tomorrow afternoon with his wife, the femme fatale herself. She's driving me out to the birthplace of the local highwayman. It's a heritage site, apparently.'

'I must say, you get around.'

'Thanks for being here, Dave,' she said seriously, as he held the pub door open for her. 'It's a load off my mind, knowing you're to hand.'

'Glad to be of service, ma'am,' he replied.

Fifteen

Rona woke the next morning with a heavy feeling in the pit of her stomach, presage of her visit to DI Barrett. She'd decided against phoning for an appointment, in the hope that if she presented herself in person, it would be more difficult for him to refuse to see her.

'You won't need to take the diaries, will you?' Nuala asked over breakfast. 'I'd hate to think of the police pawing them and poking fun.'

'Not in the first instance, anyway,' Rona said. 'They don't contain any positive ID; my main task will be convincing them they could be important.'

The foyer of the police station seemed as large and forbidding as before, and the walk to the desk immeasurably longer. This time, it wasn't a question of handing across a packet and making her escape; this time, she had to beard the lion in his den.

'Yes, ma'am?' the desk sergeant said pleasantly. 'How can I help?'

'I was wondering if Detective Inspector Barrett is free?' she began.

'Is he expecting you?'

'No, but I've something important to tell him.'

'Concerning?'

Rona's mouth was dry. 'Concerning the murder of Barry Pollard.'

There was a brief silence. Then the sergeant said, 'I believe I'm right in thinking that case was closed some time ago?'

'I have new information,' Rona insisted. 'Please, it's really important that I see him.'

'Your name, ma'am?'

'Rona Parish.'

'One minute, please.' The sergeant turned away and picked up a phone. A child, being dragged across the foyer by its mother, had started to scream, and Rona missed what was being said. Once, the sergeant looked back at her over his shoulder, as though checking something.

'Unfortunately Mr Barrett's tied up at the moment,' he told her, returning to the desk. 'Perhaps you could phone and make an appointment?'

Rona's temper snapped. 'No, I couldn't. I'm only here till tomorrow, and I need to see him. *Now* – if he's available.' She held the man's eyes, leaving him in no doubt that she knew he was.

He lifted the phone again, and only then did she realize the line was still open and Barrett must have heard her. No doubt it would have endeared her to him still further.

The sergeant finished speaking into the phone, and behind her, the child lapsed into sobbing hiccups.

'Very well, ma'am; the DI can spare you ten minutes, if you'll wait in Interview Room One.' He nodded to a door across the hallway.

Rona drew a deep breath. The first hurdle was behind her. 'Thank you,' she said.

Barrett, who arrived with his sergeant in tow, nodded at her unsmilingly. 'Ms Parish.'

Rona said evenly, 'It's good of you to see me, Inspector. I'll keep this as brief as possible.'

He indicated a chair and she sat down, the two men seating themselves across the table from her.

'So –' Barrett clasped his hands on the table – 'who do you think has been murdered this time?'

She ignored the jibe. 'Have you finished with my transcript?'

'Yes, thank you, I've given orders for it to be left at the desk; you can collect it on your way out.'

'Was it of any use?'

He shook his head. 'Shadows in the dark. Quite literally. As I suspected, you read too much into the ramblings of an old lady who was close to death.' He paused. '*Natural* death. Did you ever recover your tape?'

'No.' She'd no intention of telling him Clive Banks had it. 'You might reconsider its value when you hear who those shadows belonged to.'

He threw himself back in his chair, clearly exasperated. 'Is this your "important information"? Ms Parish, we're not *Hello!* magazine—'

Rona said sharply, 'Will you do me the courtesy of hearing me out?'

The sergeant – Tyson, wasn't it? – moved uncomfortably on his chair.

Barrett lifted a resigned hand. 'Go ahead then.'

'They were Alan Spencer and Helena Maddox.'

Tyson whistled softly through his teeth. Barrett remained impassive.

'Even supposing this allegation isn't slanderous, what possible significance could it have?'

What indeed? In his presence, the fragile case she'd so painstakingly built up suddenly crumpled, and she wondered despairingly why she had come. All right, she told herself, switch from the two of them and concentrate on Spencer, the crux of the matter.

'Well?' Barrett pressed, when she didn't reply. 'Your time's running out, Ms Parish.'

She braced herself to meet his eyes. 'Alan Spencer didn't murder Pollard,' she said.

The expected onslaught didn't come. Instead, Barrett pursed his lips and surveyed her, still without expression.

'I heard you'd been spreading rumours,' he said at last. 'Visiting the prison and generally making a nuisance of yourself. Let me tell you, Ms Parish, the job of the police is hard enough without people like you sticking your oar in. God knows there are plenty of cases we can't crack, but when we do, and it's all behind us, it's especially galling to have it raked up again.'

'Even if you have the wrong man?' she countered.

His eyes narrowed. 'Since we last met, I've discovered who you are: none other than the woman who turned the Harvey case on its head, got his widow killed in the process and was nearly killed herself. Well, it may come as a surprise to you, but sometimes the police *do* get it right, even without your help.'

Rona's nails dug into her palms. 'What about the hate mail?'

Barrett shrugged, his eyes never leaving her face. 'Occupational hazard, specially where a kid's involved.'

'At the beginning of a sentence, perhaps, but surely not all the way through? Someone using red ink wrote to him till the day he was released. Did you look into that?'

'Of course we bloody looked into it. Since Pollard was killed within days of his release, his last weeks were gone over meticulously, though why the hell I'm telling you this, I don't know. And where did you come up with the red ink, anyway? That was restricted information.'

'He told his friends at the Cat and Fiddle.'

Colour came into Barrett's lean cheeks. 'You really have been ferreting around, haven't you?'

'Did you trace the letter-writer?' she persisted.

She thought for a minute that he wasn't going to reply, but then he said flatly, 'We'd nothing to go on; Pollard hadn't kept them, and by that time they were pretty academic anyway; Spencer himself was the most obvious candidate, and we already had him behind bars.'

Rona changed tack. 'What about the letter asking him to go to the pub?'

'What letter?' Barrett shot back. 'We've only his word it

ever existed. Instead of showing it to his wife, as any normal person would, he made up some cock-and-bull story about meeting friends. The whole thing was an invention, to explain his presence at the scene.'

'But he needn't have bothered to explain it. He could have killed Pollard and got the hell out, not phoned nine-nine-nine and stayed till help arrived.'

'Double bluff,' Barrett said shortly.

She produced her trump card. 'How did the knife get into the garage?'

She saw the flash of anger, and guessed this unexplained point still rankled. 'He had an accomplice,' he answered, deliberately offhand. 'All right, we weren't able to trace him, but we'd enough to nail Spencer without that.'

There was a brief silence, then he said abruptly, 'Very well, I'll humour you. If you're so damn sure he's innocent, who would you put in the frame?'

'It could have been Richard Maddox,' Rona said, aware of how thin her case was.

Barrett stared at her for a minute, then threw back his head with a burst of laughter. Spencer's own reaction, she remembered. 'Really, Ms Parish, I have to hand it to you! First you think an old lady's been murdered to hush up a love affair, then you accuse one of the most respected men in the county – the *country*, even – of being a killer! I must say, I can't wait to hear what you come up with next. My only hope is it's a million miles from Buckford.'

Rona leant forward. 'You said you'd humour me, Inspector. Then *please*, as discreetly and circumspectly and tactfully as you like, find out where Maddox was that evening.'

'And how exactly do you propose we do that, after a gap of more than two years, and without arousing his suspicions or being accused of harassment?' He also leant forward, so that their faces were only inches apart. 'Read my lips, Ms Parish: a) Spencer had Pollard's blood on him, b) The murder weapon was found hidden on his premises, and c) the man had killed his child. What more do you want?'

Rona's heart was beating high in her chest. 'All right, you think I'm a know-all and too big for my boots and all the rest of it, and you might even charge me with wasting police time. Fair enough, but I just *know* Spencer didn't do it. What's so frustrating is that I can't seem to convince you.'

'And just why are you so sure? Because he told you? He'd hardly hold his hand up, would he, to a journalist anxious to clear him?'

She shook her head, dismissing the conjecture. 'Seriously, though, there's something off-key about Richard Maddox. If he'd discovered his wife was having an affair—'

'With Spencer, if I heard you right. It can't have escaped your notice that *he's* still alive.'

No point even mentioning her theory of mistaken suspicions; it would be annihilated without mercy.

She tried again. 'We were discussing it yesterday, at Sports Day – I went with Beth Spencer. As soon as the case was mentioned, he got very tight-lipped, and—'

'No doubt on Mrs Spencer's behalf.'

'No, it was she . . .' Rona broke off. What was the use? He was never going to believe her. Feminine intuition was something he'd laugh to scorn, and basically it was all she had.

She stood up, momentarily at an advantage as she looked down into his hostile grey eyes. 'Thank you for seeing me, Mr Barrett. We can only hope that the killer doesn't strike again while he's still at large.'

And before he could think of a retort, she turned and left the room.

The bright sunshine stung her eyes, and she realized there were tears of frustration in them. Well, she told herself, impatiently dashing them away, she'd done all she could. It looked as though Alan Spencer would after all have to 'sit it out', as he'd put it, until his time was up.

Dave was waiting by the entrance to the mall, and she crossed the road to join him.

'No joy, I take it?'

'Positively none. Oh, damn! I didn't pick up my transcript; it's been left for me at the desk.'

He eyed her astutely. 'And you don't want to go back for it? I'll get it.' And before she could protest, he had crossed the road and disappeared through the swing doors, emerging a minute later with the packet under his arm.

'Now,' he said as he rejoined her, 'let's go into the mall and have a coffee. You look as though you could do with it.'

The mall was, as usual, seething with people, and they seated themselves in a fenced-off area from where they could watch the passers-by moving in a constant stream in front of them.

Their coffee arrived, and as they drank it, Rona recounted her conversation with the inspector.

'To be fair,' Dave said reflectively, when she'd ended by summing up her less than favourable opinion of him, 'he did at least give you your say. He didn't have to see you.'

Rona sighed. 'I suppose,' she said dispiritedly.

'You've had enough of Buckford, haven't you?'

'It's just that I've become more involved than I expected, which is hardly professional. It'll do me good to have a few solid weeks at home, before coming up for a final blitz. In the meantime, I'll cut my losses and drive back in the morning. If I hadn't been meeting Helena, I'd have set off straight away.'

Dave smiled. 'Don't let the DI get to you. From what you've said, you've made friends up here.' He looked at his watch. 'It's only eleven o'clock; what are you doing the rest of the morning?'

Rona shrugged, unable to shake off her despondency.

'If you've nothing planned, how about playing hooky? Drive out into the country somewhere and have a pub lunch?'

She looked at him gratefully. 'Dave, I'd love to!'

It had been just what she needed, Rona reflected as, back in her room, she prepared for the afternoon outing. Though Dave was more than ten years her junior, they had a lot of similar interests, and it was refreshing to hear the views of a different generation.

She checked that there was a new tape in her recorder – though she wasn't sure she'd need it – and slipped it into her bag before running downstairs. The radio reached her from behind Jack Stanton's door, and Nuala was vacuuming the sitting room. Dave was right, she thought, letting herself out of the house; she *had* made friends up here, and she would miss them.

Helena Maddox came swishing round the corner in a red sports car with the top down. Her hair was restrained by a wide chiffon band, and she was wearing tortoiseshell sunglasses.

'Lovely afternoon for a drive,' she said, leaning over to open the passenger door. 'Sorry I'm a little late; for some reason, Richard wasn't too happy about our jaunt. He was trying to talk me out of it until the last minute.'

'Why was that, do you think?' Rona asked carefully, fastening her seat belt.

Helena shrugged, starting up the engine, and they whooshed into a three-point turn. 'He kept insisting you weren't really interested and I was wasting your time. Such a fuss over one afternoon!'

Rona realized almost at once that this wouldn't be a comfortable ride. She was already holding on to her seat as they zoomed at forty-five miles an hour through the busy streets, and wondered apprehensively how long it would take to reach Kit Tempest's birthplace.

'Magda's catalogue's on the back seat,' Helena said, above

the roar of their passage. 'Don't let me forget to give it to you.' She turned to look at Rona, who wished fervently that she'd keep her eyes on the road. 'I gather you two have known each other some time?'

'Since we were ten,' Rona confirmed, pushing her flying hair back from her face. 'She's been a good friend over the years.'

'You're lucky,' Helena commented. 'I've never had a friend like that.'

'Surely you had "best friends" at school?'

She gave a quick shake of her head. 'My family moved around a lot – my father was in the army – and I was never at any one school for more than a year or so. I've no brothers or sisters, so it was a lonely as well as a disrupted childhood. I was determined that when I grew up I'd have a large family to make up for it, but it didn't work out that way.'

Rona, remembering Magda's comments, remained silent. They had reached the outskirts of Buckford and were driving along the road that passed the college. Helena's speed had increased to seventy-five, and Rona had to force herself to keep her eyes off the speedometer.

'You seem quite friendly with Mrs Spencer,' Helena remarked, overtaking a lorry and just missing a bus coming in the other direction. 'I gathered at the funeral that you'd visited her husband, but I was surprised to see you together at Sports Day.'

Rona, trying to ignore the blaring horns, moistened dry lips. 'She asked if I'd go with her, because she felt conspicuous without him.'

Helena gave a light laugh. 'Oh, come on! She was after your sympathy! A lot of the fathers weren't there, with it being on a Monday.'

Thinking back, Rona realized this was true; though many fathers *had* managed to be present, there'd been several groups of mothers on their own. Possibly it was Beth's particular circumstances that made her feel like an outcast.

'She's rather too earnest for me,' Helena went on dismissively, 'though I only knew her on a parent/teacher basis, from giving Lottie piano lessons. I'm sorry for her, of course; in fact, I often wonder how she manages to go on. There can't be anything worse than losing a child.'

That didn't stop you going after her husband, Rona thought. Aloud, she said – as though she'd not known – 'You taught Charlotte the piano? Wasn't she rather young?'

'The younger the better,' Helena replied, 'and she already had a good ear. She was a lovely little girl, bubbling and full of fun. You couldn't be cross with her, even when she played up, as she quite often did. I've been fond of all my pupils, but I loved Lottie like my own. I used to fantasize, sometimes, that she was.'

Another sidelong glance, while the car swerved and then righted itself. 'Sorry if that sounds maudlin. The fact is, I had a breakdown some years ago and I still have bouts of depression. Lottie was like a beacon at those times; I was always the better for seeing her.'

It occurred to Rona that this conversation was more suited to friends than casual acquaintances, and she wondered apprehensively if Helena was suffering from depression at the moment; even more worryingly, if she was on medication of some kind. Perhaps that's why Richard hadn't wanted her to come, though surely he'd have acted more authoritatively if she'd been unfit to drive.

In an attempt to lighten her mood, Rona asked brightly, 'Where exactly are we heading?'

They were out in open country now, fields of crops and scattered farmhouses beginning to give way to wilder heathland and more hilly terrain.

'Lammerden,' Helena replied after a minute, seeming to accept the change of subject. 'It's a little hamlet near the Bedfordshire border. There's nothing there, really – or wasn't, before they built the centre. Now, it's quite a tourist attraction. Tempest was a bit of a Robin Hood character, but that didn't save him from the gallows. He was hanged at the crossroads above the hamlet.'

'How long will it take us to get there?'

'Another half-hour or so.'

At least, Rona thought philosophically, the traffic was thinner up here and they were less likely to bump into anything more substantial than a sheep. The wind was stronger, too, and her hair was continually whipping across her face, making her cheeks sting and her eyes water.

Breaking into her thoughts, Helena said suddenly, 'Alan Spencer and I were lovers, but I've a feeling you know that?'

Rona caught her breath; this was not at all what she'd expected. 'How could I possibly?'

Helena raised her shoulders. 'I've been thinking about old Miss Rosebury and her night walks. She could have seen us, and you interviewed her, didn't you? Did she tell you?'

'No,' said Rona honestly.

'Well, I'm telling you now.' Rona noted uneasily the staccato quality in her voice, surely indicative of tension. 'It started soon after Charlotte's death, and I can imagine what you're thinking, but you're wrong. Alan was so wretched he couldn't bear to be in the house, and one night, when I was walking back to my car after a recital, we bumped into each other. We'd barely met before, but he'd a great look of someone I used to be very fond of. Since we couldn't avoid speaking, I said something conventional like how sorry I was about Charlotte. Then, to my total horror, I broke down and couldn't stop sobbing. I'm always emotional after a concert, and his looking like Edgar could have added to it, but it was all highly embarrassing.'

She half-smiled. 'Poor man, he didn't know what to do. Eventually, probably to shut me up, he put an arm round me.'

She gave a loud blast of the horn, making Rona jump and an ambling sheep skip smartly out of the way.

'When I'd calmed down a bit,' she continued, 'we sat on

the wall of the car park and talked for an hour or more. He hadn't realized how fond I was of Lottie and I think he was touched. He poured out the whole story, about her skipping ahead and that maniac Pollard mounting the pavement and crushing her, and by that time we were both crying and trying to comfort each other. He kept saying he could hardly face his wife, because she blamed him for Charlotte's death.

'Well, eventually we separated and went to our respective homes, and I thought that was that. But about a week later he phoned and asked if I'd any more recitals coming up. It was obvious what he meant. As it happened, the music society I belonged to had arranged a series of weekly concerts throughout the winter, and they proved the perfect alibi. Richard has no interest in music, and never checked what time they ended.

'So it became a weekly arrangement. I went to the concerts – it would have caused comment if I hadn't – and Alan had his meal with the family and spent the evening at home. Then, at ten o'clock, he'd go out for his "walk before bed". He said later that I was his salvation, that he couldn't have survived without me.

'The first three or four times, all we did was walk and talk, talk, talk. But it was getting steadily colder by then, so I suggested sitting in my car. By the time we arrived there, it was often the only one left – most people use the multi-storey – and I started parking it over in the far corner, away from the lights. And, of course, things progressed from there.'

She gave an unexpected gurgle of laughter. 'I never thought I'd still be making love in the back of a car when I was in my forties!'

'Not this car, I presume?' Rona suggested, with a glance over her shoulder at the narrow back seat.

'No, no, I had a much more sedate – and roomy – one then. I know what you're thinking,' she said again. 'Yes, I *was* cheating on my husband, but our marriage is a sham. He married me because he needed a wife for the headship,

I married him because I was sure I'd never fall in love again and I desperately wanted children. Of the two of us he got the better deal, achieving both his aims, while I – well, as it turned out we didn't have children, and although Richard had two sons, they were already in their teens and never accepted me as their mother. And to crown it all, I *did* fall in love again, very, very deeply. Alan loved me too, there's no doubt about that, and since Beth was no comfort at a time when he desperately needed it, I just couldn't accept that what we did was wrong.'

They drove in silence for several minutes, Helena obviously lost in the past. Rona was longing to know what happened next, but there was no way she could prompt her. Nor could she ask if Richard had found out about the affair.

Finally, Helena spoke again. 'You went to see him, didn't you? How did he seem?'

'I think the word is "resigned".'

She sighed. 'How could anyone possibly blame him?'

Rona looked at her quickly. 'You think he did it?' Somehow, she'd not expected that.

'Of course,' Helena answered, and there was surprise in her voice, too. 'Who else could it have been?'

Rona was thankful that the question was rhetorical; she could hardly have answered, *Your husband?*

As they rounded a bend, a brown heritage sign indicated that Lammerden lay two miles down a side road to their left. Helena swung into the narrow lane, with Rona hoping they wouldn't meet a tractor coming in the opposite direction.

The Kit Tempest Display and Exhibition Centre, as Helena had implied, dominated the unremarkable little hamlet. One of the cottages, no different in appearance from the rest, had placards in its garden proclaiming it to be his birthplace, and a few people were standing on the path, reading leaflets. Outside the village shop stood a cardboard cut-out of a figure in highwayman's garb, with a sweeping hat, a mask and a pistol in each hand.

However, all this was dwarfed by the large glass-fronted building set back from the road with a car park in front of it and flagpoles flying a variety of international banners. Helena swerved into it and turned up one of the aisles, looking for an empty space.

Suddenly, she slammed on the brake, sending Rona hurtling forward, restrained only by her seat-belt from hitting the windscreen.

'What is it? What's the matter?' she demanded, struggling upright.

Helena was staring at a large grey Daimler parked in one of the slots. 'That's Richard's car,' she said, and before Rona had processed the thought they shot forward again, gravel flying under their wheels as they screeched up the aisle, down the next one, and straight out onto the village street. An approaching car screamed to a halt with inches to spare and a barrage of furious honking, and, with the way home temporarily blocked, Helena veered instead to the left and went speeding through the village and up the hill on the other side.

'We'll look at the gibbet first,' she said jerkily, as though that explained everything.

'But – why do you want to avoid your husband?' Rona asked in bewilderment and growing unease.

'He thinks you know something,' Helena said, and then, before Rona could question her further, 'I'm not entirely sure where this road leads. There's an Ordnance Survey in the glove compartment – could you get it out for me?'

Rona leant forward and as she extracted the map, something rolled out of the compartment on to the floor at her feet. It was a red ballpoint pen.

Sixteen

'Well, don't just sit there staring at it!' Helena said impatiently, and Rona's heart jerked. Then she realized she was referring to the map and as Helena, after a quick check in the mirror, drew in to the side of the road, she numbly handed it over. There must be millions of red ballpoints in circulation, she was telling herself, and yet . . .

She heard herself say, 'Did you write to Barry Pollard in prison?'

Helena's hands stilled on the map. Then she gave a forced little laugh. 'Talk about non sequiturs!' she said. 'Whatever brought that up?'

Rona released her belt and bent down to retrieve the pen. 'This; someone wrote to him regularly in red ink.'

'You really are the most amazing woman! How in hell do you know that?'

'He said so.'

'He—?' Helena removed her sunglasses and turned to stare at her.

'Not to me, of course, but to some friends at the pub. Hate mail, he called it.'

'Oh, it was certainly that,' Helena said slowly. 'I'll never stop hating him, even though he's dead. May he rot in hell.'

The words rang incongruously in the still, hot afternoon and Rona shivered. In front and behind them stretched the deserted country road, glinting in the sunlight, and on either side featureless expanses of scrub and low bushes stretched to the horizon. Oh Dave, Rona thought suddenly, where are you?

Helena was still speaking, and Rona felt inside her handbag and surreptitiously switched on her recorder. 'I told you how much I loved Charlotte. She was the little daughter I never had; I was able to see her regularly, spend time with her, watch her grow, and that more than made up for all the disappointments and failures. Then, suddenly, her life was snuffed out, extinguished like a candle, all because that bastard not only couldn't hold his drink, but had the criminal insanity to get behind a wheel. And the really incredible part –' her breath was coming in great, tearing rasps – 'was that no one seemed to take it seriously. He was sentenced to eighteen months – *eighteen months* – for murder – because that's what it was. And not satisfied with that, they let him out in nine! Can you believe it? So I vowed that for every week of those months, he'd be reminded of what he'd done.'

She turned to face Rona defiantly. 'So yes, the answer to your question is that I did write to Barry Pollard in prison. Making him suffer was the only comfort I had.'

Rona swallowed drily. 'Did Alan know about it?'

She shook her head. 'That was something I never told him. It was my own, private revenge.' She swung the car door open. 'Let's go for a walk. I'm tired of being cooped up in here.'

Rona was also glad to stretch her legs. 'Is it safe to leave the car with the top down?' she asked.

'We're not going far, and there's no one within miles.' Helena looked about her at the empty landscape. 'The gibbet's not on this road; we must have taken a wrong turning. According to the Survey this is a dead-end, and only leads to a farm. Bring your bag, though, just in case.'

Rona, aware of the almost inaudible humming of the recorder, had every intention of doing so. She accepted she was being unethical, but assured herself she'd own up later, and obtain Helena's permission before making use of it.

They set off, walking parallel to the road on the springy turf. It was easier on their feet than the hard surface which, in any case, was starting to melt in the heat. Bees hovered overhead and far away over the hill a dog could be heard barking incessantly. They might have been the only two people left on earth. Then, mingling with the hum of the insects, another noise impinged on them, and with one accord they turned. Away in the distance the sun glinted off glass – a windscreen – that was rapidly approaching, growing larger even as they watched.

'Run!' Helena shouted. She seized Rona's arm and began pulling her away from the road towards the stunted bushes, stumbling and tripping in her high-heeled sandals. Rona tried to hold back, but the pressure was insistent.

'It's probably someone going to the farm,' she protested, as the brambles scratched her ankles. 'And there's no point in running – there isn't anywhere we can hide.'

'He mustn't catch up with us,' Helena gasped, dragging on her arm. 'Come *on*! Can't you go faster?'

Down on the road a car skidded to a halt – presumably behind theirs. A door slammed, and a man's voice called, 'Helena! For God's sake, darling, come back!'

'Keep going!' Helena panted. 'He might give up if we put a fair distance between us.'

It seemed to Rona that Richard Maddox wasn't the man to give up on anything, but she'd no breath to argue. Her mouth was dry and her heart hammering, partly from their headlong flight, partly from fear, though of what, she wasn't sure. The footsteps were gaining on them and behind her, bewilderingly, she heard another car stop, another door slam.

Helena's urgency infected her, but as she increased her pace her foot caught in a rabbit hole and she went flying, landing heavily on the uneven ground and temporarily winding herself. The earth beneath her vibrated with running footsteps, and heaving herself on one elbow, Rona turned to see Richard Maddox bearing down on them and, a few yards behind him, Dave Lampeter giving chase. Then, within feet of them, Richard drew up sharply, staring past her, and Dave went cannoning into him.

Jigsaw

Puzzled by their sudden stillness, Rona looked up at Helena's motionless figure and saw, unbelievingly, that there was a knife in her hand, its blade glinting blindingly in the sunlight.

For an instant their four figures could have been carved from stone. Richard, suddenly pale, was the first to move, holding out a cautious hand. 'Darling, please,' he said, his voice ragged and uneven from his running, 'let's be sensible about this.'

'Go away.' Helena's voice was shaking. 'Go back to your cars, both of you.' Suddenly she bent forward, seized Rona's hair and forced her head back, holding the tip of the blade against her throat. 'If you don't go, I'll kill her.'

Frozen, still unbelieving, Rona glimpsed Dave's horrified face over Richard's shoulder. At another level, she was aware that her hand was pressing on a nettle, and almost welcomed its vicious sting.

'Darling, give me the knife! It's all right – no damage has been done. Just give me the knife, and we can talk things over calmly.'

Helena did not respond, and, seeing the helplessness of the two men, Rona realized the next move must be hers. Very, very slowly, she raised a hand to Helena's and gently pushed it away. In the same instant Richard sprang forward, wrenched the knife from his wife's hand, and hurled it into the bracken. Dave came running to Rona and helped her up, though she could hardly stand and was glad of his supporting arm. Together, they turned to look at the others. Helena was sliding very slowly to the ground, her gaily coloured skirt billowing round her. Richard knelt beside her and pulled her into his arms.

'My poor love,' he said softly. 'Why didn't you tell me things were so desperate? I could have helped.'

'No one can help,' Helena said in a flat, expressionless voice. 'I killed—'

'No!' Richard's hand went quickly over her mouth. 'Don't say anything. We'll go home and—'

She shook him away. 'I killed Barry Pollard,' she said clearly, 'and I'm glad I did.'

For a minute there was total silence as her words echoed and re-echoed in their heads. Then Rona said hesitantly, 'And – Alan?'

Helena looked up then, her face anguished. 'I loved him so much!' she cried, and Rona saw a spasm of pain cross her husband's face. 'But in the end he left me, just as Edgar had. How could he do that to me?'

She looked wildly from one face to another as though expecting an answer. 'Gradually,' she went on quietly, when no one spoke, 'I came to hate him for deserting me, till in the end I hated him as much as I did Pollard. He had to be punished too, but in his case letters wouldn't be enough.' Rona felt Dave glance quickly at her, but her eyes were intent on the beautiful, vengeful face below her.

'I wanted – *needed* – to hurt him,' Helena went on in a low voice, 'to make him suffer as much as he'd made me. Then it came to me, the perfect way to deal with both of them at once, and avenge Lottie at the same time.'

Richard, his attempt to quieten her having failed, had sunk back on the grass, still holding her hand and with his dark, troubled eyes intent on her face. It was Rona who prompted gently, 'How did you get hold of the knife?'

Helena glanced up briefly. 'I knew his wife went to work and was unlikely to be home when the boys got back from school, so there had to be a key somewhere.' She was speaking quite calmly now, as though the crisis inside her had been resolved and there was nothing more to worry about.

'So one day I went round and searched for it. It wasn't in an obvious place, I'll give her that; it took me nearly an hour to find it, balanced on top of a drain by the garage door. In fact, there were two keys on a ring, one for the back door and one for the side door of the garage – so the boys could get their bikes out, I suppose. That was a bonus; it gave me the idea of leaving the knife there instead of in the house. I took them straight to an ironmonger's out at Sunningdean, had copies made, and put them back in their hiding place, with no one any the wiser.'

A plane droned lazily overhead, part of another, more normal, world. The dog had long since stopped barking. The three of them waited, unmoving, until Helena started speaking again.

'All I had to do then was wait for Pollard to be released. I was outside the prison when he came out, saw him get into a friend's car, and followed them back to his house. After that, I tailed him every day – to the job centre, to the bank – and to the pub. He went there every evening, and caught the ten thirty bus home. His routine never varied in the week I followed him; it was almost too easy.

'There was a meeting of the Music Society coming up, so I wrote to Alan, pretending to be Pollard and asking him to meet me that evening, at just the time he'd be coming out of the pub. Then, the day before, I went back and helped myself to a knife from the Spencers' kitchen. I'd left it to the last minute, in case it was missed.'

In the silence that followed, Rona heard a tiny click as the tape recorder switched itself off. She'd forgotten all about it, and realized with a sense of shock that she'd recorded the entire confession. This was not, she felt, the moment to own up.

Richard slowly rose to his feet and helped Helena to hers. She stood listlessly, staring down at the ground. All the life seemed drained out of her and she looked like a beautiful doll.

Richard turned to Rona, and she was shocked by the change in his face; he seemed to have aged ten years in as many minutes.

'Miss Parish, this is a total nightmare and I haven't even begun to take it in. However, it's clear I owe you a very sincere apology for what's just happened. Obviously, I hadn't the slightest inkling of what was going on – perhaps I should have had. I have, though, been increasingly worried over the last few weeks; Helena's always been highly strung, but her behaviour has become increasingly erratic. I was afraid she was heading for another breakdown.'

'You tried to stop her coming this afternoon,' Rona said. 'Why?'

'Because her attitude towards you worried me. She said a couple of times, "That girl knows something." And once she said, "She has to be stopped." I'd no idea what she meant. As to this afternoon, I thought I'd dissuaded her, but as luck would have it, I glanced out of a window just as she was driving off. I knew you were going to Lammerden, so I came straight here and, since she went to collect you first, arrived ahead of you. Having searched the centre, I came out just in time to see the car shoot off through the village.' He turned to Dave. 'I'm sorry, I don't think—'

'Dave Lampeter,' Dave supplied. 'I've been – helping Rona.'

'I presume you followed me here?'

'Yes. I was thrown when they drove into the car park and then straight out again, and by the time I reached the exit there was no sign of them. I was hesitating, wondering which way to go, when you drove quickly past me and turned left. I recognized you from the funeral and guessed you must be after them, so I tagged along. Not,' he added ruefully, 'that I did much good; Rona diffused the situation herself.'

Richard nodded. 'We'd better be getting back,' he said heavily.

Throughout these explanations Helena had stood docilely, eyes still downcast. Richard held out his hand to her, she took it as trustingly as a child, and they all retraced their steps to the waiting cars. Richard let Helena into the Daimler, then went to pull up the hood on the red sports car, with the comment that he'd send someone out to collect it. Magda's catalogue was still on the back seat, but Rona hadn't the heart to retrieve it.

She and Dave waited as Richard also got into his car, made

a wide, sweeping turn, and, with a lift of his hand, set off back towards Buckford.

'Poor bugger,' Dave said softly. 'He really loves her, doesn't he?'

Rona nodded. Another part of the jigsaw she'd got wrong. 'What'll happen to them, do you think?'

'God knows.' Dave grinned suddenly. 'But I sure would like to be a fly on the wall when your friend Barrett hears about all this!'

It had been a relief, when they arrived at the police station, to find CID too busy dealing with the Maddoxes to have time for them. Rona wrote the DI a brief note, explaining that she'd forgotten the tape was switched on, but if he could make use of it, he was welcome to do so. She doubted, since it had been recorded without Helena's knowledge, that it would be admissible evidence, but in all likelihood she'd have no objection to going over it again.

Back in her room, the first thing Rona did was to phone Lew Grayson at the *Courier.* 'I have a scoop for you,' she told him. 'One good turn deserves another!'

Barrett would bless her for that, but she'd discharged any duty she might owe him, and Grayson's reception of the news was worth incurring further displeasure.

It wasn't until Will was in bed that she told Nuala and Jack the story. They were completely thunderstruck.

'Mrs Maddox!' Nuala kept repeating, shaking her head. 'I can't believe it! She was always so poised and in command of herself.'

'At a cost,' Rona said soberly.

'So Auntie was right after all. The lovers *did* have a connection with the murder.'

'It wouldn't have made any difference, though, if she'd gone to the police,' Rona commented. 'They'd never have believed her; look at the reception I got.'

* * *

Before going to bed, she phoned Max. 'We've had quite a dramatic turn of events,' she told him.

'Why aren't I surprised?'

'I'll tell you about it tomorrow, but all is well.'

'I'm glad to hear it; it seems pointless to tell you to take care.'

Rona laughed. 'Oh, I will, I will.'

She was exhausted, she realized as she switched off the phone and started to undress; but although this was the last night she'd spend in this little room, her work here was far from finished. She'd still not been to St Stephen's, nor visited the court house, nor the *Courier* archives. As to what she *had* achieved, she thought sleepily as she climbed into bed, it was a mixed bag: she'd been wrong about Edna's death and about Richard Maddox, but at least she'd helped Beth and Alan Spencer, and Richard and Helena were not, thank God, her problem.

Which was not to say she hadn't others of her own: her father and Catherine Bishop; Lindsey and Hugh; even, perhaps, the fluttery Adele Yarborough, whose welfare so concerned Max. For the moment, though, all she wanted was to drift into sleep and forget the lot of them. Tomorrow, after all, was another day.

DISCARD